"…one of the most important SF writers of the 20th century…"
— *Publishers Weekly*

"Aldiss is a master at cracking open the mundane shell of the ordinary."
— *Washington Post*

"Mr. Aldiss is (now) in competition with no one but himself."
— *New York Times Book Review*

"Aldiss shares with J.G. Ballard the distinction of being a science fiction writer whose intelligence, wit, and flawless prose style have enabled him to enter the mainstream and then to divert its course."
— *Literary Review*

"…a man who loves the English language with a profound and contagious passion."
— James Blish

"…one of SF's most gifted veterans."
— *Booklist*

"Few SF writers possess as fine a prose style as Aldiss…. Aldiss's voice is assuredly his own, and his style is elegant, sometimes elegaic, always carefully honed, never affected."
— *New Encyclopedia of Science Fiction*

"Aldiss is simultaneously fierce, and sad, and happy, and he has said almost everything that can be said in SF."
— John Clute

"He is probably our most all-around literate science-fiction author, measured by his command of language and his critical facilities. He has written a literary history of imaginative fiction (*Billion Year Spree*); co-published a small critical review long before science-fiction criticism was taken seriously by the rest of the world; and for many years he was a regular critic for the *Oxford Mail*. Moreover, Aldiss is unique in that he moves just as easily in higher levels of the literary establishment as he does among fellow science-fiction writers."

    – Charles Platt, *Dream Makers: Science Fiction & Fantasy Writers at Work*

"Aldiss's surreal universe is his way of introducing both quirky comedy and an obstinate humanity."

    – *New Statesman*

"[arguably] the most significant English writer of science fiction since H.G. Wells."

    – *St. James Guide to Science Fiction*

CULTURAL BREAKS

SELECTED WORKS BY BRIAN ALDISS

Cultural Breaks

BRIAN ALDISS

TACHYON PUBLICATIONS
SAN FRANCISCO

SF

Tachyon Publications
1459 18th Street #139
San Francisco, CA 94107
(415) 285-5615
www.tachyonpublications.com

Series Editor: Jacob Weisman

ISBN: 1-892391-26-0

Printed in the United States of America
by the Maple-Vail Book Manufacturing Group

First Edition: 2005

9 8 7 6 5 4 3 2 1

To All my Friends
who attend the
Conference of the Fantastic,
In particular
Bill Senior, Chip Sullivan,
Don Morse, David Lunde,
    &
Donna and Steve Hooley

CONTENTS

The Crocodile's Apprentice

ANDY DUNCAN

BY NOW, none of us should expect a wonderful writer to be wonderful in person as well, but isn't it glorious when that happy accident actually comes to pass?

I have loved Brian W. Aldiss the writer for most of my reading life, but in the past few years I have come to love Brian W. Aldiss the person as well. I met Brian through an annual event we both attend, the International Conference for the Fantastic in the Arts, held each March at an airport hotel in Fort Lauderdale, Florida. (See *www.iafa. org.*) Note the aplomb with which I toss off "we both attend," as if we were peers, old cronies from *New Worlds* before that kid Moorcock took it over. In fact, Brian was a living legend, with the ICFA title of Permanent Special Guest, when I first showed up a decade ago as an unknown graduate student clutching my entrée to Olympus, a paper on "The Cold Equations" that had earned me an A. I'm slightly better known now than I was then, at least at ICFA – like Jack Benny's character in *To Be Or Not To Be,* I am "world famous in Poland" – but Brian in the meantime has gone from strength to strength, and remains world famous across the actual world.

Moreover, I have read and admired his books since I was a kid, when I first plucked them off the shelves of the public library in Batesburg, South Carolina, where the librarians had helpfully stamped each one – even *Billion Year Spree,* which I read with delight, cover to cover, at age twelve – with the little red rocketship that meant "science fiction." So being in his presence still reduces me to awe, to the level of the whining schoolboy, with his satchel.

Of course, every convention, like Hell, has circles within circles, and my ultimate entrée into Brian's circle at ICFA was not my "Cold Equations" paper; after all, let's be honest, "The Cold Equations" is about as relevant to Brian's career as the lightning bug is relevant to the lightning. (Brian has learned more from Borges than from John W. Campbell.) No, my letter of transit was my then-girlfriend, now wife, Sydney, who caught Brian's eye as readily as she had mine and whom he promptly recruited into the unofficial stock company that peopled the one-act plays he staged each year. One year, I remember, there were several rehearsals, and at each rehearsal Sydney's part got bigger. Some of the script pages were handwritten. Brian was going back to his hotel room and writing whole monologues just for Sydney. "If Sydney's in it," Brian likes to say, "it's fireproof!" Since I was hanging around anyway, Brian was good enough to toss me a role occasionally. As a result, Sydney and I got to play the robot child's troubled parents in Brian's own stage version of *Super-Toys Last All Summer Long*, years before what's-her-name and what's-his-face played the roles in Spielberg's AI.

One of Brian's ICFA plays was *Drinks with the Spider King*. Brian and I both were typecast, he as the Spider King and I as a brainless minion. My role was to sit at his feet, gnaw an imaginary haunch of meat and gaze up at him with fearsome adoration. This I found easy to do. I had ample time – for it was a rather long play – to study, up close, Brian's marvelous face. I was fascinated by its creases, jowls, and bristles, and the zest with which Brian animated them. It is an old vaudevillian's face, a face that can be instantly read from the cheapest seats in the house. It has many stories yet to tell, that face.

In recent years, Sydney has been spending her summers at Oxford University, as a teacher and administrator in the Alabama at Oxford program. Oxford is, of course, Brian's hometown, so Sydney and I have been fortunate enough to visit him repeatedly in much more congenial settings than a convention hotel. When we go to dinner or to a pub, we don't even wear name tags! How liberating. On a number of memorable occasions, Brian has been the most welcoming and gracious host one could imagine, and a marvelous tour guide to his beloved Oxfordshire.

With Brian, we lounged on the lazy banks of the Windrush in the ragged shadow of the dismantled Minster Lovell Hall, where a vault once was opened to reveal a skeleton sitting upright at a writing-table, surrounded by books. (No wonder Brian loves the place.) With Brian, we navigated country lanes to the old stone village of Langford (in which, I am assured, Dave Langford has no economic interest), and a fabulous pub called the Bell Inn, where the lamb was divine and the conversation even better. With Brian, we had a long and luxurious cream tea at a sidewalk café in Burford, which Brian's young son, in the wake of Brian's 1969 novel *Barefoot in the Head*, christened Burford-in-the-Head. ("I thought that was rather good," Brian says, still the proud papa thirty-six years later.) Our Burford tea party was so lush and attractive, we actually drew bees. We also attracted a passerby who asked, "Excuse me, aren't you Brian Aldiss?" – a first in my writerly experience, and an instance of Brian's celebrity in his homeland.

On another occasion, as he and I sat side by side on a rough-hewn bench in an extraordinary Oxford seafood restaurant called Fishers (it's in St. Clement's Street, just over Magdalen Bridge), Brian delighted me with a long, impassioned, funny, profane denunciation of a new critical anthology – to which I had contributed, hence my delight – while the two of us munched fistfuls of deep-fried whitebait, with lemons and sea salt. Normally I am squeamish about eating things that reproach me with their eyes, but there we were, the crocodile and his apprentice, welcoming the little fishes in with gently smiling jaws.

Best of all, I think, has been our chance to see Brian's house, his study, his library (which is pretty much coexistent with his house), and his amazing garden – a vast, lovingly tended tangle full of surprises, into which the wanderer quickly disappears. Goldfish thrive in the murk of what only a soulless cynic would call an abandoned pool.

Speaking of pools: In closing, I offer an ICFA anecdote that Brian doubtless does not remember, as it occurred before I met Sydney, and before he even knew my name. Late one night, I sat poolside with a group of my fellow graduate students. By ones and twos, the group drifted off to bed, leaving only two of us, a young man and a young woman, deep in a high-octane critical conversation about something or other (I hope, God help me, it wasn't "The Cold Equations"). We both gradually became aware of the sound of someone in the pool, gently swimming toward us – at 2 A.M. We looked up. Bobbing there, a few yards away, was the conference's distinguished Permanent Special Guest, gray hair plastered across his head, beaming at us. When he spoke, his voice was barely a murmur, but the acoustics of the pool ferried it directly into our ears, like a confidence. "Come on," Brian cooed. "Don't be shy. Come in. Come into the water." He then winked, turned, and glided away, as graceful and amoral as an otter. You were right, Brian. The water's fine. Happy birthday.

CULTURAL BREAKS

Tarzan of the Alps

AN OLD AND WEARY VAN, travelling southwards across the plains of Patagonia, stopped ten kilometres outside the village of Esperanza. The driver of the van, a corpulent man by the name of José Pareda, climbed out and walked slowly round his vehicle. He looked under the bonnet. He scratched his head and returned to the steering wheel.

When he started the engine and went into gear, alarming noises sounded. Pareda switched off the engine.

Again he climbed out, to stand on the shady side of the vehicle, where a faded sign read, "Pareda's Mobile Cinema." He scanned the horizon hopefully.

The horizon was flat and unpromising, bereft of trees or foliage. However, movement soon appeared on it. Pareda waved his hat and shouted to attract attention.

A heat haze made the distant figures uncertain. As they drew nearer, a man could be seen with a dog and perhaps a dozen head of cattle. The man left his hound to guard the cattle and came on alone.

He was middle-aged and presented a dusty appearance.

"What are you doing here?" he asked. "What made you stop in this barren place?"

Pareda explained he was hoping to get down to the city of Rio Gallegos, but his clutch was broken.

"You're in luck, friend," said the other. "My son Pedro works in a

3

garage in Esperanza. He can fix the problem. Leave your vehicle here. Come with me to my house." He said his name was Alejo Galdos.

So Pareda went with Galdos. Galdos had eleven thin cattle. They drank at a spring, after which Galdos and his dog drove the herd back to his estancia. As they were securing the animals, Galdos's wife, Maria, came out of their dwelling to enquire about their visitor.

Maria was warmly consoling regarding the broken clutch and pressed Pareda to come into their house and make himself comfortable.

The house was poor and built of adobe, and showed many signs of neglect, but the two men sat themselves down on benches while Maria fed the dog, after which she produced a jug of thin red wine for her husband and their guest.

She was a well-built woman, matronly of figure, who complained of sciatica and failing eyesight. Almost the first thing she said to Pareda was that they were down on their luck. The men also had their complaints, and warmed to one another when they found they had something in common: the stupidity and failure of their fathers.

Pareda's father had owned a flourishing cinema in the brilliant city of Comodoro Rivadavia. Unfortunately, he had allowed the cinema to be burnt down. The fire had spread to the whole street. He was sued for a great deal of money and threatened with death by several irate householders. In desperation, he hanged himself. Pareda, then a teenager, had managed to save a good many reels of film from the blaze. With them, he escaped from town and had established his travelling cinema.

"But, alas, these days people have television and computers and no longer wish to see my films. Admittedly, some are very old, but are not old things valuable?"

Galdos agreed that old things were better than new and sipped his wine sparingly.

"And old dreams are better than new ones," said Maria, but her husband would not go as far as that.

Alejo Galdos admitted that he and Maria lived very poorly. They had recently bought a PC with an e-mail facility, but had never possessed a television set. It was all the fault of his father. This terrible man with gold teeth had become rich from banking in the distant capital, Buenos Aires, and had amassed a fortune through his liaisons with a corrupt governor. The governor had been shot and now there was a lawsuit over the money which had been going on for years – the very money Galdos claimed was his by right.

So Galdos was parted from wealth and the comfort wealth could bring. He had taken up ranching, but his heart was not in it. His life and Maria's had become more and more empoverished. After many hard years, he had even forgotten how to read or write, and it was all the fault of his beast of a father with the gold teeth.

The two men shook hands across the table. Fathers were a bad lot. But they were now friends, and already Maria had emailed their son Pedro at the garage in Esperanza to repair Pareda's clutch, and to give the vehicle a general overhaul.

Pareda was more than grateful and tucked into the meat dish Maria provided.

"We unfortunates must live without hope," he said, with a gallant flourish of his knife. "Despair is a noble thing!"

"Yes, exactly!" Galdos agreed. "It is the Argentinian philosophy!"

He passed round some slender cigarillos. All three of them lit up and drank down the thin wine and felt happy in each other's company.

And so it was that young Pedro fixed up the old van and "Pareda's Mobile Cinema" was once more a going concern. Since Pareda had spent two nights at the Galdos estancia, enjoying their hospitality and getting quite drunk with Galdos, he determined to repay them with a free film show.

He drove his vehicle close to the porch of the adobe dwelling and set up his canvas screen so that Maria and Galdos could watch from their bench on the porch. When dusk was fading fast into darkness, and the stars were appearing richly overhead, he began to project his film.

Maria and Galdos were immensely excited. Here was a little good fortune at last.

It was an old film, shot in black and white. The title came up on the screen with a blast of music.

"What does it say, Maria? What does it say?" asked Galdos in extreme agitation.

Maria screwed up her poor eyes and read. "This film is called..."

"Yes, yes, what is it called, my dearest?"

"It is called *Tarzan of the Alps*. Yes. That's it! *Tarzan of the Alps*."

They watched the film enthralled. Mighty Tarzan swung through the great jungles from tree to tree. He gave his magical call. He was surrounded by elephants trumpetting and pushing down giant trees, by monkeys who were comical and loveable and obeyed Tarzan's call, and by superb parrots who alighted on Tarzan's shoulder. Tarzan also had a beautiful mate. She lived in a tree with him.

Tarzan outwitted a bunch of nasty white men. He fought with a lion and tamed it. He fought with a crocodile and killed it, wrenching its jaws apart.

And all this happened in the wonderful tall jungles of the Alps, which seemed to stretch on to eternity. There, it was clear, one might be forever wild, forever free, and never ever have to herd cattle.

By the time the film finished, Galdos and Maria were in tears, overcome with emotion at the brilliance of the film.

Pareda packed his equipment away. They implored him, weeping, to stay another night, but he would not. After fond farewells, the "Pareda Mobile Cinema" van trundled away and soon was lost in the gloom of the night.

But Alejo and Maria Galdos never forgot the impact of the film they had viewed. Night after night, they would close their door on the bleak open spaces surrounding their estancia and talk about the resounding cry of that great athlete, Tarzan, as he swung on lianas through the trees. They would try to recreate the call of the lumbering elephants and to mimic the chatter of the monkeys. And above all they would remind each other of the wonderful forests covering the Alps.

They had heard of the Alps. They knew those mountains stretched across part of distant Europe. But never had they dreamed that those mountains were home to such splendid wildlife, such splendid wildernesses of jungle.

Often in his longing for that fecundity, Galdos would swear he would sell their poor herd of cattle and go to visit those alpine forests. Alas, he knew in his heart that the cattle would not raise enough money even to get him and his wife back to Buenos Aires.

Worn out at last, Alejo Galdos died. Maria held his hand until he breathed no more. His last word, delivered in a sigh, was "Tarzan."

Maria mourned her husband deeply. She resolved to keep on the cattle as long as she could. And then, amazingly, luck changed. The long-protracted lawsuit in the capital was settled in favour of Galdos's estate. A man in a suit, driven by a chauffeur in a smart car that never broke down, called on Maria Galdos and gave her, as her husband's surviving widow, a large suitcase full of money.

"What shall I do with all this?" she asked, surveying the miraculous inheritance.

"You could travel," suggested the man in the suit, as he moved rapidly back to his automobile.

Maria felt she was too old to travel. She called Pedro on the e-mail, summoning him to her.

"Pedro," she said, when he arrived at the estancia, "You must have this money. You must fulfill your father's wish. You must go to see the forests of the Alps."

Pedro embraced his mother and swore he would tell her everything on his return. He went to the capital, bought himself a new alpaca suit and booked himself a seat on the next flight to Europe. At last the family dream would be fulfilled. He would feast his eyes on those eternal forests depicted in that wonderful film his mother called *Tarzan of the Alps*.

Tralee of Man Young

IN MY GARDEN, doing a flower-watch, I was fascinated to see the daisies grow. An industrious bee was moving from blossom to blossom, presumably under orders from headquarters. One understands that bees are enormously good at communication.

This it was which prompted me to catch the bee and try to educate her still further. I used great kindness. Patience was also needed. I was aware all the while that I was entering realms where no one had been before. Although the bee worked hard, strong empathy developed between us: so much so that the bee, whom I christened Bea, would eat honey from my hand. Once Bea had mastered the alphabet, she showed she was ready to tackle the masterpieces of English literature. She suggested we start with Leo Tolstoy's *War and Peace*. I had to inform her – I trust without too much condescension – that this novel was in fact Russian, in origin if not in translation. She so immediately went off the idea that I suspected racial prejudice, rarely found in a bee, although she claimed never to have heard of Russia.

We finally settled on an English classic. Bea would read nothing less than Jane Austen's *Pride and Prejudice*.

We settled down comfortably, one lovely summer evening, with the open book. I had chosen a paperback edition with good print. With the scrupulousness that was one of my trademarks, I had placed grains of sugar between each word, by way of encouragement.

Bea settled on the first page. She began a slow crawl over the first sentence. Rather to my disappointment, she insisted on working from right to left, Hebraic fashion. I wondered what she would make of it.

"...in man single a that, acknowledged..."

These words were travelled in the first hour.

In the second hour, after a rest, we got only as far as

"...universally truth a..."

Bea then rested. I felt that "universally" had exhausted her. I could not help wondering how she would manage with "possession" in the second line.

She indicated to me that she was extremely disappointed with the literary quality of the piece. I sympathised. We spent the rest of that evening watching television, although there was little enough about apiary to hold our attention.

It is a tribute to the tenacity of Bea that, come the next evening, she was eager to start reading Jane Austen again. She set off along the page at a fair pace, this time choosing to read the second line of text, although once again – perversely, to my mind – choosing to travel from right to left.

In the first half hour we had reached

"...wife a of want in be..."

Here she came to a halt. I could tell by the flutter of her wings that she was annoyed. Finally she explained: "bee" was misspelt. I attempted to tell her that this word, "be" with one "e" had no reference to her kind, but was merely a part of the verb "to be," as in Hamlet's soliloquy, "To be or not to be."

This proved an unfortunate example to have chosen. She could not understand what Hamlet meant; her argument – perfectly logical in its way – was that either one was or was not a bee, and that there could be no confusion about the matter. Even a wasp was clearly not a bee; though she admitted that there may have been some period in past prehistory when bees and wasps shared a common ancestry.

How was it, Bea asked, that this rubbish from Hamlet could be so highly prized? I found it hard to answer.

We came as near to quarrelling as we had ever done, Bea and I. However, after a while she kindly announced I was an honorary bee, albeit wingless, and she was prepared to go on with her reading of Jane Austen.

So on the third day, Bea triumphantly reached

"...truth a is it..."

and pronounced it good.

A simple physiological fact stood in Bea's path to full enjoyment of Jane Austen's work. Her memory always died at sunset. It lasted only one day. It was renewed on the succeeding sunrise, completely fresh and blank. All traces of her yesterdays, of her experiences good or bad, had vanished. This discovery touched me deeply. How pleasant, I thought, to awaken every morning to an entirely new world! – No horrid memories of childhood, no memories of bills to be paid, no memories of work to be done: just a total blank, full of childlike expectation, on which a new sun shone. Even if it ruined one's appreciation of Jane Austen.

Many explanations passed between us. Finally, Bea curled up in my ear exhausted.

It became clear to me that what was needed was a short prose piece through all of which Bea could travel in one day, thus receiving it whole. A prose piece or...a poem!

So I turned to my favourite verse form, the limerick.

Bea was immediately enthusiastic about the new project.

It was on a Sunday morning when we set to work on the limerick book. I opened it at random, and flattened out the page. Almost at once, Bea began to make steady progress through the first line of the first limerick we came across, this time without grains of sugar between each word.

"...Tralee of man young a was there..."

Only then did I realise that the second line was
"Who had an affair with a – "

No, no, I could not let my innocent friend read that filth! How could I ever explain its implications to the virgin Bea?

She was resting after her exertions, but was about to approach the second line, of which, from her point of view, was inevitably....

– but I could not let it happen!

"Bea, my dear," I said, "it has come time for us to part, alas!"

I let her go. She flew away with many a backward look. I waved until she disappeared into a distant flowerbed. Tears stood in my eyes.

That dear little winged being remains for ever in my heart. Never again can I open a novel by Jane Austen without thinking of her. Or a book of limericks.

The Eye Opener

ON THE FIRST DAY, the Head was visible only to armies. Many armies of many kinds ceased to advance or retreat. Men crawling on their bellies stood to view. Boy soldiers eased their bandoliers and looked up.

It created a far greater disturbance than war. As it happened, I was up on the moor as usual. I saw the Head first by moonlight on a cloudless night, when it most resembled a giant cactus.

Of course its effect was fearsome. For a start, it was enormous. It seemed at first to fill the whole quarter of the western skies, as later it came to fill our lives. What we have never experienced always stands in our path like a land mine. Like the first time you have an enemy in your gunsight. However, I speak for many when I say that apprehension was accompanied by a sense of relief. Without consulting others, I knew that here was a different mode of life for everyone, a spot of adventure just when you were growing a bit long in the tooth....

Between the stark alternatives of Life and Death, a third force was interposed – if that doesn't sound too grand.

It is not too much to say that I just stood there, transfixed. Couldn't keep my eyes off the thing. Extraordinary. Bizarre. There were no words for it.

What I didn't realize was that all round the world everything was grinding to a halt. Pretty well the entire human race was staring upwards. Not a posture you usually hold for long.

In the first hours of its manifestation, no one had any conception of time as it related to the Head: was it a transitory phenomenon, or was permanence one of its unknown characteristics? The appearance of the Head was in itself so enigmatic, like a private dream, that other considerations took a while to dawn. Although I had been used to trouble all around the world, this was something entirely new.

My resolve was to stay observing the Head until moonset and daybreak. As the light changed and the moon in its third quarter sloped towards the west, the face of the Head became less well defined, while the bulbous nature of the skull became more pronounced. In saying this I do not express what my inner feelings were at the time. So novel was this grotesque thing, so far beyond nature, that I remained for some while uncertain as to whether we had received a visitation from a Head or a vegetable growth roughly resembling a Head. It occurred to me that this might be a new psychological weapon, launched by some unknown enemy – in which case, it might come in handy for some astronomical target practice!

Despite the mixture of elation and misgiving which filled me, I fell asleep on the moor. When I woke, a new day had barely begun; Earth's dewy shadow still lay over the moor. The Head was still there, immense in the pallid sky, bathed in sunlight.

I should explain that my worldly fortunes had varied greatly. I had joined the army at an early age. My family connections entitled me to early promotion. During the war with Groznia, I was made general, when my courage and grasp of strategy were instrumental in winning a swift victory. After the war, I entered politics on a tide of popularity. In two years I was made a junior minister and in five appointed Minister of Defence. Unfortunately, my so-called "illegal dealing in arms," undertaken purely for the good of my country, was brought to light and misinterpreted; this, coupled with my brief affair with the Kirghis princesses, brought about my downfall.

Disillusioned, I purchased a few hundred acres of this moor, to become a farmer of sorts, a calling some of my mother's ancestors had followed. At least it kept me outdoors. There I reared the black-faced horned sheep common in this part of the country. I had the odd stag to pot at now and again, to relieve the boredom. Of course I retained my connections with the highest in the land. And with other lands.

After a swig from my hip flask, I rose to my feet and stared into the sky. Nearby, the sheep rooted about between heather and bracken, eyes to the ground, in the manner of all grazing animals. I looked up, in the manner of carnivores. All that interested my animals was what passed between their black lips.

The Head was turned full face in my direction. With all else that was strange, this did not strike me at the time as particularly strange. Wispy clouds partly obscured the immense Head. I saw brutish lips, a large squashed nose, and eyelids heavy like unbaked pastry covering the closed eyes. The expression, it seemed at first, was one of an unutterable contempt. Yet at a later moment, as the vapours drifted, I perceived – or thought I perceived – an expression of calm resignation to sorrow. What sorrow I knew not. I'm not an imaginative man, I'm happy to say.

Such nobility as the face might possess was negated by a nest of stiff "hair" (so I must call it) surrounding it. The chin sank into a neck much resembling the trunk of a sequoia. A suggestion of shoulders was obscured by the mists of the horizon.

I stared up at this apparition. I was alone on the moor, without even my dog for company. A sudden emotion seized me. Awe of an unprecedented nature, I suppose, but something more; *a dark sense of the artificiality of human life....*

As if I had been living on half-rations all my natural life.

What in hell had we all been up to, all these thousands of years?

Just supposing those eyes opened and it saw me....

Somehow, just to look up at that thing made you feel mighty

small. So I ran, ran towards the nearby lane where my all-terrain stood. Kicking it into gear, I drove furiously back to my house in the valley.

Once there, I dashed inside and snatched up my binoculars.

The binoculars gave me a better view of the immense thing in the sky: better, yes, but more enigmatic. It scarcely appeared to have a face: the features I thought I had seen proved almost as imaginary under higher magnification as the canals on Mars. The mouth was but a vast furrow, the nose and closed eyes were mere protuberances on a wrinkled surface. That surface seemed to be constituted of a material like dried mud, impenetrably surrounded by what resembled a forest destroyed by fire, of which only blackened stumps remained. The thing was some kind of vast vegetable growth, only to my anthropomorphic imagination resembling a human being.

Yet lowering the glasses brought back that face of gloom and resignation. It is typical of my limited thinking that I try to puzzle out these minor details while the major puzzle remains. How did this monstrous thing arrive? What order of monstrous thing was it?

Was it meant to be a caricature of someone living? I knew a Major Trapido once in Belize who looked somewhat similar. Couldn't help wondering what Cynthia (just temporary) would say about the thing.

Re-entering the house, I switched on my computer.

Already the Internet was buzzing. Reports of sightings were coming in from all over the world. At least the Head was no solitary creation of my own imagination, as I had almost been tempted to believe! It was clear no one knew more than I did.

I fed in a private number and spoke to well-placed friends in other parts of the world. Disquieting facts emerged.

Most estimates placed the Head in the upper ionosphere, where the ionosphere fades into the exosphere. Which is to say, about 250 miles above the earth's surface. This figure was arrived at by observing the times at which the Head entered and quitted earth's shadow.

To an observer, the Head filled an angle of 22.5 degrees. By triangulation, it was established therefore that it measured all but one hundred miles across. So much for mensuration.

But numbers and figures, for long mankind's consolation, were soon to provide no comfort. My contact in Vladivostok, Vladimir Mironets, reported that he saw the Head full-face. Colin Steele from Canberra gave the same report. From Leslie Howle in Seattle came the same answer: the Head was seen full-face. Always full-face, from any vantage point on Earth.

Perhaps you will understand the mixture of bewilderment and despair which overcame my psyche at this point. Perhaps you remember feeling the same yourself. No stolid Victorian preacher, confronted with the truths of Darwinism and facing the knowledge that he was descended from apes and mistier creatures back in time, could have suffered a greater sense of betrayal. The Head by its very presence set all scientific knowledge at nought.

I reached the conclusion that this could not possibly be an enemy psychological weapon. No nation had technology advanced enough to project such a thing into Earth's skies.

There were others who did not despair. More disconcerting news revealed that the Head could not be photographed. As Count Dracula showed no reflection in a mirror, so the Head did not register on any kind of film.

Whilst I was sitting in a limbo of thought, Cynthia Goodwin-Jones came downstairs, wearing her white satin wrap, her hair entangled in towelling.

"You've seen it?" I asked.

"The product of a hangover. I need orange juice, aspirin, black coffee, sympathy. Not necessarily in that order." She disappeared in the direction of the kitchen. I made some phone calls.

As I was getting myself a drink, Cynthia returned, coffee mug in hand, and sprawled on my chaise longue.

"The bloody thing's about a hundred miles across — from ear to ear, as it were. The size of one of Jupiter's moons."

She said, "You were on the phone. Not calling any of Claude's friends, I hope?"

Goodwin-Jones was a cabinet minister, currently indulging in an affair with a female American rock singer half his age, name of Babbles. How he kept these affairs out of the tabloids I shall never know.

"Why are you always paranoid as soon as you get up? You should take more exercise."

She hugged her coffee cup. "Why go on about Jupiter's moons? That object up there is not an astronomical object. Surely you can understand that? It's just an image of some sort."

"Image?"

"It expresses religious anxiety, guilt – all the things people wallow in at present, me included. Not to mention sexual dilemma."

"You mean, like someone giving you head?"

She ignored my wit. "UFOs having had their day, along comes this new image. Who knows what? End of human egotism? Some hopes!" A tiresome woman in some ways, but with a good bone structure. Goodwin-Jones had never appreciated Cynth enough. After a silence, she said, "The dawning of the age of philosophical life? Is that what it means? Or maybe it will come down here and eat us all...."

"I got on to Purvis in Washington. Remember him? They're going to send a shuttle up."

She gave her high-pitched laugh. "Claim this bloody cranium in the name of the UN? Trust the Yanks! How crazy can you get?"

"You have to do something. You can't just sit around, can you?"

Her expression said, Don't bore me with your male platitudes.

Later, we went out and observed the Head together. The cloud had cleared as the morning advanced. The Head took on an appearance of pewtery lambency, as if lightly powdered with aluminium.

"In my opinion, for what it's worth, you could land a shuttle on it," I said.

———

I had to go to London on business in the week. Cynthia stayed in sole possession of the house. I managed to get a half-hour's conversation with Claude Goodwin-Jones in his Whitehall office. He sat at his desk, turning a pen over and over in his paper-thin hands. He said the government was consulting with other EU leaders and with the Americans. There was much to be optimistic about. For example, the Head had advanced no nearer Earth, as had been feared it might. It had caused no meteorological upsets, as might have been anticipated. And astronomers reported absolutely no gravitational disturbance to Earth's orbit. The Head had no detectable substance.

"Meaning in fact it doesn't exist."

"Wouldn't say that, old chum." He spun his chair round to stare gloomily out of the window. "That might frighten the populace. Bit too much for them. The populace can see, or thinks it can see, that the bloody thing exists, whatever instrumentation says to the contrary. Personally, I can tell you the PM regards the Head with a pinch of affection – takes everyone's minds off the financial crisis. Let's just say that whatever it is – well, you've seen the line we are putting out for general consumption – it exists in a different dimension of space-time from the rest of the universe."

Trying to put him in his place, I said, "It probably spells the end of human egotism."

Claude gave me a penumbral glance. "Where would that leave you, old chum?"

As I rose to leave, he treated his pen to another twiddle and asked after Cynthia. "I do feel bad about her, you know."

Handing in my pass, leaving the building, I thought to myself, So you damned well should, old chum.

"The Ghost from Outer Space"... Was it first a headline in the *Miami Sun-Sentinel*? Wherever the phrase came from, it caught on. Thus the unfamiliar, the outré, the monstrous, became familiarized – a kind of a joke, a child's bogeyman, a cultural reference. "Ordinary life" is an obsessive habit: something which must continue, even in the midst of war or catastrophe. Women in cities devastated by earthquake, their houses in ruin, still peg out their washing to dry in the sun. I've seen them at it.

"Political life" also continued. Pronouncements were issued on all sides of the spectrum. The pronouncements always sounded like distortions of the truth, rather in the way that the most innocent person feels he or she is lying when talking to a policeman. Religious leaders, as was inevitable, called upon sinners to repent. They handle any kind of crisis that way. I suppose it must work for a day or two.

I liked a quotation from Thoreau, which a friend in Alma-Ata sent me via the net: "Men can be wise only with the wisdom of their age; they also share its ignorance. Even the greatest minds must yield in some degree to the suppositions of their age." (I translate roughly from the Turkic.) True, I thought, though happily it did not apply to me.

Then there was Bishop Archer, with his pronouncements. A pompous fellow. I had bumped into him several times in my more palmy days. It was said of him he had slept with his mother. More than once, I mean. There were other evil rumours too, of which I took no notice. "The Head is a manifestation of all mankind's unlived days...." And so on. Enough to make you sick. "Those who don't know how to use their lives...."

I continued to manage my farm. The Head loomed high above the moor. I studied it often. This is purely subjective, but it seemed to me that the face was undergoing subtle alterations as the season unfolded. The eyes remained closed, the mouth held its contemptuous pout. But a slow refinement crept over the features; even the "hair" seemed less barbaric. It may have been that I was growing accustomed to the Head, so that now I could see in it almost a kind of beauty. The way people used to talk about seeing the Man in the Moon.

When I said as much to Cynthia, I added – I thought modestly – that possibly I was alone in perceiving this beauty.

"You always were a conceited old thing," she said. "What makes you think you're unique? From the start, commentators have pointed out a delicate resemblance between that enigmatic face and certain races in the South Seas. It's a beauty to which we are going to grow accustomed if it remains there for long... You miss a great deal, reading those boring old military journals of yours."

With admirable patience, for the woman was still in a nervous state, I asked what I should be reading. *Home Chat*, for instance?

Cynthia tapped the magazine she was carrying. She liked to make out she was a bit of a thinker.

"This chap Brady has an interesting lead article in this month's *Art and Illusion*. He points out that every transitional age produces a major disturbance – wars, revolutions, or just deep psychological changes. We may be undergoing such a transitional period now. Faith in technological progress has reached its nadir. We are now, Brady suggests, leaving the Technological Age. What is coming cannot be foretold, but he claims that the Head may be produced by a kind of mass myth-wish, as he calls it. The Head poses no threat beyond its mystery. Indeed, the threat of something coming from outer space has been one of the psychoses haunting the Technological Age."

"So what does this chap believe this thing is? What could it be, if not a threat?"

She gave me one of her tiresome you-dummy smiles. "Try and hear what I am saying. Brady believes that the Head is connected with our moral life, which could be re-awakening."

"Then moral life is fast asleep!" I laughed. "I like that!"

"For those who can receive it, the Head speaks a secret language, the language of meditation. Some see human features on the face, others merely natural features. In short, the Head is there, quite separate from our physical world, as an object of contemplation. It is by its nature necessarily and testingly obscure: not an answer but a question."

"Whose question, for heaven's sake?"

"Our question, of course. 'Une grande porte ouverte sur le mystère éternel...'"

"Ha ha! When in doubt, lapse into French..."

"Brady has his reasons. He likens the Head to a French symbolist painter called Odilon Redon. Redon painted isolated Heads, male and female, according to an inscrutable private code, intended to convey to those who might understand, 'les esprits de silence,' and – "

"Oh, turn it off, Cynthia. This is all high-flown tosh, and you must know it. Besides, the Head's male, not female."

She arched her fine brows and regarded me with a hard gaze. "I certainly see it as female."

I said, "Anyhow, enough of all this. The Americans are sending up a shuttle next Thursday."

It was so vexing. I wanted to end the argument. Instead, another one blazed up. This time, it was about the feasibility of launching the u.s. exploratory shuttle. Supposing, she said, the vehicle burst the illusion and the Head disappeared? Excellent, I said. Rubbish, she said. She said she liked it. Really, there are times when I can see how old Claude chucked her over.

Thursday approached. And on the Tuesday, President Yeltsin – never the most reliable of men – sent up three SS-20s from his vast stash of nuclear missiles.

Two of the missiles spiralled off into space, as you might expect. The third detonated somewhere near the bridge of the thing's nose.

Nothing happened. Absolutely nothing. The Head was unscathed.

Yeltsin quit the following Monday. Now lives in Oklahoma City, tending the Alienated People's Penitential Church.

I was out late that night, rescuing a ewe stuck in a ditch. Cynthia was having another of her fits of whatever it was, and I had phoned her sister, Judith, to come down to stay, thinking that the two of them looking after each other would make life a bit easier. Cynthia and I drove down to the railway station to collect her.

The all-terrain was bumping back to the house when the Moon rose, freeing itself from cloud.

Cynthia made us stop to look at the Head. Judith was keen.

There it was, immense as ever. I was growing pretty fond of it, to tell the truth. The resemblance to Major Trapido in Belize was always pretty remote. And a change was overtaking it. Even I could see that.

It was becoming a female Head. Altering in outline, becoming female. Or was that it? Perhaps the thing was disintegrating.

Of course I said nothing of the sort to the women, but in my heart I felt a deep sorrow to think it might be about to disappear. After all – ever since the war, really – the world had become pretty flat. Prosaic.

There had been something missing, an extra dimension it used to possess. A vacuum not exactly filled by black-faced sheep.

We stood there by the vehicle, the three of us, watching. Luckily, we had a flask of coffee with us, plus my hip flask. Judith has not got half her sister's style. Smells pretty good, though.

The transformation taking place was uncertain. In the darkness, details were elusive, but it appeared that the hair was no longer hedgehog-like but smooth and flowing, outlining a more graceful shape of head. A woman? A man of a somewhat hippie type? Hard to tell. The sisters discussed it while I kept pretty mum, butting in only when Cynthia became too pretentious.

She was telling Judith of this fellow Brady's criticism in her magazine. Judith agreed most of the time. I took a swig of whisky.

"We aren't meant to understand," Judith said. "I have to say I have become quite a different person under its influence, less worldly. I used to be a Capricorn, too. To my mind, the Head represents some-

thing different to everyone who looks at it. To me, it's just a big conundrum, like – oh, like family problems – like the conundrum of
human existence. I don't really feel I'm up to modern life."

People say things like that when they get on the moors by moonlight.

Long before dawn visited our part of the world, sunlight lit upon the
Head. We saw now a more classical countenance. Long straight nose,
small mouth, large eyes, closed as ever and shielded by pale oval lids.
Hard to tell whether it was male or female. Neither, maybe. The ladies went on about Christ and the Buddha.

"Do you think she looks a bit like Mother?" Judith asked, anxiously. "Something about the mouth...."

I could see a suspicion of a bare shoulder. The immense torso rose
from a mist, pale and yellowish, much like thin cream, but with a
hint of motion as if troubled. It was something newly born, awesome
yet full of pathos. Unblemished, I'd say.

Now the new light softly illuminated the left side of the face. The
temple, the cheekbone, the corner of the lips, that side of the chin,
making the right side obscure. Something in that expression with
the closed eyes made a picture of endurance and meditation and –
well, I found myself so moved I had to turn away for another swig
of the Glenfiddich. It would have been too ridiculous to have shed a
tear. And for what, exactly?

The women were weeping, heads on each other's shoulders.

The first birds began to twitter about us. The bracken remained
dark. The sheep were grazing as ever, looking down all the while,
munch, munch, munch. Silly things, sheep.

"You see, she's rising out of the seas of the unconscious," said
Cynthia. "Oh, it's so sexy! She's – oh, I always hoped – I mean, to be
redeemed – no, it's impossible, but – "

She stopped in midsentence. Without thinking, we seized each other and stood huddled, the three of us close, staring upwards in hope and fear at the great change taking place in the sky.

The thing's eyes were opening.

Then it spoke to us about those unlived days.

Aboard the BEATITUDE

IT IS AXIOMATIC *that we who are genetically improved will seek out the Unknown. We will make it Known or we will destroy it. On occasions, we must also destroy the newly Known. This is the Military Morality.*

— COMMANDER PHILOSOPHER HIJENK SKARAMONTER
IN *BEATITUDES FOR CONQUEST*

THE GREAT BRUTE PROJECTILE accelerated along its invisible pathway. The universe through which it sped was itself in rapid movement. Starlight flashed along the flank of the ship. It moved at such a velocity it could scarcely be detected by the civilizations past which it blasted its course – until those civilizations were disintegrated and destroyed by the ship's weaponry.

It built on the destruction. It was now over two thousand miles long, travelling way above the crawl of light, about to enter eotemporality.

Looking down the main corridor running the length of the structure you could see dull red lurking at the far end of it. The Doppler effect was by now inbuilt. Aboard the *Beatitude*, the bows were travelling faster than the stern....

<< Much of the ship is now satisfactorily restored. The hardened hydrogen resembles glass. The renovated living quarters of the ship

shine with brilliance. The fretting makes it look like an Oriental palace.

<< In the great space on C Deck, four thousand troops parade every day. Their discipline is excellent in every way. Their marching order round the great extent of the Marchway is flawless. These men retain their fighting fitness. They are ready for any eventuality. >>

It paused here, then continued.

<< The automatic cleaners maintain the ship in sparkling order. The great side ports of the ship, stretching from Captain's Deck to D Deck, remain brilliant, constantly repolished on the exterior against scratches from microdust. It is a continual joy to see the orange blossom falling outside, falling through space, orange and white, with green leaves intertwined.

<< All hand-weapons have been well-maintained. Target practice takes place on the range every seventh day, with live ammunition. The silencing systems work perfectly. Our armoury-systems are held in operational readiness.

<< Also, the engines are working again at one hundred-plus percent. We computers control everything. The atmosphere is breathed over and over again. It could not be better. We enjoy our tasks.

<< Messing arrangements remain sound, with menus ever changing, as they had been over the first two hundred years of our journey. Men and women enjoy their food; their redesigned anatomies see to that. Athletics in the free-fall area ensure that they have good appetites. No one ever complains. All looked splendidly well. Those dying are later revived.

<< We are now proceeding at FTL 2.144. Many suffer hallucinations at this velocity. The *Beatitude* is constantly catching up with the retreating enemy galaxy. The weapons destined to overwhelm that enemy are kept primed and ready. If we pass within a thousand light-years of a sun, we routinely destroy it, whether or not it has planets. The sun's elements are then utilised for fuel. This arrangement has proved highly satisfactory.

<< In ten watches we shall be moving past system x377 at a proximate distance of 210 light-years. Particular caution needed. *Computer SJC1*>>

Ship's Captain Hungaman stood rigid, according to Military Morality, while he waited for his four upper echelon personnel to assemble before him. Crew Commander Mabel-Mo Hole was first, followed closely by Chief Technician Ida Precious. The thin figure of Provost-Marshall of Reps and Revs Dido Shappi entered alone. A minute later, Army Commander General Barakuta entered, to stand rigidly to attention before the ship's captain.

"Be easy, people," said Hungaman. As a rep served all parties a formal drink, he said, "We will discuss the latest summary of the month's progress from Space Journey Control One. You have all scanned the communication?"

The four nodded in agreement. Chief Technician Precious, clad tightly from neck to feet in dark green plastic, spoke. "You observe the power node now produces our maximum power yet, Captain? We progress toward the enemy at 2.144. More acceleration is needed."

Hungaman asked, "Latest estimate of when we come within destruction range of enemy galaxy?"

"Fifteen c's approximately. Possibly fourteen point six niner." She handed Hungaman a slip of paper. "Here is the relevant computation."

They stood silent, contemplating the prospect of fifteen more centuries of pursuit. Everything spoken was recorded by SJC2. The constant atmosphere control was like a whispered conversation overhead.

Provost-Marshall Shappi spoke. His resemblance to a rat was increased by his small bristling moustache. "Reps and revs numbers reduced again since last mensis, due to power node replacement."

"Figures?"

"Replicants, 799. Revenants, 625."

The figures were instantly rewired to sJc1 for counterchecking.

Hungaman eyed Crew Commander Hole. She responded instantly. "Sixteen deaths, para-osteoporosi-pneu. Fifteen undergoing revenant operations. One destroyed, as unfit for further re-tread treatment."

A nod from Hungaman, who turned his paranoid-type gaze on the member of the quartet who had yet to speak, General Barakuta. Barakuta's stiff figure stood like a memorial to himself.

"Morale continuing to decline," the General reported. "We require urgently more challenges for the men. We have no mountains or even hills on the *Beatitude*. I strongly suggest the ship again be enlarged to contain at least five fair-sized hills, in order that army operations be conducted with renewed energy."

Precious spoke. "Such a project would require an intake of 10^6 mettons new material aboard ship."

Barakuta answered. "There is this black hole 8875, only three thousand LY away. Dismantle that, bring constituent elements on board. No problem."

"I'll think about it," said Hungaman. "We have to meet the challenges of the centuries ahead."

"You are not pleased by my suggestion?" Barakuta again.

"Military Morality must always come first. Thank you."

They raised ceremonial flasks. All drank in one gulp.

The audience was ended.

Barakuta went away and consulted his private comp, unaligned with the ship's computers. He drew up some psycho-parameters on Ship's Captain Hungaman's state of mind. The parameters showed ego levels still in decline over several menses. Indications were that Hungaman would not initiate required intake of black hole material for construction of Barakuta's proposed five hills.

Something else would need to be done to energise the armies.

———

Once the audience was concluded, Hungaman took a walk to his private quarters to shower himself. As the walkway carried him down his private corridor, lights overhead preceded him like faithful hounds, to die behind him like extinguished civilizations. He clutched a slip of paper without even glancing at it. That had to wait until he was blush-dried and garbed in a clean robe.

In his relaxation room, Barnell, Hungaman's revenant servant, was busy doing the cleaning. Here was someone with whom he could be friendly and informal. He greeted the man with what warmth he could muster.

Barnell's skin was grey and mottled. In his pale face, his mouth hung loosely; yet his eyes burned as if lit by an internal fire. He was one of the twice-dead.

He said, "I see from your bunk you have slept well. That's good, my captain. Last night, I believe I had a dream. Revs are supposed not to dream, but I believe I dreamed that I was not dreaming. It is curious and unscientific. I like a thing to be scientific."

"We live scientific lives here, Barnell." Hungaman was not attending to the conversation. He was glancing at his standalone, on the screen of which floated the symbols *miqoesiy*. That was a puzzle he had yet to solve – together with many others.

With a sigh, he turned his attention back to the rev.

"Scientific? Yes, of course, my captain. But in this dream I was very uncomfortable because I dreamed I was not dreaming. There was nothing. Only me, hanging on a hook. How can you dream of nothing? it's funny, isn't it?"

"Yes, it's very funny," agreed Hungaman. Barnell told him the same story once a mensis. Memories of revs were notoriously short.

He patted Barnell's shoulder, feeling compassion for him, before returning down the private corridor to the great public compartment still referred to as "the bridge."

———

Hungaman turned his back to the nearest scanner and reread the words on the slip of paper Ida Precious had given him. His eye contact summoned whispered words: "The sJC1 is in malfunction mode. Why does its report say it is seeing orange blossom drifting in space? Why is no one else remarking on it? Urgent investigation needed."

He stared down at the slip. It trembled in his hand, a silver fish trying to escape back into its native ocean.

"Swim away!" He released his grasp on the fish. It swam across to the port, swam through it, swam away into space. Hungaman hurried to the port; it filled the curved wall. He looked out at the glorious orange blossom, falling slowly past, falling down forever, trying to figure out what was strange about it.

But those letters, *miqoesiy* – they might be numbers ... *q* might be 9, *y* might be 7. Suppose *e* was = ... Forget it. He was going mad.

He spread wide his arms to press the palms of his hands against the parency. It was warm to the touch. He glared out at the untouchable.

Among the orange blossom were little blue birds, flitting back and forth. He heard their chirruping, or thought he did. One of the birds flew out and through the impermeable parency. It fluttered about in the distant reaches of the control room. Its cry suggested it was saying, "Attend!" over and over.

"Attend! Attend! Attend!"

They were travelling in the direction of an undiscovered solar system, coded as x377. It was only 210 LYS distant. A main sequence sun was orbited by five planets, of which spectroscopic evidence indicated highpop life on two of its planets. Hungaman set obliteration time for when the next watch's game of Bullball was being played. Protesters had been active previously, demonstrating against the obliteration of suns and planets in the *Beatitude's* path. Despite the arrests then made, there remained a possibility that more trouble might break out: but not when Bullball championships were playing.

———

This watch, Fugitives were playing the champions of F League, Flying Flagellants. Before 27 and the start of play, Hungaman took his place in the Upper Echelon tier. He nodded remotely to other Uppers, otherwise keeping himself to himself. The dizziness was afflicting him again. General Barakuta was sitting only a few seats away, accompanied by an all-bronze woman, whether rep or real Hungaman could not tell at this distance.

The horn blew, the game started, although the general continued to pay more attention to his lady than to the field.

In F League, each side consisted of forty players. Numbers increased as leagues climbed towards J. Gravdims under the field enabled players to make astonishing leaps. They played with two large heavy balls. What made the game really exciting – what gave Bullball its popular name of Scoring 'n' Goring – was the presence of four wild bulls, which charged randomly round the field of play, attacking any player who got in their way. The great terrifying pitiable bulls, long of horn, destined never to evolve beyond their bovine fury.

Because of this element of danger, by which dying players were regularly dragged off the field, the participants comprised, in the main, revs and reps. Occasionally, however, livers took part. One such current hero of Bullball was fair-haired Surtees Slick, a brute of a man who had never as yet lost a life, who played half-naked for the FlyFlajs, spurning the customary body armour.

With a massive leap into the air, Slick had one of the balls now – the blue high-scorer – and was away down the field in gigantic hops. His mane of yellow hair fluttered behind his mighty shoulders. The crowd roared his name.

"Surtees... Surtees..."

Two Fugs were about to batter him in midair when Slick took a dip and legged it across the green plastic. A gigantic black bull known as Bronco charged at him. Without hesitation, Slick flung the heavy ball straight at the bull. The ball struck the animal full on the skull.

Crunch of impact echoed through the great arena (amplified admittedly by the mitters fixed between the brute's horns).

Scooping up the ball, which rebounded, Slick was away, leaping across the bull's back toward the distant enemy goal. He swiped away two Fug revs who flung themselves at him and plunged on. The goalkeeper was ahead, rushing out like a spider from its lair. Goalkeepers alone were allowed to be armed on the field. He drew his dazer and fired at the yellow-haired hero. But Slick knew the trick. That was what the crowd was shouting: "Slick knows the trick!" He dodged the stun and lobbed the great ball overarm. The ball flew shrieking toward the goal.

It vanished. The two teams, the Fugitives and the Flagellants, also vanished. The bulls vanished. The entire field became instantly empty.

The echo of the great roar died away.

"Surtees... Surtees... Sur..."

Then silence. Deep dead durable silence.

Nothing.

Only the eternal whispered conversation of air vents overhead.

Hungaman stood up in his astonishment. He could not comprehend what had happened. Looking about him, he found the vast company of onlookers motionless. By some uncanny feat of time, all were frozen; without movement they remained, not dead, not alive.

Only Hungaman was there, conscious, and isolated by his consciousness. His jaw hung open. Saliva dripped down his chin.

He was frightened. He felt the blood leave his face, felt tremors seize his entire frame.

Something had broken down. Was it reality or was it purely a glitch, a seizure of his perception?

Gathering his wits, he attempted to address the crew through his bodicom. The air was dead.

———

He made his way unsteadily from the Upper Echelon. He had reached the ground floor when he hear a voice calling hugely, "Hungaman! Hungaman!"

"Yes, I'm here."

He ran through the tunnel to the fringes of the playing field.

The air was filled with a strange whirring. A gigantic bird of prey was descending on him, its claws outstretched. Its aposematic wings were spread wide, as wide as the field itself. Looking up in shock, Hungaman saw how fanciful the wings were, fretted at the edges, iridescent, bright as a butterfly's wings and as gentle.

His emotions seemed themselves almost iridescent, as they faded from fear to joy. He lifted his arms to welcome the creature. It floated down slowly, shrinking as it came.

"A decently iridescent descent!" babbled Hungaman, he thought.

He felt his life changing, even as the bird changed, even as he perceived it was nothing but an old tattered man in a brightly coloured cloak. This tattered man looked flustered, as he well might have done. He brushed his lank hair from his eyes to reveal a little solemn brown face like a nut, in which were two deeply implanted blue eyes. The eyes seemed to have a glint of humour about them.

"No, I said that," he said, with a hint of chuckle. "Not you."

He put his hands on his hips and surveyed Hungaman, just as Hungaman surveyed him. The man was a perfect imitation of human – in all but conviction.

"Other life-forms, gone forever," he said. "Don't you feel bad about that? Guilty? You and this criminal ship? Isn't something lost forever – and little gained?"

Hungaman found his voice.

"Are you responsible for the clearing of the Bullball game?"

"Are you responsible for the destruction of an ancient culture, established on two planets for close on a million years?"

He did not say the word "years," but that was how Hungaman understood it. All he could manage by way of return was a kind of gurgle. "Two planets?"

"The Slipsoid system? They were 210 LYS distant from this ship – offering no threat to your passage. Our two planets were connected by quantaspace. It forms a bridge. You destructive people know nothing of quantaspace. You are tied to the material world. It is by quantaspace that I have arrived here." He threw off his cloak. It faded and was gone like an old leaf.

Hungaman tried to sneer. "Across 210 LYS?"

"We would have said ten metres."

Again, it was not the word "metres" he said, but that was how Hungaman understood it.

"The cultures of our two Slipsoid planets were like the two hemispheres of your brain, I perceive, thinking in harmony but differently. Much like yours, as I suppose, but on a magnificently grander scale....

"Believe me, the human brain is, universally speaking, as obsolete as silicon-based semiconductors..."

"So...you...came...here..."

"Hungaman, there is nothing but thinking makes it so. The solid universe in which you believe you live is generated by your perceptions. That is why you are so troubled. You see through the perception, yet you refuse to see through the deception."

Hungaman was recovering from his astonishment. Although disconcerted at the sudden appearance of this pretence of humanity, he was reassured by a low rumbling throughout the ship: particles from the destroyed worlds were being loaded on board, into the cavernous holds.

"I am not troubled. I am in command here. I ordered the extinction of your Slipsoid system, and we have extinguished it, have we not? Leave me alone."

"But you are troubled. What about the orange blossom and the little blue bird? Are they a part of your reality?"

"I don't know what you mean. What orange blossom?"

"There is some hope for you. Spiritually, I mean. Because you are troubled."

"I'm not troubled." He squared his shoulders to show he meant what he said.

"You have just destroyed a myriad lives and yet you are not troubled?" Inhuman contempt sounded. "Not a little bit?"

Hungaman clicked his fingers and began to walk back the way he had come. "Let's discuss these matters, shall we? I am always prepared to listen."

The little man followed meekly into the tunnel. At a certain point, Hungaman moved fast and pressed a button in the tiled wall. Metal bars came flashing down. The little man found himself trapped in a cage. It was the way Barakuta's police dealt with troublemakers on the Bullball ground.

"Excellent," said Hungaman, turning to face the intruder. "Now, I want no more conjuring tricks from you. Tell me your name first of all."

Meekly, the little man said, "You can call me Manifold."

Manifold was standing behind a leather-bound armchair in a black gown. Hungaman was on the other side of a desk, the top of which held nothing but an inset screen. He found he was sitting down on a hard chair. A ginger-and-white cat jumped onto his lap. How the scene had changed so suddenly was beyond his comprehension.

"But – but how – "

The little man ignored Hungaman's stutter.

"Are you happy aboard your ship?" Manifold asked.

Hungaman answered up frankly and easily, to his own surprise: it was as if he was glad to find that metal bars were of no account. "I am not entirely happy with the personnel. Let me give you an example. You realize, of course, that we have been making this journey for some centuries. It would be impossible, of course, without AL – aided longevity. Nevertheless, it has been a long while. The enemy galaxy is retreating through the expanding universe. The ship is deteriorating rapidly. At our velocities, it is subject to strain. It has constantly to be rebuilt. Fortunately, we have invented xhx, hardened hydrogen, with which to refurbish our interiors. The hull is wearing thin. I think that accounts for the blue bird which got in."

As he spoke he was absentmindedly stroking the cat. The cat lay still but did not purr.

"I was consulting with Provost-Marshall Shappi about which revs and reps to use in this Bullball match, which I take it you interrupted, when a rating entered my office unannounced. I ordered him to wait in the passage. 'Ah,' he said, 'the passage of time.' It was impertinent to answer back like that. It would not have happened a decade ago."

The little man leaned forward, resting his elbows on his thighs and clasping his hands together. Smiling, he said, "You're an uneasy man, I can see. Not a happy man. The cat does not purr for you. This voyage is just a misery to you."

"Listen to me," said Hungaman, leaning forward, unconsciously copying the older man's attitude. "You may be the figment of a great civilization, now happily defunct, but what you have to say about me means nothing."

He went on to inform his antagonist that even now tractor beams were hauling stuff into one of the insulated holds, raw hot stuff at a few thousand degrees, mesons, protons, corpuscles, wave particles – a great trail of material smaller than dust, all of which the *Beatitude* would use for fuel or building material. And those whirling particles were all that was left of Manifold's million-year-old civilization.

"So much for your million-year-old civilization. Time it was scrapped."

"You're proud of this?" shrieked Manifold.

"In our wake, we have destroyed a hundred so-called civilizations. They died, those civilizations, to power our passage, to drive us ever onward. We shall not be defeated. No, I don't regret a damned thing. We are what humanity is made of." Oratory had hold of him. "This very ship, this worldlet, is – what was that term in use in the old

Christian Era? – yes, it's a *cathedral* to the human spirit. We are still young, but we are going to succeed, and the less opposition to us there is, the better."

His violent gesture disturbed the cat, which sprang from his lap and disappeared. Its image remained suspended in midair, growing fainter until it was gone.

"Mankind is as big as the universe. Sure, I'm not too happy with the way things are aboard this ship, but I don't give a tinker's cuss for anything outside our hull."

He gave an illustrative glance through the port as he spoke. Strangely, the Bullball game was continuing. A gored body was being elevated from the trampled field, trailing blood. The crowd loved it.

"As for your Slipsoid powers – what do I care for them? I can have you disintegrated any minute I feel like it. That's the plain truth. Do you have the power to read my mind?"

"You don't have that kind of mind. You're an alien life-form. It's a blank piece of paper to me."

"If you could read it, you would see how I feel about you. Now. What are you going to do?"

For response, the little man began to disintegrate, shedding his pretense of humanity. As soon as the transformation began, Hungaman pressed a stud under the flange of the desk. It would summon General Barakuta with firepower.

Manifold almost instantaneously ceased to exist. In his place a mouth, a tunnel, formed, from which poured – well, maybe it was a tunnel mouth for this strange concept, *quantaspace* – from which poured, *poured* – Hungaman could not grasp it ... poured what? – solid music? ... wave particles? ... pellets of zero substance? ... Whatever the invasive phenomenon was, it was filling up the compartment, burying Hungaman, terrified and struggling, and bursting on, on, into the rest of the giant vessel, choking its arteries, rushing like poison through a vein. Alarms were sounding, fire doors closing, conflagration crews running. And people screaming – screaming in sheer disgusted horror at this terrible irresistible unknown overcoming them. Nothing stopped it, nothing impeded it.

Within a hundred heartbeats, the entire speeding *Beatitude* worldlet was filled completely with the consuming dust. Blackness. Brownness. Repletion. Nonexistence.

Hungaman sat at his desk in his comfortable office. From his windows – such was his status, his office had two windows – he looked out on the neat artificial lawns of academia, surrounded by tall everlasting trees. He had become accustomed to the feeling of being alive.

He was talking to his brainfinger, a medium-sized rep covered in a fuzzy golden fur, through which two large doggy eyes peered sympathetically at his patient.

Hungaman was totally relaxed as he talked. He had his feet up on the desk, his hands behind his neck, fingers locked together: the picture of a man at his ease, perfect if old-fashioned. He knew all about reps.

"My researches were getting nowhere. Maybe I was on the verge of an NB – you know, a nervous breakdown. Who cares? That's maybe why I imagined I saw the orange blossom falling by the ports. On reflection, they were not oranges but planets."

"You are now saying it was not blossom but the actual fruits, the oranges?" asked the brainfinger.

"They were what I say they were. The oranges were bursting – exploding. They weren't oranges so much as worlds, whole planets, dropping down into oblivion, maybe meeting themselves coming up." He laughed. "The universe as orchard. I was excited because I knew that for once I had seen through reality. I remembered what that old Greek man, Socrates, had said, that once we were cured of reality we could ourselves become real. It's a way of saying that life is a lie."

"You know it is absurd to say that, darling. Only a madman would claim that there is something unreal about reality. Nobody would believe such sophistry."

"Yes, but remember – the majority is always wrong!"

"Who said that?"

"Tom Lehrer? Adolf Hitler? Mark Twain? Einstein McBeil? Socrates?"

"You've got Socrates on the brain, Hungaman, darling. Forget Socrates! We live in a well-organised military society, where such slogans as 'The majority is always wrong' are branded subversive. If I reported you, all this – " he gestured about him " – would disappear."

"But I have always felt I understood reality-perception better than other people. As you know, I studied it for almost a century, got a degree in it. Even the most solid objects, chairs, walls, rooms, lives – they are merely outward forms. It is a disconcerting concept, but behind it lie truth and beauty.

"That is what faster-than-light means, incidentally. It has nothing to do with that other old Greek philosopher, Einstein: it's to do with people seeing through appearances. We nowadays interpret speeding simply as an invariant of stationary, with acceleration as a moderator. You just need a captain with vision.

"I was getting nowhere until I realised that an oil painting of my father, for instance, was not really an oil painting of my father but just a piece of stretched canvas with a veneer of variously coloured oils. Father himself – again, problematic. I was born unilaterally."

The brainfinger asked, "Is that why you have become, at least in your imagination, the father of the crew of the *Beatitude?*"

Hungaman removed his feet from the desk and sat up rigidly. "The crew have disappeared. You imagine I'm happy about that? No, it's a pain, a real pain."

The brainfinger began to look extra fuzzy.

"Your hypothesis does not allow of pain being real. Or else you are talking nonsense. For the captain of a great weapon-vessel such as the *Beatitude* you are emotionally unstable."

Hungaman leaned forward and pointed a finger, with indications of shrewdness, and a conceivable pun, at the brainfinger.

"Are you ordering me to return to Earth, to call off our entire mission, to let the enemy galaxy get away? Are you trying to relieve me of my command?"

The brainfinger said, comfortingly, "You realise that at the extra-normal velocities at which you are travelling, you have basically quit the quote real world unquote, and hallucinations are the natural result. We brainfingers have a label for it: TPD, tachyon perception displacement. Ordinary human senses are not equipped for such transcendental speeds, is all..."

Hungaman thought before speaking. "There's always this problem with experience. It does not entirely coincide with consciousness. Of course you are right about extra-normal velocities and hallucination.... Would you say wordplay is a mark of madness – or near-madness?"

"Why ask me that?"

"I have to speak to my clonther shortly. I need to check something with him. His name's Twohunga. I'm fond of him, but since he has been in Heliopause HQ, his diction has become strange. It makes me nervous."

The brainfinger emitted something like a sigh. He felt that Hungaman had changed the subject for hidden motives.

He spoke gently, almost on tiptoe. "I shall leave you alone to conquer your insecurity. Bad consciences are always troublesome. Get back on the bridge. Good evening. I will see you again tomorrow. Have a nice night." It rose and walked toward the door, narrowly missed, readjusted, and disappeared.

"*Bad conscience!* What an idiot!" Hungaman said to himself. "I'm afraid of something, that's the trouble. And I can't figure out what I'm afraid of." He laughed. He twiddled his thumbs at great speed.

The *Beatitude* had attained a velocity at which it broke free from spacial dimensions. It was now travelling through a realm of latent temporalities. Computer SJC1 alone could scan spacial derivatives, as the ship-projectile it governed headed after the enemy galaxy. The

Beatitude had to contend with racing tachyons and other particles of frantic mobility. The tachyons were distinct from light. Light did not enter the region of latent temporalities. Here were only eotemporal processes, the beginnings and endings of which could not be distinguished one from another.

The sJc1 maintained ship velocities, irrespective of the eotemporal world outside, or the sufferings of the biotemporal world within.

Later, after a snort, Hungaman went to the top of the academy building and peered though the telescope. There in the cloudless sky, hanging to the northwest, was the hated enigmatic word – if indeed it was a word – *hiseobiw...hiseobiw*, smudgily written in space fires. Perhaps it was a formula of some kind. Read upside down, it spelt *miqoesiy*. This dirty mark in space had puzzled and infuriated military intelligentsia for centuries. Hungaman was still working on the problem, on and off.

This was what the enemy galaxy had created, why it had become the enemy. How had it managed this bizarre stellar inscription? And why? Was *miqoesiy* aimed at the Solar system? What did it spell? What could it mean? Was it intended to help or to deter? Was it a message from some dyslexic galactic god? Or was it, as a joker had suggested, a commercial for a pair of socks?

No one had yet determined the nature of this affront to cosmology. It was for this reason that, long ago, the *Beatitude* had been launched to chastise the enemy galaxy and, if possible, decipher the meaning of *hiseobiw* or *miqoesiy*.

A clenched human fist was raised from the roof of the academic building to the damned thing. Then its owner went inside again.

Hungaman spoke into his voxputer. "Beauty of mental illness. Entanglements of words and appearances, a maze through which we try to swim. I believe I'm getting through to the meaning of this enigmatic sign....

"Yep, that does frighten me. Like being on a foreign planet. A journey into the astounded Self, where truth lies and lies are truth. Thank god the hull of our spacevessel is not impermeable. It represents the ego, the eggnog. These bluebirds are messengers, bringing in hope from the world outside. TPD – must remember that!"

Hungaman, as he had told the brainfinger to little effect, had a clonther, a clone-brother by the name of Twohunga. Twohunga had done well, ascending the military ranks, until – as Steel-Major Twohunga – he was appointed to the www, the World Weaponry Watch on Charon, co-planet of Pluto.

So Hungaman put through a call to the Heliopause HQ.

"Steel-Major here...haven't heard from you for thirty-two years, Hungaman. Yes, mmm, thirty-two. Maybe only thirty-one. How's your promotion?"

"The same. You still living with that Plutottie?"

"I disposed of her." The face in the globe was dark and stormy, the plastic mitter banded across its forehead. "I have a rep – a woman-droid – for my satisfactions now. What you might call satisfactions. Where are you, precisely? Still on the *Beatitude,* I guess? Not that that's precise in any way..." He spoke jerkily and remotely, as if his voice had been prerecorded by a machine afflicted by hiccups.

"I'm none too sure. Or if I am sure, I am dead. Maybe I am a rev," said Hungaman, without giving his answer a great deal of thought. "It seems I am having an episode. It's to do with the extreme velocity, a velocillusion... We're traversing the eotemporal, you know." He clutched his head as he spoke, while a part of him said tauntingly to himself, You're hamming it up....

"Brainfinger. Speak to a brainfinger, Hungaman," Twohunga advised.

"I did. They are no help."

"They never are. Never."

"It may have been part of my episode. Listen, Twohunga, Heliopause HQ still maintains contact with the *Beatitude.* Can you tell me if the ship is still on course, or has it been subjugated by life-forms from the Slipsoid system which have invaded the ship?"

"System? What system? The Slipsoid system?"

"Yes. x377. We disintegrated it for fuel as we passed."

"So you did. Mm, so you did. So you did, indeed. Yes, you surely disintegrated it."

"Will you stop talking like that!"

Twohunga stood up, to walk back and forth, three paces one way, swivel on heel, three paces the other way, swivel on heel, in imitation of a man with an important announcement in mind.

He said, "I know you keep ship's time on the *Beatitude,* as if the ship has a time amid eotemporality, but here in Sol system we are coming up for Year One Million, think of it, with all the attendant celebrations. Yep, Year One Million, count them. Got to celebrate. We're planning to nuclearize Neptune, nuclearize it, to let a little light into the circumference of the system. Things have changed. One Million... Yes, things have changed. They certainly have. They certainly *are...*"

"I asked you if we on shipboard have been subjugated by the aliens."

"Well, that's where you are wrong, you see. The wrong question. Entirely up the spout. Technology has improved out of all recognition since your launch date. All recognition... Look at this."

The globe exploded into a family of lines, some running straight, some slightly crooked, just like a human family. As they went, they spawned mathematical symbols, not all of them familiar to Hungaman. They originated at one point in the bowl and ricochetted to another.

Twohunga said, voice-over, "We used to call them 'black holes,' remember? That was before we domesticated them. Black holes, huh! They are densers now. *Densers,* okay? We can propel them through hyperspace. They go like spit on a hot stove. Propelled. They serve as weaponry, these densers, okay? Within about the next decade, the next decade, we shall be able to hurl them at the enemy galaxy and destroy it. Destroy the whole thing..." He gave something that passed for a chuckle. "Then we shall see about their confounded *hiseobiw*, or whatever it is."

Hungaman was horrified. He saw at once that this technological advance, with densers used as weapons, rendered the extended voyage of the *Beatitude* obsolete. Long before the ship could reach the enemy galaxy – always supposing that command of the ship was regained from the Slipsoid invader – the densers would have destroyed their target.

"This is very bad news," he said, almost to himself. "Very bad news indeed."

"Bad news? Bad news? Not for humanity," said Twohunga sharply. "Oh no! We shall do away with this curse in the sky for good and all."

"It's all very well for you to say that, safe at Heliopause HQ. What about those of us on the *Beatitude* – if any of us are there anymore...?"

Twohunga began to pace again, this time taking four paces to the left, swivel on heel, four paces to the right, swivel on heel.

He explained, not without a certain malice, that it was not technology alone which had advanced. Ethics had also taken a step forward. Quite a large step, he said. He emitted a yelp of laughter. A considerably large step. He paused, looking over his shoulder at his clonther far away. It was now considered, he stated, not at all correct to destroy an entire cultured planet without any questions asked.

In fact, to be honest, and frankness undoubtedly was the best policy, destroying any planet on which there was sentient life was now ruled to be a criminal act. Such as destroying the ancient Slipsoid dual-planet culture, for instance....

As Captain of the *Beatitude,* therefore, Hungaman was a wanted criminal and, if he were caught, would be up for trial before the TDC, the Transplanetary Destruction Crimes tribunal.

"What nonsense is this you are telling – " Hungaman began.

"Nonsense you may call it, but that's the law. No nonsense, no! Oh no. Cold fact! Culture destruction, criminal act. It's you, Hungaman, you!"

In a chill voice, Hungaman asked, "And what of Military Morality?"

"What of Military – 'What of Military Morality?' he asks. Military Morality?! It's a thing of the past, the long long past! Pah! A criminal creed, *criminal*... We're living in a new – In fact, I should not be talking to a known genocidal maniac at all, no, not a word, in case it makes me an accessory after the fact."

He broke the connection.

Hungaman fell to the floor and chewed the leg of his chair.

It was tough but not unpalatable.

"It's bound to be good for him," said a voice.

"They were an omnivorous species," said a second voice in agreement – though not speaking in speech exactly.

Seeing was difficult. Although it was light, the light was of an uncomfortable wavelength. Hungaman seemed to be lying down, with his torso propped up, enabling him to eat.

Whatever it was he was eating, it gave him strength. Now he could see, although what he could see was hard to make out. By what he took to be his bedside two rubbery cylinders were standing, or perhaps floating. He was in a room with no corners or windows. The illumination came from a globular object which drifted about the room, although the light it projected remained steady.

"Where am I?" he asked.

The two cylinders wobbled and parts of them changed colour. "There you are, you see. Typical question, 'Where am I?' Always the emphasis on the Self. I, I, I. Very typical of a human species. Probably to be blamed on the way in which they reproduce. It's a bisexual species, you know."

"Yes, I know. Fatherhood, motherhood... I shall never understand it. Reproduction by fission is so much more efficient – the key to immortality indeed."

They exchanged warm colours.

"Quite. And the intense pleasure, the joy, of fission itself..."

"Look, you two, would you mind telling me where I am. I have other questions I can ask, but that one first." He felt the nutrients flowing through his body, altering his constitution.

"You're on the *Beatitude*, of course."

Despite his anxiety, he found he was enjoying their colour changes. The colours were so various. After a while he discovered he was *listening to the colours*. It must, he thought, be the something he ate.

Over the days that followed, Hungaman came slowly to understand his situation. The aliens answered his questions readily enough, although he realised there was one question in his mind he was unable to ask or even locate.

They escorted him about the ship. He was becoming more cylindrical, although he had yet to learn to float. The ship was empty with one exception: a Bullball game was in progress. He stood amazed to see the players still running, the big black bulls still charging among them. To his astonishment, he saw Surtees Slick again, running like fury with the heavy blue ball, his yellow hair flowing.

The view was less clear than it had been. Hungaman fastened his attention on the bulls. With their head-down shortsighted stupidity, they rushed at individual players as if, flustered by their erratic movements, the bulls believed a death, a stillness, would resolve some vast mystery of life they could never formulate.

Astonished, Hungaman turned to his companions.

"It's for you," they said, colouring in a smile. "Don't worry, it's not real, just a simulation. That sort of thing is over and done with now, as obsolete as a silicon-based semiconductor."

"To be honest, I'm not sure yet if *you* are real and not simulations. You are Slipsoids, aren't you? I imagined we had destroyed you. Or did I only imagine I imagined we had destroyed you?"

But no. After their mitochondria had filled the ship, they assured him, they were able to reestablish themselves, since their material was contained aboard the *Beatitude*. They had cannibalised the living human protoplasm, sparing only Hungaman, the captain.

It was then a comparatively simple matter to redesign quantaspace and rebuild their sun and the two linked planets. They had long ago mastered all that technology had to offer. And so here they were, and all was right with the world, they said, in flickering tones of purple and a kind of mauve.

"But we are preserving you on the ship," they said.

He asked a new variant of his old question. "And where exactly are we and the *Beatitude* now?"

"Velocity killed. Out of the eotemporal."

They told him, in their colours, that the great ship was in orbit about the twin planets of Slipsoid, "forming a new satellite."

He was silent for a long while, digesting this information, glad but sorry, sorry but glad. Finally, he said – and now he was rapidly learning to talk in colour – "I have suffered much. My brain has been under great pressure. But I have also learned much. I thank you for your help, and for preserving me. Since I cannot return to Earth, I hope to be of service to you."

Their dazzling bursts of colour told Hungaman they were gazing affectionately at him. They said there was one question they longed to ask him, regarding a matter which had worried them for many centuries.

"What's the question? You know I will help if I can."

There was some hesitation before they coloured their question.

"What is the meaning of this *hiseobiw* we see in our night sky?"

"Oh, yes, that! Let me explain," said Hungaman.

He explained that the so-called letters of *hiseobiw*, or preferably *miqoesiy*, were not letters but symbols of an arcane mathematics. It was an equation, more clearly written – for the space fires had drifted – as

$$M\pi 7\omega \varepsilon \ [\ = \ ] \ X!_9.$$

They coloured, "Meaning?"

"We'll have to work it out between us," Hungaman coloured back. "But I'm pretty sure it contains a formula that will clear brains of phylogenetically archaic functions. Thereby, it will, when applied, change all life in the universe."

"Then maybe we should leave it alone."

"No," he said. "We must solve it. That's human nature."

The Man and a Man with His Mule

MY TRAIN WAS CARRYING ME away from the ruins of Arroyo Alegro towards the West and civilization. The ruins had bored me; now I was eager to immerse myself in the novel I was reading, the classic Mexican novel *El Señor de la Costumbrista,* published in the early years of the twentieth century. I had reached Chapter Five, and the passage where the heroine, Christina, standing clutching the hand of her adopted daughter, Hira, is confronting General Lopez in the deserted cattle station.

Opposite me in the railway carriage sat a bearded man of worn, stern countenance. He had an arm about the shoulders of a younger, rather stupid-looking woman, who writhed occasionally under the confinement of the other's naked arm. It seemed they were related. I took no notice of them beyond a cursory glance.

Unexpectedly, the man leaned forward and tapped me on my left knee.

"I suffer what it is humiliation to travel by this Hard Class," he said in a grating voice.

I told him stiffly that I had not noticed. But the exchange was not concluded.

"Once I travel always in First Class, in greatest luxury. Now see what is befallen me to be here."

Saying nothing, I reflected that the man should have been grateful for his earlier good fortune. As I turned again to my novel the man said, "Okay, so I see you have no pity. You are one of the hard-heart men."

By agreeing, as I immediately did, I hoped the fellow would fall silent. Instead, he seemed to take my words as a challenge. "My name is Vlasco Ibanez," he told me, staring at my face. "My family suffer more than their fair share of misfortune. When I am only a boy, my father falls by accident from a bridge and is kill quite dead. So I must to go immediately to work. I have no more than four years in age. Work it is heavy."

While I reflected that such things must always happen now to those who can master only the present tense, his talk flowed on.

"My mother is make insane by the disaster. Her sister also is mad many years. Both have the eye problems. When aged, she studies pataphysics. It's a sickness caused. My uncle also is crazy and short-sighted. He break his spectacle and never can he swim."

Interupting Ibanez, I said, with more indignation than I had intended, "I cannot swim either."

To which he replied coldly, drawing himself up, "Some people do these things deliberately."

At this juncture, the woman by his side, who had not spoken or shown any sign of listening, decided to take part in the conversation.

Her milky eyes indicated she was blind.

Waving her hand for emphasis, as if conducting a symphony, she said in a shrill voice, "This person to whom I sit next is my adopted guardian, Sr. Ibanez – a good man but often cruel. He is not educate like me. His history is strange. You should hear it. For years he worked without wages on a coffee plantation. That is a place where coffee is planted. Hence the name 'plantation,' as you might for instance say 'tea plantation,' a place where tea is planted, but Sr. Ibanez never worked on one of that kind. Do I make it clear?"

As her blind eyes stared at me, Ibanez said, angrily, "Let me tell this fool this story." As he spoke, he slapped the woman on the face. He called her Hora the Whore.

She hit him back. I stared out of the window at the passing scenery which, frankly, was not interesting. I shall not bother to describe it.

"By age of fifteen," Ibanez said, when the fight was over, "I reach puberty and desperation. They will not have me in the ranch house. The porridge is made with water. The beans of coffee are not selling more. Mr. Charles Bush, the estate-owner, he is anxious. Things are now become so bad I must to pay them to work there.

"Then comes the miracle. One day I see a very fine film which is showing to us. It is an allegory – "

The woman butted in to explain to me what an allegory was. "It is like a story that means one thing but not another. Say for an instance I say I am falling down a well, it can be just an image and what is not real is more important than – "

He smacked her across the mouth and continued with his tale. "This film she is call *Tarzan of the Apes*. A brilliant film. By working among apes in the jungle, this man Tarzan, he discover he is really a distant lord. He stay naked.

"From this time, I invent the famous 'A Man with His Mule.' I take it to Mr. Charles Bush. He cease to drink and is in delight with my idea. Oh yes, you may sneer, but what a success am I with 'A Man with His Mule'!"

The train was going slowly now. I thought of throwing myself out of the window, though not, perhaps, before I had finished Chapter Five and found what happened between Christina and General Lopez.

Unfortunately, I could not resist asking Ibanez what exactly this "A Man with His Mule" was. Ibanez told me at length.

He had never invented anything before, he said, until the day it came to him that the sale of packaged coffee beans was impersonal.

It was like remaining in Tarzan's jungle. How could there be personal contact between grower and customer, perhaps hundreds of miles distant? The answer was to have a short letter from a grower himself to the coffee-drinkers.

"I invent a man who is been German but now he share our nationality. His mule I call him August, and the man himself I call him Sancho Panzer. It is a genius stroke." Ibanez struck his forehead to show where the genius was kept.

"Sancho he say in his short letter such like, 'Dear Faraway Coffee Drinker, I am your friend and I long to see you drink and enjoy my coffee. But I must work here on the plantation with my mule August. It is a lonely life but we enjoy hard work. You must come and see to me by yourself one day. The mule is well, as I hope you are. Your firm friend, Sancho Panzer.'

"Each little letter went into each bag of coffee. That is the start for my brillant success. Meanwhile, my demented relations they grow more bad."

He shot an angry look at his adopted daughter as he spoke.

"Soon, what I never expect – the little letters of Sancho Panzer they have answer. Coffee drinkers everywhere, they fall in love with this clever nice man who loves them. So Sancho has to tell more about this place – which of course I make up to be nice – and also of his mule August – how many hands high he is and such details. If Sancho Panzer has a wife, they ask. So I make up a wife Carmen who is a mad thing and bitch. More letters are coming in with great sympathy for this poor man. I tell you my tears spring forth when I write his letters for him."

He paused to see if tears would spring forth on this occasion. Instead, he allowed his expression of perennial gloom to fade somewhat as he said, "How the sales of the coffee grow upward! Now I have fame. Well, some fame, because the distant coffee friends do not realise that Sancho Panzer is not real man. But then one day is coming a phone call from people in the city who are rulers of television. This is after the revolution. I am so please. Here something is I do not expect.

"The television people wish to make a series of the man Sancho Panzer and the mule August. A kind of comedy, they say. I tell he does not exist ever. They say they will find among actors both of these people, also Carmen, the mad wife. I must write what they call the scripts."

Ibanez looked down at his hands which dangled between his knees. In a reflective tone, he said, "Once, I am rich to have a shirt to my backside. I even hire a blackman-servant to wash the shirt. This boy, he does a lot what he calls 'strokin' de black mamba,' but he is otherwise useful to me."

Listening, I realised my finger had gone dead. I had stuck it into my novel to mark the beginning of Chapter Five of *El Señor de la Costumbrista*.

Sucking my finger, I say as best I can, "Well, what good fortune for you. Congratulations! Now I must get on with my book."

As I bent my head to it, Ibanez shouted in a loud voice, "At that very day of success, when I give party and boast so much, my insane mother-in-law, Monika, she jump from her bedroom window. The panes of glass are shatter. The zinnias below are crush. But Monika has only a broken leg. I am furious. I go to her bed in the hospital and I hit her. Because now it is in the news that the great celebrity Vlasco Ibanez, triumphant author and inventer of 'A Man with His Mule,' is of a relation with a mad woman who throws herself always from windows.

"I kick out the blackman-servant with his mamba. I am broken man. I take this silly blind woman here and go to live in a drain pipe. Many people say I am mad. The friends, they hurl the stones."

The train stopped with such a sudden jerk that I was thrown forward, my face burying itself in Hora's lap.

"Raise yourself at once!" called Ibanez. "You pig dog!"

"Let him be!" shrieked Hora

"She's mine!" shouted Ibanez.

As they began a quarrel, I jumped out of the train.

We had stopped at a small wayside halt called Erasmoso. I bought an ice cream and stuck my nose into Chapter Five of *El Señor de la Costumbrista*. Although I stood at the end of the platform, a whining voice soon told me I had been discovered by Hora. She seized my arm, declaring she would always be true.

I perceived that she was in love with me.

"This was a brief love affair, already over," I told her.

"I know my way around, mister."

"What? Although you are blind?"

"I am not virgin, mister. Sex is not of the eyes only."

"Sorry, I am trying to read."

"Why you don't have sex?"

"Because I edit a small literary magazine, *The New Impostor*," I explained. "I don't suppose you people have ever seen an issue."

"I read every issue. Is my favourite."

"Rubbish! You're lying. You're blind."

Again I turned to that tempting Chapter Five, eager to see what the General Lopez would say to poor Christina in that desolate room.

Ibanez came up. Seeing the girl so close to me, he said, grabbing my bicep, "I give her to you. One hundred dollar only!"

"I don't want her."

"Fifty dollar, then."

"I told you, I don't want her."

"She good girl. She virgin. Thirty-five and she yours."

I pointed to a printed notice on the side of the shelter. It read in rather contorted language, THE HABIT OF SOLDING PEOPLE ON THIS PLATFORM IS TO BE PROSECUTED.

"It was before the Revolution," Ibanez explained. "Now we are all capitalists. Thirty dollars."

At that moment, the train began slowly to pull out of the platform.

Ibanez screamed. "Run! Or we spend our lives all in Erasmoso!"

Plainly, he exaggerated: yet I ran. We piled together into the last carriage, gasping.

Really at that moment I had lost patience with the entire country. Indeed, I had nearly lost my novel.

"Why did the train not even toot?" I asked furiously.

"I know well the driver. He is bastard."

We lapsed into silence, breathing heavily. For five minutes I enjoyed the peace. Then the woman, Hora, said, "So, once more, eternally and for ever-lasting and all the future of this bad world, the train carries me into more misery and humiliation and my wretched life of a dog."

"I'm sorry to hear it, Hora."

"No, you are not, or you would not go to a hotel where capitalists live."

"Are you disappointed that I would not marry you?"

"Maybe yes, maybe no. Who can tell? But I do not like you. Rather, I hate you, maybe. And also I hate your lousy language."

"Always she complains," said Ibanez. "Is no gratitude. A bad woman, probably crazy. Is why I hit her. My suffering is much greater. My father he fall from the bridge and get kill because he drink. He should not be at all on the bridge. My mother go insane by this disaster but she already is much unstable in her mind, like her crazy sister. My uncle is much a dope fiend. He is born missing a tooth. That's why he can not swim although he has the job as swimming instructor. All have the eye problems and whole family is crazy like my grandmother."

At last we arrived in the city. I at once took a taxi to the Hilton Hotel. In my comfortable suite I enjoyed a shower, washing away the idiot company of Sr. Vlasco Ibanez and his unattractive charge, Hora. Downstairs, I sat in the comfortable lounge, ordered a waiter to bring me a glass of Chardonnay, and settled down to read Chapter Five of *El Señor de la Costumbrista*.

It was fascinating. General Lopez holstered his revolver. He revealed to the fair Christina that he came from a mad family. His father had died when he was young, his mother became crazed by grief and never spoke again. Both his aunt and uncle were on drugs. There was also a form of inherited blindness in the family. He had been forced to join the military in order to support his unfortunate relations.

As the general confessed, tears ran down his bronzed cheeks. Christina, listening, also shed tears, her adopted daughter likewise. It was all most affecting to read. One could empathise with their sorrow, conveyed in faultless prose. The general fell against a counter, weeping uncontrollably. Christina put an arm about his shoulders. I could tell she would fall in love with him in Chapter Six.

It is well there is a distance between life and art.

Dusk Flight

ONLY THIS WEEK, I read in the newspapers the obituary of the re-markable writer Clementine Bigsohn, known to her friends as Clara. I fear I had lost touch with her some years ago. She was always elusive.

The obituarist was brief and chilly in his comments, saying that Clara in her writings "opted for obscurity." She had no choice. There was something obscurantist in her nature, by which she designed to shield herself from the horrors of her childhood. Her great book, *Dusk Flight,* sums up in its very title something of the early miseries from which she sought escape.

All her books are difficult to classify. There is the slight *Smoke in the Spinneys,* long out of print. *Dusk Flight* is the great book which eludes classification.. When I met Clara, she was still writing *Dusk Flight* – writing and rewriting – composing page after page, only to erase them one by one, later to resurrect them in different form. She still wrote the old-fashioned way, with a cartridge pen in an A5 note-book. The tiny black ink lettering, interspersed with sketches, spread decoratively across the page. She wrote in English, having left her Russian origins behind – or as far behind as she was able.

Yet there was something Russian about her passion for the English tanner beetle. For something like twenty years, Clara pursued this species of beetle in all its various forms. She refers to it once as "a parenthetical detail in the encompassing biomass." This phrase was mocked as pretentious by more than one critic; yet on the new edition of *Dusk Flight* the phrase is emblazoned on the dust jacket.

The tanner, a member of the *Cerambycidae*, is an increasingly rare British beetle. In its adult form, it is quite a large insect, confined in the main to Cheshire and Flintshire, where there remain extensive ancient parkland and woodland. The beetles live in rotting timber. In general, they make their flights as dusk descends.

Clara describes her beetle as "dignified," and of a "distinguished taxonomy," with its dark-greenish wing case and long saw-toothed antennae. Clara writes always as someone enjoying her newfound liberty in the riches of the English language; she speaks of her mighty volume as "the marmoset's pursuit of an immemorial morsel." In her discursive account, itself like one of the thickets she haunted, we submerge ourselves in the historic woodlands, encountering deer, squirrel, hare, and other animals, as well as the assorted human refugees from regulated civilization who eke out an existence within its glades.

It required an author, not to tell tales, but to listen to tales muttered by these fallen Robin Hoods when, late into the night, in drink-sodden eloquence, they recounted their bizarre and sorrowing falls from society.

Much of *Dusk Flight* is filled with fantastic life stories. "I made the histories up when they were not fantastic enough to satisfy me," Clara told me once, when we were bivouacking in a wood near Malpas.

She let her hair grow long and ragged. Her clothes were black and formless; she might look strange to the outside world, but in these surroundings, she was no less than its resident spirit. Her face was long and stern. There was little of the female about her. Only her eyes were beautiful; I remember them as a light grey. Her book is filled with the dusky light of forest life, that intense secret microcosm, full of uncertainties and whispers. Her hand-drawn maps included in *Dusk Flight* are intended as much to mislead as lead. Day by day, week by week, she travelled through the elderly woodlands, following the trail of her beckoning beetle.

At one point, she made off in the middle of our evening meal – dropping the turkey bone she was gnawing – to pursue a tanner beetle in its wheeling flight from tree to tree.

"Why?" I asked. "Why?"

She said that "Why" was the world's most sensible word. There was no answer to it because it was itself an answer in response to the world and all that the world held in its complexity. This mysticism and obscurity lies at the profound heart of *Dusk Flight*. The book it most resembles is Melville's *Moby-Dick*, with the pursuit of a small beetle as momentous as the pursuit of the great white whale.

"It's a quiet and harmless being, of long endurance," she told me. She was showing me one of the beetle larvae, a little whiteish grub, squirming in the palm of her hand, which she had uncovered at the roots of a dying oak. "It lives in the death of this tree. It will take at least a year to mature. It's a symbol of eternity." Then she gave a brief cackle. "Can we claim as much?"

But she, the elusive and forbidding Clara – she had her own life cycle. I woke one morning and she was gone. Vanished. I was furious and betrayed – I who alone was prepared to publish her gigantic book. By the time I was back at my office desk, I had forgiven her. Clara was unlike me or the rest of us: she was part feral! Feral – yet a scholar.

The habit of such vanishings must have been formed early in her life. It was only with difficulty I drew from her a few details of her previous existence. Clara was born of Jewish parents in a town not far from Moscow in the nineteen-thirties. She was attending school when the Nazi Wehrmacht invaded Russia during the Second World War. The invaders perpetrated unspeakable horrors on the population. Vast stretches of the countryside became a slaughterhouse. Both of Clara's parents were killed brutally before her eyes. Only narrowly did she escape their fate.

———

Clara had an English grandfather who was working as an architect in Moscow. It was this wealthy grandfather who had had the baby girl christened Clementine, an English name he hoped would shield her from the prevalent anti-Semitism.

He sheltered the girl. Clara was traumatised and withdrawn. She lived for over a year in a wardrobe in his bedroom, emerging at night for food and exercise. A "nocturnal adolescent," she called herself.

It was this grandfather, her saviour, rather than the Nazis, who assaulted her sexually. Clara went on the run again. It was another of her vanishing tricks. The Russian KGB got on her scent and pursued her. She escaped – eventually reaching England and safety. Safe, that is, from all but the past. The past remained to haunt her.

Now Clara is dead. I shall be there to attend her funeral. And whatever my critics may say, I never made any money from Clara's book; nor, for that matter, did she. Scarcely anyone knew her personally: only the beetles and wild things, you might say. She has left behind her dizzying book, a profound volume, a work of undaunted scholarship, and of myth, of life itself – and of the life cycle of this one rather obscure beetle, this small and mainly peaceable life form, one of the "whys" of our complex world.

"Did you light on this beetle because you felt for its obscurity?" I asked her when the book was at the printers. (Of course the reviewers mocked *Dusk Flight*; they considered it "as impenetrable as her thickets"; my edition never sold and was eventually remaindered. It was too good for them. The years passed. Tastes changed. Now it is a Penguin Classic.)

Clara never really answered my question. What she did say remains in my mind.

"For years I was pursued. So I can write only a book of pursuit."

Commander Calex Killed, Fire and Fury at Edge of World, Scones Perfect

AN ENGLISH DREAM

ALL WAS confusion. Somehow, I had to return to Ingushetia. Finally I came out of hiding and ran down a side street. Broken glass clattered beneath my feet. I found a tripcar in a courtyard. I pulled the tarpaulin off it and smashed the window.

As I climbed in, angrils winged overhead. They plunged down the narrow street and were gone.

Once I had been a beautiful significant person. Now the car would not start. The inputer told me it was completely out of gas.

My de-entropiser to the rescue! One shot and the engine was purring. I flung the car forward, knowing the angrils would be back.

I drove up to the second floor, which continued to the end of town.

The place was a tip. Some angrils were fluttering down to feast. They had a preference for warm living flesh. In the car I was reasonably safe. I speeded up. The radio suddenly announced that Commander Calex had been killed by the patagais. His force had surrendered. It was the end of organised human resistance. You might almost say, the end of civilization.

I wept as I drove. Radioscan picked up a foreign station radiating from near Tblisi. Using the linguadux, I heard a professional voice repeating the news of the Commander's death. They said he was being eaten by patagais. They announced that patagais and angrils were one and the same species, larval and imagal forms being stages of the same loathesome creature's life cycle. Useless knowledge, I thought. The world beyond my screen certainly looked as if civilization had ended. Broken trees stood or fell everywhere. Cataracts of mud plunged down the mountainsides. Despite the heavy rain, a castle burned, the red eyes of its windows flickering, its smoke pouring heavily downwards. I swerved along the road to avoid boulders.

When the asteroid struck – had that been only ten days ago? – it ploughed into the plateau in central Spain. Madrid was immediately destroyed, lock, stock and barrel. The shock wave started the world burning. The angril brood was released from the interior of the asteroid. Angrils hatched from the heat.

Their rate of reproduction was phenomenal. It had not yet been precisely calculated – and probably never would be.

I passed what had been a camp. Crushed human bodies gleamed like fish in the wet. From some corpses, a white whiskery fungus grew. The savage invaders would feast on it in due course.

My speed slowed. I was climbing into a more extensive mountain region. Featureless geology surrounded the vehicle. Rivulets spewed from gulleys onto the road. As I rounded a curve between enclosing cliffs, a lone figure ran into the road ahead, waving its arms.

This might be a decoy for hidden brigands. But there was no place here for men to hide. My impulse, nevertheless, was to run the gaunt creature down.

"Stop!" said the punchiputer. It cut the engine.

The tripcar slithered to a halt. The gaunt creature came along side, wrenched open the passenger door, and climbed barefoot and sobbing into the passenger seat. It oozed water.

I regarded it with distaste. It mopped its face with the hem of its black robe. It smoothed back its disordered hair. It revealed itself as a female.

Opening its gown, it revealed two slender breasts, shiny with moisture. The skeletal being was a woman, and no mistake. She also produced a short dagger, pointing it at me to show her nudity was no invitation.

"I have no intention of touching you," I said. "Who are you, anyway? Where have you come from?"

She responded swiftly in a tongue I did not understand. The linguadux was no help; her dialect was unlisted. It was a tribal tongue, lost somewhere here on the fringes of Daghistan.

The woman slumped back in her seat, taking from her inner pocket an object she began to gnaw. Disgusted, I saw it was a severed human hand. Two fingers had already been eaten to the bone. Tales of cannibalism in these wilds had reached me.

I spun open the window and gestured strongly to her to throw the revolting object away. She growled and spat.

"There's better food where we are going!"

I snatched the hand and flung it into the howling dark. She curled up sulkily in her seat.

I shouted at her a Caucasian saying I remembered: "The world is carrion and he who seeks it a dog!"

A rain shower struck our windscreen. It turned rapidly to hail. The hail also disappeared as we climbed. Now it was snow, flying at speed almost horizontally through the passes.

"Commander Calex is dead," I said aloud.

"Commander Calex," she repeated.

As tears began again to trickle down my cheeks, she too started to cry. Her grief had a passionate intensity. I laid a consoling hand on her shoulder, whereupon she wailed the more strongly. I stopped the tripcar.

We huddled together, mourning the loss of everything once valued, I and this lost woman. She was ageless, her long face with its acquiline nose betrayed years of struggle drawn on its sallow cheeks. When the snowstorm died, we could see there was fire at the edge of the world. A sullen steady fire, with centuries to burn in.

An eagle fluttered like transistorised tissue before our windows.

I glimpsed an angril on its back. Cascading feathers, the bird plummetted down into the abyss, to be lost in spume and weather.

Fatigued though I was, I decided to drive on. We had not too far to go now.

Both weather and terrain grew even wilder. A thunderstorm blew up. I turned on the silencer. At one stage, we passed a village perched as insecurely as a bird's nest between towering crags. Rain water gushed from its gutters into the depths below. A banner waved from its walls. Then it was gone as we rounded the next curve. The woman slept from exhaustion, her damp head against my shoulder.

Darkness was on us – a darkness stitched with flickering light.

All through that night I drove. The woman slept on, breathing heavily through open mouth. Towards dawn, when ragged signals of day tore through the eastern skies, I pulled into a side gap and was instantly asleep.

Morning came clad in a sullen green. The wind had died to a breeze.

Our limbs were stiff. We climbed out of the car and pissed, one on one side of the vehicle, one on the other. Then on, on.

When the day was half-used, the weather blew itself out. Droves of drab-hued angrils flew overhead, like machines in a wretched dream.

The terrain became less broken, although signs of destruction were everywhere. We came on a notice, half-broken, which read INGU. The frontier hut had been burnt down, and was deserted. But we had unmistakeably arrived in Ingushetia.

It was nearly teatime when we drove into the capital. This quiet little place – a refuge when the Russian-Chechen war was in force – had suffered serious destruction. A mosque survived, a whole terrace of houses, an office block. Yes, much remained intact, and no angrils were about. Not a single soul was to be seen.

"Smarten yourself up," I told the woman. Suiting the action to the words, I went to the rear, washed my face and hands, combed my hair. I passed the comb to the woman. She came, meekly enough, washing her face and hands, combing her long hair. I found a ribbon, a red ribbon, and tied back her hair. She made no protest.

We then drove a little farther, turning down a side street. There I parked the car. Taking the woman by her arm, I led her to the tea shop.

The tea shop! Its window box was still bright with geraniums, its windows clear, its door freshly painted! In one corner of the window was an unobtrusive notice: "Devonshire Cream Teas." What a beacon amid a world of desolation! The bell tinkled as always as we entered.

We were greeted by that delicious homely smell of baking cakes. And there was Wun Luk to meet us, sprucely dressed as ever, bow tie in place. He called to Fiona to appear as he came, hands outstretched.

"Guess who's here, Fiona!" There was a smile on his broad cheeks as he clutched my hand.

Wun Luk was a renegade Tibetan monk. He had married his Scottish Fiona five years previously. They had set up this teashop in the Islamic city, and made a great success of it. A Hovis sign on the wall read, "No Politics, No Religion, No Gloom. *Please!*" People from five continents came here for a cup of Fiona's tea.

Fiona herself came bustling forward, wiping her hands on her apron. She embraced me warmly. She had put on a little weight, which suited her.

I introduced the woman at my side. Fiona and Wun Luk gave her a warm welcome – as indeed they did all their customers.

"How's business?" I asked.

Wun Luk beamed and pointed upwards. "Chunks of Madrid still flying over. So folks stay in the doors..."

Fiona shrugged and smiled. "Aye, it's wee bittie slack the noo.

Ye ken, the world falling apart – it distracts yon customers." She laughed. "Canne help it."

"What can't be helped must be endured," said Wun Luk jovially. We all laughed at that.

The room looked beautiful. Music I thought I recognised as one of Percy Grainger's compositions played softly in the background. There were hunting prints hanging on the walls, together with pictures of Highland cattle. Candles glowed under red shades on every table. A turbanned man was sitting with a woman in a head scarf at one table; she was laughing quietly at something he had said.

How Fiona and Wun Luk managed all this I will never know.

Fiona took my strange woman by the arm, leading her with gentle gestures to a private back room. I discussed with Wun Luk his difficulties in obtaining fodder for his cow.

Fiona returned escorting a vision in a light blue gown. She had a blue ribbon in her hair. It was a transformation! She herself was aware how good she looked.

"Her old clouts were gey mankey," Fiona explained, laughing. In an aside to me she said she had confiscated the woman's dagger for a wee while.

"Sit yersens down and make yersens at home," said Fiona. "I will bring ye a bite of tay."

Hardly had we settled ourselves down that she appeared beside us with a loaded tray. This was her "bite"!

Her service was as prompt as ever. What a spread we enjoyed, this unknown woman and I!

Of a sudden, she said, "Cream tea!" Those were the first words of English she spoke. She gazed at me with eyes of love. Wiping my lips on my linen napkin, I leaned forward and kissed her. "Yes, cream tea, darling...."

Our pot of tea, snug under its knitted tea-cosy, the scones baked to perfection with crisp serrated edges, the little pots of raspberry jam, the generous helpings of clotted cream... All served with refinement on patterned crockery.

What a feast we had! – Well worth travelling a thousand miles for....

The Hibernators

THE TIME *of the Great Darkness was approaching,*
when oblivion would descend and Time itself stand still.

MOTHER FLEEBIS OF ROCKADOOF took a final bowl of nutrition to
her mating partner, Castener of Rockadoof.

He looked up, pulled the plug from his ear, and smiled his tired
old smile at her. He accepted the bowl with both hands.

She said, "It is time to take the children to the hibernatorium
now, Cast. Our appointment to enter is due. It is safer inside, than
remaining here at home. Will you not change your mind and come
with us?"

He gestured towards his apparatus. "How can I leave my scanners
at such a crucial time? I feel I am on the edge of something. I must
pursue it till I fall asleep."

Without rancour, she asked him if his scanners were more precious to him than the children.

"My dear Fleebis," he replied, "would not life on our world be a
kind of prison if we did not believe that we might change and develop: that for instance our mental and spiritual lives might never
expand, that there might never come a time when those future ver-
sions of ourselves would scarcely credit our present state?"

She replied with a sigh that he was always thinking of the future.

He said, "My dear, that is more profitable than thinking always of the past."

"But we are a part of nature, Cast, aren't we? How can we change? Our annual long sleeps —"

"We have changed," he said quickly. "Our conception of ourselves has changed radically in the last hundred years. No longer do we see ourselves devoured by a great black monster when darkness comes. That anthropomorphism has been banished by our new awareness that we are accidental by-products of vast events in space and time. We now understand eclipses. We are the dust and ashes of dead suns and exploding novas–the very products of distant sequencing."

Castener leant forward, addressing his mating partner with intensity.

"But that's just our bodies. How did human consciousness develop on Moorn? When? We don't know. We may be the only species with consciousness in the universe. But that consciousness is in some way apart from our bodies. Maybe in future – the far future – we will be able to live only in consciousness, separate from our bodies, free from physical need. Then when the Great Darkness comes, we will no longer fear it."

He realised as he was speaking that he had treated Fleebis to such lectures before.

"Time's getting on," she said. "I wanted to shampoo my hair before we left for the Hibernatorium." As she adjusted the hair at the back of her head, Castener's mouth shut like a trap.

"Off you go, then!"

It was her turn to be offended. "Aren't you going to come up and kiss Guthram and Miney good-bye?"

"I must resolve this equation."

"Well... Good-bye then."

"I'll come up if I can. How is Guthram?"

She said over her shoulders as she started up the stair, "Too late."

———

To the inhabitants of Moorn, it seemed like a paradox: that the sun was nearly at zenith, and yet the Great Darkness was about to descend on them. The sky was blue and almost cloudless, yet a wind screamed down the streets. Tarrell, the primary, could not be seen. Yet its approach was inevitable, and immanent.

Transportation had already ceased. Fleebis planned to walk to the local hibernatorium. She was vexed because Guthram had insisted on going down to say good-bye to his procreator.

"Will you be all right?" Castener asked the boy, scrutinising his face. "You are almost a man."

"I don't feel sleepy, dad."

"Seems there are two sorts of people, those who hibernate and a much smaller number, the freaks who don't hibernate. I don't hibernate. Possibly it is an evolutionary effect. Maybe you won't hibernate. You used to do so as a baby."

"I'm not a baby any more."

Tears filled his eyes. He knew it was true. "Sure. Growth is one of the miracles of time and space...."

He kissed his son. "Take care of yourself, dear boy. I'm anxious for you."

As he embraced his father, arms thrown about his neck, Guthram asked, "Dad, what really *is* space?"

"Space is one of the two all-embracing things we live in, Guth, the other thing being time."

"So what really is time? You can't see it, can you?"

"No, but you can feel it."

"I can't."

"Biologically speaking, we are all products of time."

Castener watched his son disappear up the stairs, thinking with regret that perhaps he should have kept the boy with him. But then— there would have been all the bother of feeding and amusing him, interfering with work.

Sighing, he turned back to his scanners.

———

The local hibernatorium stood on the edge of Vurndrol City. Its massive structure loomed windowless over the low houses of the population. It could have been mistaken for a gigantic rock. Made anthill-like by its immensity, it sported a long tail, a trail of people wending their way to shelter in its multitudinous cells. They entered the brightly lit entrance and were swallowed up, the chill wind whistling at their rear.

Fleebis was leading her children to the shelter. They were entering into the embrace of the hibernatorium's shadow.

"But I still don't feel at all tired, ma," said Guthram, lagging behind the bulk of his mother.

"Of course you do," cooed his mother in consolatory tones. "Just you wait till we are settled down."

She was clutching to her bosom Guthram's sister, Miney, who was already half asleep.

"I can't sleep, ma. I want to keep out of here."

She looked with concern into his troubled face. "This is no time to be outside, dear."

"Ma, I want to keep out of here! I really dislike this place."

Feeling the resistance in Guthram's hand, which she was clutching, Fleebis uttered more words of encouragement. "Once we get snuggled down in our cell, you'll be asleep in no time. I'll sing to you."

The crowd, of which they formed a part, entered the building. Fleebis had their tickets checked by an official.

Miney roused long enough to say, "I'm asleep already...."

Guthram inhaled the warm sickly sweet smell of the interior. The hibernatorium had stood empty for six months; now it was heating up to sustain its sleepers during the Great Darkness. He felt something close to fear at the thought of surrendering his being to sleep for all but half a year.

Fleebis kept firm hold of his hand as a minion escorted them in a slow-moving elevator all the way up to their cell on the forty-fourth floor. The lighting here was dim. People draped in blankets jostled about like aged peasants in an oil painting. They spoke in subdued tones, as if the world of sleep were an eerie forest. A sort of murmurous complaint arose from them, a united breath of human resignation.

"After all, we've got to be what Nature intends us to be," Fleebis said to a woman she pushed against.

"I'll be glad of the rest, myself," was the half-whispered answer.

They struggled into their padded cell, and lay down on the couches, Guthram still faintly protesting that he was not tired.

"Don't be a nuisance, there's a dear," said Fleebis. Putting her arm round the lad, holding him suffocatingly close, she sang him a song, whiskery with tradition.

> Comets and starlight
> Comets and starlight
> Time's come to sleep tight
> You too shall sleep tight
> Sandman is waiting
> Once Moorn is mooring behind big Ma Tarrell
> Big big Ma Tarrell big as a barrel
> Sleeping is right sleeping is fun
> While we're all hibernating
> Right away from the sun
> Away from the sun

Miney fluttered into sleep, thumb in mouth. As Fleebis uttered the last notes of her song, she too closed her eyes and slept. And so they would both lie, unknowing, sleeping away the six months during which the parent body of the gas giant Tarrell obscured the sun from the satellite Moorn, and chill prevailed over the face of their little world.

In the dozy cell, a bulkhead light gleamed. It too, like most human consciousness, would be extinguished when Moorn entered Tarrell's shadow in a few hours' time. By its light, Guthram surveyed his mother's face. Although Fleebis was not yet in hibernation proper, already her face was assuming a disquieting blankness.

A wave of loneliness filled Guthram's being. He worried that he felt no prompting to sleep. What was wrong with him? Cautiously, he began to extricate himself from under his mother's protective arm.

Once free, he crawled from the door of the cell and began his descent through the great building, squeezing past people who were still seeking their numbered cells. Small blue lights lit the way. Floors were carpeted. Everything was muffled. Every storey was filled with a myriad quiet snuffles, as thousands surrendered their souls to the Great Sleep.

At last he gained the entrance to the Hibernatorium. Stragglers were still entering, producing or fumbling for their tickets before merging into the dimness of the interior. The boy slipped out into the brighter world beyond.

He stood for a moment, breathing the purer air, letting the wind pluck at his clothes. His one thought was to return to his father and then make some sort of plan for himself.

Scanning the sky, still a hard blue, he could see at first no sign of Tarrell in the last afternoon sunlight. But it would be there, nearing, nearing. Then he caught sight of it, blue, indistinct, occupying almost thirty degrees of sky, drawing close to taking its first bite from the sun.

As he began his walk, a stronger gust of wind caught the tall tukkas trees lining the route. Their spear-shaped leaves came rattling down, to slither along the paved way at his feet.

An occasional light showed in the houses along the road. People who were too poor to afford a cell in the hibernatorium were having to accommodate themselves in their own homes, barricading themselves as best they could against the forecast snows and floods.

A howler-bowler sounded in the distance. Guthram quickened his pace as the rattle of wheels came closer. Soon the vehicle would be upon him. He looked back. Dim round eyes of headlamps were rapidly drawing near. He discerned the two howlers pulling the carriage, a light two-wheeler. The howlers' necks were stretched forward. They ran with their usual high-stepping gait. Their scant plumage rippled with movement. Behind the first bowler came a second.

Guthram stepped back hurriedly into a sheltering doorway to avoid being run over. The first howler-bowler sped past. As the second howler-bowler came up, it slowed with a screech of brakes. The howlers howled in protest. They gave forth a deep brassy beige note.

The carriage door was flung open. An immense man, clad from head to foot in black fur, jumped out. He rushed at Guthram and seized the boy.

Guthram yelled and struggled. The man wrenched at him so violently that he lost his balance. He was carried kicking and screaming into the recesses of the bowler. The door slammed, a whip cracked, and they were at once off at a great pace.

The man clamped a black hand over Guthram's face to stop his cries.

"Keep quiet, kid! You're mine now, to do what I like with!"

A paralysing blow landed on the back of his neck.

Guthram was never entirely unconscious. He was aware of a firework display behind his eyelids, where pain and fear collided. He was aware of a monstrous body against his, causing something deeper even than pain. Through a great threshing blackness into an abyss he was thrown.

Something moved. He managed to open one eye. Opening the other eye, he struggled to bring both of them into focus. He discovered he was lying against long brown sticks, his head and part of his body propped against a yielding warmth which occasionally moved.

He groaned in misery.

The noise started some movement above him, beyond his sight. There came a kind of high singing, to which he had scarcely the strength to listen. He could not grasp its meaning. After a while, it died away.

Stirring, he got to his knees. There was blood between his legs. He shivered with cold and apprehension. Crawling forward, he found his trousers. Although they had been torn, he managed to draw them on. The high singing began again.

Guthram stood on his own two feet. Light filtered dimly through a grating. He had been lying against two howlers, in a confusion of legs – those brown sticks! – and beaks. Now the great birdlike steeds raised their necks to scrutinise him. Their eyes were large, with slitted pupils. They sang at him. The songs came directly into his head without passing through his ears.

He had never met a howler. Since they had not harmed him when he was powerless, he saw no reason to fear them. He put out a hand to pat the head of one of them; the head was quickly withdrawn.

"I won't hurt you," he said.

They sang the words back at him. "I won't hurt you." This time, he understood the song.

"But you can't speak. You only howl."

"Howling is for misery, for misery. Although we cannot speak, yet you hear our voices."

He was mystified and pleased in a way. But there were more important things on his mind. He wanted to know what had befallen him, and where he was.

The howlers seemed to tell him they were all at the Science Lord's castle. He could not understand very well; what they sang was so obscure.

They were trying to tell him they had come originally from a great distance. Failing to understand, he began to bang on the door of his prison. He thought, If only my father would come and save me....

The door was suddenly flung open. There stood the gigantic man, the very man who had seized Guthram and dragged him into the howler-bowler. And after that, when he was helpless... The howlers at once sprang up to their feet and began howling in unison.

Ignoring them, the man said in a deep voice, "So you're recovered, are you? Good. Come on with me, lad, and I will feed you."

This was said not unkindly. Although Guthram shrank back, his hand was seized and he was pulled into the open. The door slammed behind them, shutting off the howling.

Light dazzled him after the dimness of the stable. He shielded his eyes with his free hand.

In response, the man said, with a sort of laugh, "You'll get all the dark you want soon enough."

Still clutching the youth's hand, he set off at great speed across what seemed to Guthram to be a great blank space barricaded with large dark buildings to one side. Every step was such pain for him, he imagined the blood was starting to well up again in his trousers.

"I can't go so fast, sir. My bottom parts are terrible stiff."

"That's to knock the self-image out of you."

Since the pace did not slow, he managed to gasp, "I didn't think I had one of those, sir."

"Well, we'll see."

"Who is the Science Lord, sir?"

"You'll see."

The man was staring ahead at his goal, walking even faster, but he turned his head to give Guthram a smile.

Guthram saw the man's teeth were grey and irregular. He felt a twinge of liking for him because of that.

They came to a stone building, to enter at a canter. Roaring sounds indicated that the place was full of people. It was not at all like the hibernatorium. The two of them clattered up a flight of spiral stairs, Guthram tripping at every step, until they arrived at a confusing chamber with people running about and dishes being carried and a good deal of shouting, mainly from large-sized men at pint-sized youths.

Sunlight flooded into the room through arched windows. Guthram's captor roared at a man for bowls of food, to which the man said respectfully, "Yes, Althuron," before scurrying off.

Althuron sat his grand frame down on a bench and dragged Guthram down against him. He indicated with a sweep of his hand that he should look out of the window.

The sun had a bite out of it. Already, its light was diminishing. Althuron grunted that that bite was the cruel planet Tarrell, just as two bowls full of a yellow mash were set down in front of them.

Guthram stared in awe as the bite increased and the sun diminished. A hush had overwhelmed the room. Everyone was now crowding to the windows. Tarrell was immense, immense and black. Another moment and its great bulk had totally obscured the sun. Darkness rushed in. The world beyond the window went blank. A gust of a united sigh of apprehension escaped from the throats of the watchers.

Electric lights came on in the room, hesitant and dim. Moorn was a small world, short of minerals, and generators were consequently scarce.

"Six months of this lousy dark," said Althuron. "Now we must fight." As he spoke, he began ladling the yellow stuff into his mouth, between the grey teeth.

"Can't I go back to my father?" asked Guthram in a whisper.

"I'm just the Conscriptor, son. Keep your mouth shut."

A flimsy pale youth, overhearing this unpromising exchange, eased himself along the bench so that he could speak in Guthram's ear.

"I want my progenitor too. He's a powerful man. He'd get me out of here. It's so unfair."

"We'd better make the best of things," said Guthram, tucking into his soup.

"But it's so unfair," said the pale youth, whom Guthram was already designating mentally as "the whining boy."

Although he felt some contempt for the whiner, his conscience prompted him to offer what consolation he could find.

"Look at it this way," he said, "at least while we're here we don't have to comb our hair."

"It's what happens," Althuron said, evidently thinking in the abstract, between mouthfuls, nodding his head at the whining boy. "We're short of those who don't hibernate. You're needed to fight the enemy."

"Fight!" shrieked the youth. "I've never fought in my life. My progenitor would never allow me to fight...."

"Keep your trap shut, kid," the Conscriptor advised. "Get on with your food. Calories protect you against the cold."

With a sob, the whining boy turned away.

Althuron gave Guthram a conspiratorial nudge in the ribs.

"Better look out. I'm glad you're not a wimp. Someone's coming."

Certainly someone was coming, someone of consequence. Bugles announced his coming. Before his arrival, four servitors rushed into the long chamber, savagely making everyone stand up quietly by their tables. No more eating, no more talking. Even Althuron had to drop his spoon and stand rigid.

Out of the corner of his mouth, he said, "Science Lord...."

Entering through a wide door came a strange figure, gaunt and black robed, escorted by two women bearing flambeaux and two men bearing naked swords. Guthram believed at first that this figure wore a mask. As it drew nearer he realised that the man's skull, ravaged by disease, bore scarcely any flesh. It resembled a death mask, and was as pale as death. The figure halted in the middle of the chamber. It spoke in an assertive and sepulchral tone, its voice magnified by a hidden microphone.

"For those wretches who do not know me, my name is Holy

Clathertam, known as the Invincible. Beware, for you shall know me! I am Lord of Science of Moorn. Now that the Great Darkness is come upon us, we shall arise and protect those who are without power in hibernation.

"You are here, you youths, as pawns in the battle to come. You are called the Expendables. You all have been marked. We shall fight with and overcome the Powers of the Predators. You will meet the Predators in good time.

"Now you will file from here to the parade ground outside. There you will be mustered into squads. We shall then proceed to the ancestral battle field, where stands the great Insulator. This is the order given by me, Holy Clathertam the Invincible. Proceed."

No sooner had the deep ringing voice died away than the occupants of the chamber, Guthram among them, began to leave the shelter of the building. Only Althuron remained behind, arms folded across his chest, saying not a word. Guthram glanced back at him: Althuron smiled his old grey smile, but did not move.

Outside, in the open, over the great parade ground, temperatures were already falling. Frost glittered on the ground. Minute beads of cold fell from the unclouded air. They called it *glit*.

Widely spaced flares partly illumined the expanse of the parade ground. It was marked out in squares, each hardly two hand-spreads in either dimension. The youths each assigned themselves a square, as if preordained. Guthram followed suit.

Orderlies came, bearing thick mantles, one to a youth – to a pawn, as the Invincible had called them. They were quickly handed out, and as quickly thrown over shoulders. As his eyes adjusted to the murk, Guthram saw that, separately, a great body of men stood silent not far distant. Something about them glittered: their helmets and possibly their spears, held rigidly at their sides. There was something about their very silence, their motionlessness, that was chilling.

Came a great howling, the sound echoing against the facades of the buildings. Howler-bowlers came rushing on the scene, each bearing two men, one of them standing clutching the reins and clearly a commander of some sort. When they drew to a halt, the howlers ceased their noise, bowing their beaks to the ground in submission.

The commanders dismounted and began issuing orders. With them went ferocious dogs, snarling and straining at their leashes.

Guthram heard the faint song of the howlers and understood: they feared the savage hounds, feeling their long legs to be in danger from them.

A hand plucked at Guthram's left arm. A whining voice said, "I don't want to be here. I'm hurting between my legs. I'm bleeding."

"Forget it," Guthram said. "There's probably worse things to come." He was addressing a pallid youth, spotty and stoop-shouldered.

He shook off the detaining hand. But the pallid youth in the neighbouring square said, "I thought we were all meant to help each other."

"What gave you that idea?"

The fellow to Guthram's right, overhearing this exchange, advised Guthram to kick the little wimp. Guthram did not respond.

Amid shouts from the commanders and furious barking from the dogs, the contingent of Expendables began to move forward. The army of men with spears marched behind with a solid thudding tramp tramp tramp. Ahead of them all went a commander in a howler-bowler, leading the way, a torch flaming and smoking in the clutch of his assistant.

The great dark body of youths and men marched ever eastward. The pace increased when they were covering level ground, and slowed when they were traversing rough land or scaling a hill. A halt was called after two hours, when most of the youths were exhausted. So cold was the ground, they could not fling themselves down to rest, as they would have wished.

Guthram stared upwards at a remarkable phenomenon. Amidst the inchoate rash of stars which formed an archway right across the sky, a strange spiral of light was rising from the eastern horizon as the army progressed. In its wider part, the ribbon was faintly green; where it thinned away into distance, it appeared more an elusive mauve or violet. He stared and stared, puzzled. No thought occured to him. Eventually, he grew dizzy from staring.

They were on the move again. The next two hour spell was more taxing than the first. Consciousness was confined to keeping the legs moving and the feet planted firmly on the deeply frosted ground, stride after stride. The cold became more intense, biting the ears, chilling the cheeks until teeth seemed to freeze. A chill wind blew, moaning among the iced bushes which impeded their march. The wasted leaves, scurrying across the ground in the breeze, tinkled stiffly against one another.

At last came the order to halt. The Expendables were made to go in file into a ruinous stone building. It could have been a castle or a palace. Its cold embraced them like a coat. It contained only relics of what had been furniture. Small insects had eaten most of it away. At least the dismal place offered shelter of a sort. Although the flagstones on which they threw themselves down were numbing to the bone, they could rest their weary limbs.

Bowls of a thick soup were served to them. They drank. The soup tasted disgusting. One of the Expendables complained to a nearby commander.

"Drink it down," he ordered. "There's medicine in it which will save your blood from freezing."

"It's disgusting."

"I said to drink it. You want to become an icicle? Temperatures are sinking down to zero."

They had no alternative but to do as they were ordered – and immediately fell asleep after drinking.

This routine of march and rest and march again was followed unbrokenly over and over, until the youths remembered nothing but the rigours of the journey. Some of them died on the way. Guthram merely became hardened. They breathed through mufflers wrapped about their faces.

Sometimes they passed through darkened villages. Here, the people were so poor they had no hibernatoria in which to flock for refuge. Instead, they had barricaded themselves into their cottages and buried themselves under rugs.

The commanders encouraged looting for food. When the cottages were broken into, scant supplies were found: the majority of Moornians passed the long eclipse in deep unconsciousness, needing nothing in the way of nourishment. Disappointed marauders quit the vulnerable homes, leaving them wide open and their sleeping inhabitants exposed to the increasingly hostile elements.

Guthram's contingent had found cans of meat stored under a counter in a small shop. They stood under a tall tukkas tree to make a hurried meal, wolfing the food down. A fire had been built from fallen branches. The contingent stood with their boots almost in the glowing embers, chewing desperately. The tukkas groaned above their heads. A sparkling fall of glit, as the local name was, occurred; it was as though the atmosphere itself was freezing.

Of a sudden, the tree split with a tremendous crack. The rapid decline in temperature had acted like an axe. From top to base, the trunk tore itself in two. The lesser half began to fall.

Yelling a warning, Guthram dropped his stolen ration and ran for safety. Others followed.

The half tree fell, slowly at first, then faster. It crashed onto the roof of a cottage and shattered into splinters, almost as if it were made of glass.

From the cottage no movement came. The hibernators inside died without knowing it.

The winter of the Great Darkness grew more intense, the strange ribbon of light rose higher in the eastern sky, to become more vivid, while, during rest periods, the howlers sang their wisps of song. Guthram tried to interpret the songs before he slept.

Moorn continued its axial rotation. Sometimes, clear sky alone ruled above them, crossed by the speedy trace of Barlits, the moon's own shard of moon. At other times, the sky remained dominated by the bulk of the gas giant Tarrell, barring them from the sun. The face of that gloomy object was lit occasionally by violent electrical storms, thousands of kilometres in extent, flashing across the equator of the planet.

Finally came a prolonged march for the assembled armies. Their way was lit by an auroral display which exploded suddenly into the skies overhead, obliterating the stars with curtains of green, red, and yellow light. The marchers halted. Some flung themselves to the frozen ground in terror. Yet almost immediately the colours overhead dulled and were gone. The darkness enveloping the Expendables seemed even deeper than before. Goaded on by the yells of the commanders in their bowlers, they continued their progress.

Their progress was always noisy, for the howling of the howlers often set the commanders' dogs barking furiously.

The terrain rose slowly, kilometre after kilometre, to a crest. Here the multitude paused, to look down into a great hollow bowl of land, stretching till the darkness hid its far limits.

Most remarkably, an immense metal object, self-illuminating, stood almost at the centre of the bowl. Its sides were as elaborately buttressed about as the exterior of a cathedral. From a projection on its upper surface curled the strange ribbon of light, up through the sky, into space, shimmering, until sight of it was lost in interstellar distance.

When they were not pulling bowlers, the howlers began their sub-audible singing, sweet to Guthram's ear. The songs of the howlers became more comprehensible the more he heard of them. Now he was beginning to understand whole phrases, although their concepts were beyond him. With many words, he could only guess at their meaning.

"In this mighty thing (?) (*somebody*) came here to this (*world*) ... Our time trail from the engines (?) shows (*us*) the way they journeyed ... This time trail will remain (blank) ... The engines (?) work (*by utilising*) time. Time is (*a greater*) power than space. Time (*permeates everything*) continually...."

Guthram lay awake, marvelling at things he could not comprehend.

The whining youth, who lay next to him, said, "You are not asleep. I bet it's because you're scared."

"Shut up."

"You'd better be scared. I'm scared. We are going to be in a battle tomorrow and I am sure I am going to be killed."

"Shut up. You will be killed if you take that attitude."

"I wish I was home with my ma."

"Well you're not, so shut *up!*"

And the howlers had another song, as puzzling as the first.

"In the mighty thing (?) came (*some creatures like us*). But small (?). They did not wish to (*travel*) here. They were merely (*things to eat*) on the way (?) They did not wish (*to be eaten*). Many were (*eaten*). After they (*landed*) here, the survivors (?) managed to (*escape*) from the mighty thing. They ran away. (*Things changed.*) Their (*descendants*) grew (?) but we were (*captured*). We are now (*miserable*) sort of (*prisoners*) (*harnessed*) to the bowlers...."

He fell asleep trying to puzzle it all out.

The eclipsing dark remained as deep as ever, the cold as intense, when what was ironically named the Dawn Call roused them.

The Expendables rose shivering, clustering together for a trace of warmth. The hot soup was served up and after that, unusually, heated helmets were issued. Then they were marched outside, where a gale was blowing. The wind bit in their clothes and their bones.

Through watering eyes, they saw that a distant body of men or youths was forming up, marked by flickering torches. It was the enemy they were about to confront.

Riding a metal encased howler-bowler, the great Invincible arrived on the scene to address his forces.

Holy Clathertam, muffled so that his skull of a face could scarcely be seen, spoke to them through a loudhailer.

"I am Holy Clathertam the Invincible. You will do well to fear me more than our enemies. I am the Lord of Science. Today you shall fight and win a battle against the Expendables of the Powers of the Predators. On the outcome of this battle depends the issue of which side shall have First Strike in a greater battle, to be fought shortly with real men.

"We the Good who fight Evil claim this territory and this mighty Space/Time Insulator machine you see here for our own.

"The Insulator arrived many years ago from a star system far distant. It was powered by a force we know only as Time-Insulation, a very advanced technology.

"The humans who manned this Insulator were all killed by the Powers of the Predators. Yes, they were easily killed even by primitive brutes like the Predators, because they did not understand evil, and so were powerless. Those humans were persons of great wisdom, acquired through the ages. Thus we lost valuable knowledge. So we fight the Predators annually, here at this neutral place, according to strict rules.

"You must be clear about the hazards of the squares on which you will fight. The ground is becoming so cold, dipping towards absolute zero, that thermal variations sink slowly lower, permitting quantum fluctuations to prevail. These minute fluctuations may induce a phase state transition between the two competing energy values of space and time. These energy values may separate out – may split away from one another like a dead tree. It is possible that time may prevail over space. There will then be a lethal phase change.

"Now. You will proceed in orderly fashion to your appointed squares. Any Expendable trying to escape this duty will be killed at once. You must conform rigidly to the rules of the battleground. You may move forward only to an empty square two squares ahead in the columns to right or left of you. You may attempt to stab and kill only an opponent on the neighbouring square to your right – unless you are positioned on the extreme right flank, when you stab only ahead. If you move through the entire square-board without being killed yourself, then you are victorious and will live to fight again.

"Remember these rules. Now collect your spears."

The whining boy stared white-faced about him.

"I don't understand. I can't understand them rules."

"What's it matter?" sneered the bully boy. "You're going to get killed anyway!"

Guthram said nothing, repeating to himself, Move to empty square two squares ahead. Stab only to the right. But who can stab me? The ones to the left or to the right?

They paraded past servitors who handed each Expendable a spear or short sword. Guthram chose a short sword as being more manoeuvrable. They moved to a vast chequerboard and took up positions, each youth to one square.

A bugle sounded. They advanced to meet the enemy, goaded forward by commanders shouting from the sidelines. The whole square was immense, stretching before the structure the Invincible had called the Space/Time Insulator.

The enemy force, the Predators, moved forward in a solid wave, square by square, spear and sword points glinting. They resembled ghosts of some kind, being garbed in white hooded cloaks. Guthram saw immediately that his side, garbed in black cloaks, had an advantage: they were less easily seen in the blackness, lit only by flares on the sidelines.

And there was another advantage. The Expendables had the

strong wind at their backs. The advancing foe faced into the wind. Some were already attempting to keep their cloaks about them, and thus not intently observing the enemy. Guthram's spirits rose.

He called to the whining boy, "Be of good courage! We shall win!"

There was no response.

The one on the right. The one on the right. Watch for the one on the left. The one ahead....

The front ranks met. Some youths on both sides fell. Rear ranks moved on, most silent, some shouting. Some wounded screaming.

The one ahead! Guthram saw his eyes glinting, preparing to strike. Instead, Guthram struck to his right, and then quickly again, moving over into a square already cleared, two ahead.

All moved like machines, like chess pieces, until they fell.

Guthram had seen that he might in four or five sideways moves gain the right flank of the board, where – under the rules of this strangely conducted struggle – he would be permitted to stab ahead. Down went another white-clad youth, dying under his blade.

An advancing opponent was about to strike. Guthram rammed his blade into the ribs of the enemy on his right, usurping his square quickly, so that his adversary had to pass him by, and quickly slipped into the next square ahead.

The formalised carnage continued, part muffled, part ringing on the frozen ground, always punctuated by the barking of the hounds on the perimeters. Both sides advanced, men sometimes being isolated ahead of their comrades. There was never time to look about. Quick wits, quick blades, a never-tiring arm, were needed.

The whining boy went down, pouring blood from a stomach wound.

Guthram slew two more pawns and gained the right hand line of squares. Here he merely had to attend to those ahead, advancing square by square towards him. Square by square he dispatched them.

So at last, in triumph, he crossed the entire board. He raised a fist in triumph or relief. He was a man!

Exhausted, he leaned against a tree, feeling his sweat freeze on his body. In horror at the whole business, he vomited up the contents of his insides. He stood there, forehead against the tree, shivering.

Only after a moment did he realise what he was doing. He tried to pull away. His forehead had already frozen to the trunk of the tree. With a mighty effort, he wrenched himself loose, tearing the skin from his forehead as he did so. Blood blinded him, until he could bind up his head with a kerchief.

Other survivors came to stand near him. He was sick with pain and could say nothing. Under half the number who had set out had survived. Nobody spoke. Several youths sobbed openly, hiding their faces in their hands.

The commanders were counting bodies, to determine which force had won.

One of the surviving Expendables nudged Guthram.

"Can you still see? Then look up yonder – on the hill! There!"

Above them, on the lip of the hollow, a half-dozen Predators were manoeuvring a cannon of some variety into position. The cannon's open snout was pointed toward where the Insulator stood.

At that moment, the commanders shouted that the Holy Clathertam had won the primary battle by causing two hundred and thirty one deaths against only one hundred and ninety deaths of his Expendables. The commanders then cheered. The surviving Expendables made not a sound, and merely looked dejected.

The newly positioned cannon roared.

The Insulator was struck fair and square by the ball.

It expanded in a white sheet of destruction. As for the great ribbon of something like light: at one moment it was writhing into space. At the next –

The controlling engines being destroyed, space and time separated violently, as foretold by the Lord of Science. White light filled everything and everywhere. It seemed to entomb the armed soldiery. They became immobile.

Time in that location was destroyed.

There remained only space, crippled by division. Everything on the dark side of Moorn was transfixed, incapable of movement or life. The fiercest warrior stood like a glass ornament on a shelf. Here, time was no more.

No longer could a clock tick or a bell chime.

Birds in flight remained suspended in the air.

Insects climbing a stone remained still as stone.

Hounds straining at their leashes continued ever to strain.

Howlers high stepping and howling remained in mid-step and mid-howl, with no sound.

There was no sound.

No sight.

Not a breath of wind.

Not a whisper of whisker grew on a chin.

All biological things were stilled. All biological action halted. Breath, heart, thought – in every human case, these functions ceased to exist. All things which inhabited space were robbed of the vitality that time alone propagated. Neither were they dead, for death also is a creature of time. They simply became without viability.

There they stood, rooted, unmoving as stalagmites. Those that looked ahead, looked ahead without seeing. Those that had opened their mouths to speak, remained with mouths open. Those whose wounds bled, stayed with wounds unbleeding. Joy, misery, triumph, defeat – all were no more.

In that place was only a mighty tableau of stillness. It might have been a great canvas painted by an artist in oils, so drained was it of reality.

This terrible stasis remained while Moorn itself continued to turn on its axis and to hasten in its orbit. Yet the scene on the battle-field remained without benefit of time, without change. Nor did the torches burn out, or their flames so much as flicker.

The solar system never ceased its various motions or its bodies their balance between motion and gravity. The Moorn Moon did not remain forever excluded from the sun by its giant primary. On its course, Moorn reached a point where once more a beam of sunlight shot from behind the shoulder of Tarrell.

It happened that the first rays of the returning sun shone direct on the Insulator where it was in stasis.

Change came. With change, time burst violently back into place.

The Insulator continued to explode as if there had been no long pause in its violence.

Birds flopped from the sky. Insects fell from stones. Howlers completed their howl. Dogs finished their bark and barked anew.

And humanity took another breath.

Guthram felt his painful forehead and looked about him in bewilderment. He turned round in a complete circle, and then turned again, completely disoriented.

Everyone of either side in the battle experienced similar confusion, and could not speak. The commanders – even the Invincible himself – were similarly struck dumb by a metaphysical shock. They knew only that something unprecedented had happened, and could not grasp it.

Slowly, people began to move; first, their lungs, then their legs. They gathered their cloaks about their living bodies, looked up at the sun – now almost fully restored to wholeness – and began to walk again. As someone hoping to learn a new subject can learn nothing if he knows nothing of it, time was a subject beyond all their understandings.

Now that again the sun was a body entire, Tarrell faded from the skies. Warmth and brilliance awoke the world. Streams and rivers began to flow once more. Fish jumped in the waters, animals moved in the forests. Birds sought again to nest. The forests began to prepare to clothe themselves in leaves again.

Guthram lifted his arms to the sunlight. Forgetting his pain, he began to cheer. Others near him joined in. The joy was contagious. Soon, everyone was cheering, raising their arms and cheering for all they were worth.

When Guthram finally made his way back to Vurndrol City, it was to find his mother and sister Miney had emerged from hibernation; they and his procreator were well. Fleebis embraced her son heartily. "You need a good wash, son," she said. "And your hair needs a good comb."

Miney said, jumping about, "Too bad you missed the great Thank—What was it called, ma?"

Her mother told her it was the Great Thanksgiving of Light.

"Too bad you missed it, Guthy. A man gave me a doll. And we had sweets. The sweets were all gold."

Castener came forward and patted the boy's shoulder affectionately. He applied some cream to Guthram's forehead.

"You're a man now, Guthram," he said, proudly. He worked in the cream with tenderness.

Guthram's jaw set stubbornly. "If being a man means looting and being subject to the orders of others, and letting the weak die, and killing people, then I have no wish to be a man."

"You need a rest, old fellow," said Castener, displeased by this outburst. And then, to change the subject, "By the way, believe it or not, a new planet has recently arrived in our system."

They went together that night, after Guthram had bathed and rested, to examine the new planet through Castener's telescope. It appeared to Guthram a miracle of beauty. Cloud moved in stately progression over its blue face. It would heed no eclipses, it would need no hibernations.

Suddenly the songs of the howlers came back fresh in his memory. Now he thought he understood them better. Their meaning became clearer.

He told his father haltingly that the visiting Insulator had been time powered – for how else could it have crossed many light-years? –and had remained connected to its parent planet by the time-ribbon stretching through space. Destroying the link had inevitably propelled the parent planet through space/time to the power site.

Castener tapped some keys on his scanner.

"I'll have to work out the physics of that," he said with a chuckle. "Clearly, it would require a de-localized wavefunction."

But Guthram thought he knew what had happened. Moreover, he recalled that that parent planet had been inhabited by beings of superior knowledge and wisdom.

"We need to get in touch with them," he promised himself.

The National Heritage

I KNEW A MAN in Playa Arenas with a strange obsession. He carried about with him a small digital recorder on which he recorded everything he said.

No conversation was too slight, no grunt edited out.

His words were recorded on disk. Towards the end of his life, he had accumulated eighty-nine of these disks. In a bar near his apartment, I condescended to talk to him. (I was wearing modish white trousers. I was famous, whereas he had never met an intellectual before.) I asked him why he considered his words to be so important, whereas in the main our remarks are as transitory as the air passing through our lungs.

"I do not consider the words important," he replied. "Rather the opposite. I am able to play back stages of my life and see what rubbish I was speaking." He was recording these utterances on Disk Ninety as he talked. "By nature I am arrogant; I try to cure this unpleasant trait by replaying my old conversations. You might well be astonished at how foolish I sound, even in my wisest utterances."

"Not at all," I reassured him.

Taking a sip from his wine glass, he added, "So this process tends to keep me humble. On such and such a day, I can see I was a complete fool."

He leant back in his chair and twiddled his thumbs. I could not but remark that he looked rather arrogant – or shall we say self-satisfied? – at that moment. That I had formed this perception I found very satisfying.

Out of curiosity, I asked him what particular facet of his conversations he considered the most foolish.

After a few minutes of deliberation, he replied that his conversations with his wife when they first met were embarrassingly silly. They included many discussions of her complexion.

"And we talked about where we might live. This involved boring questions concerning rent, the traffic, the proximity of shops, the surrounding air... It was bad enough at the time. To have to listen to it all again was murder."

His and his wife's talk became more sensible later on, when, after years of marriage, they confined their discussions to purely domestic matters, such as when the canary should be fed, or the dog exercised, or whether to give up sugar.

This interested me; indeed, I was as much interested as bored in his presence.

He went on to suggest that on the whole his silliest utterances were those on the subject of philosophy when – at the time – he had imagined he was being most profound.

This strange man died one fine July day in his ninetieth year. It so happened that I was away from Playa Arenas and heard the news of his death only several days later. I felt sorry I had never learnt to pronounce his name. It sounded something like "phosphorus." I was driven at once to his apartment, which was on the tenth floor of a run-down apartment building.

In my role as President of the Institute of Arcane Sayings, which had recently come under the umbrella of the University of Playa Arenas, I had convinced my board that the obsessive's collection of disks was of unique international importance. Never before had the entire discourse of a man's life been placed on record in this way. I pledged that, among much that was dross, gems of wisdom would be found.

Moreover, the University, which would buy the collection from the man's widow, would surely gain worldwide celebrity by writing and publishing learned monographs on the collection.

Both institute and university gave me carte blanche to go ahead. I resolved to intrude on the grief of the widow of the dead man. She had moved to the ninth floor of the run-down apartment building. This lady was surprisingly cheerful; I caught her throwing out many of her late husband's possessions. "Now at last I shall have room to breathe," she told me. "The canary and the dog are going to have to go!"

"You must be sad at your husband's death," I said, reprovingly.

She nodded. "I'm going back on the sugar again," she told me. Her manner was confidential. I suspected she fancied me as a sexual partner.

She had already put the ninety disks into a sack and thrown the sack out.

"Oh, those damned disks went first!" she said, and laughed. "They followed the corpse out the door..."

I rushed to the street to retrieve them. The sack had gone. The city rubbish collection had already called and removed the sack.

A period of litigation followed. The city council, hearing that the disks were of value, claimed them as a civic possession.

With support from the university – and here I was particularly indebted to the Governor, Humphrey Malvoso – I brought a legal case against the council. There was a benefit from the case, in that it brought both the disks, the university, and me a remarkable degree of fame, in academic circles and in more popular channels.

The council gave in at last. At last I secured possession of the disks. They had remained on a rubbish tip for ten months. Alas, disappointment followed my triumph. The disks had been stored near an electricity generating plant and, in consequence, their entire contents had been wiped and lost.

I gracefully accepted the chance to become a celebrity. I dressed better, with mauve ties, such as the upper classes wear. Addressing the TV cameras, I said, "Our country has lost a valuable resource. It is so typical of our national carelessness that this should happen. Political corruption is to blame." I felt that this last remark struck home, and repeated it. "Never before has one man – a man relatively humble and unknown – whose name cannot even be properly pronounced – produced an entire record of his whole vocal and social life. So we have forfeited the treasured wisdom of a modest and dedicated man."

I also condemned the philistinism of the President. That was how the Revolution started.

Already I had put into practice the recording of my own sillinesses. My disks form part – an important part – of our national heritage.

How the Gates Opened and Closed

A GROUP OF OXFORD STORYTELLERS was gathered round a long table in one of the local inns in Old Headington. They were convivial, exchanging stories and laughing. At the far end of the table sat a fair-haired man past his prime, an untidy man, wearing trainers, tattered jeans, and a brown sweater. He had given his name as Callow. Ken Callow.

No one of the company had heard of Callow. No one had read any of his stories. He had been sitting among them for an hour, listening, not speaking, his hands thrust into his jeans pockets. The other storytellers were drinking and smoking – *smoking* because this happened some years ago, when it was fashionable to smoke.

A woman storyteller was telling the company a story and Callow was listening. When the laughter and applause at the end of the woman's story had died down, Callow sat bolt upright. He spoke, not challengingly but with assurance.

"All your stories are choked with events, like streams choked by weeds. Stories should not be only like that. Events mean nothing unless they are there to make a philosophical point, wouldn't you agree? I would like to tell you a tale with nothing happening in it. Because my life has been empty."

"We fill our stories with events for people with empty lives," said one of the male storytellers. "Our ingenuity lies in the creation of events and their resolution."

Callow gave him a half-smile. "Oh, I admire ingenuity too. You understand that when I say my life has been empty, I mean empty of event. It has been full of drama. Of an interior kind...." His voice faded.

The people round the table responded variously to this remark. Some accepted it sympathetically, some found it pretentious, although they might have accepted it on paper. All, however, challenged Callow to tell them a story without events in it.

"Just don't bore us too much," one youth said, smiling not un-kindly.

"A story without events," said Callow, "approaches stillness and silence. And stillness and silence approach the Sacred."

This remark was considered priggish. Callow saw by their mut-tering together that the feeling of the gathering had turned against him.

"So no sex then," sighed a long-haired woman.

Callow shrugged his shoulders, waited for quiet, and began.

"My story is called 'How the Gates Opened and Closed.' It is about a old man in a remote village. He lived in a hut with his daughter and her husband. Every evening, the old man, whose name was Lee, took his three geese down to drink in the pond at the end of the village. He led one goose with a length of string round its neck, the same old string he had used for several years. The other two geese followed the first one. They walked in an orderly line."

One of the party interupted, saying, "At this point, a wolf or a fox could run out of a wood and carry off one of the geese. That would be a bit interesting!"

"No such event ever occurred in my story," said Callow. He shook his head. "The visit to the pond was always peaceful. I want you to imagine it if you can. Old man Lee, his three white geese, the dusty road to the pond, the pond itself lying in a hollow, sunlight lying aslant, shadows beginning to lengthen as evening approaches. Nothing to disturb the calm.

"Old Lee exchanged a few words with the people he met on his way there and back. As a matter of fact, this village was almost deserted. Lee had been a conscripted soldier in his time – a soldier in several campaigns. He once was forced to march six days at a stretch, in a foreign province."

"Aha, there's some action! A six-days march counts as action! Don't cheat, Callow!" one of the listening storytellers said.

"Ah, but that was all in the past, long ago. Those campaigns were almost forgotten. The country had been ravaged by war, and the famines that follow on the heels of war. I should have mentioned that the village was in ruins. Hardly a house was left intact after various armies had passed through that way, burning and destroying as they went. Most of the inhabitants had fled, or had been killed."

"You are forced to tell us of many great events in order to pad out your story, I see," said one of the women present, with a smile.

"I merely mention those happenings in passing," said Callow. "To paint the picture, you know. They are not events, merely background music. So far we have only this quiet old man with his geese, at the pond. But I should also mention that the old religion which once held the country together had died, or appeared to have died. No one visited the temple any more; it was ruinous, but no one attempted to restore it. But the temple really plays no part in my story. What I'm talking about is simply an old bent man, not in the best of health, taking three geese to the pond every evening. And not to keep you in suspense, old Lee gets safely home later, without incident – without event."

He looked round rather mischievously at the company.

"But one day his geese escape, surely?" said one of the storytellers at the other end of the table. "Otherwise, what's the point of all this?"

"Geese are friendly and intelligent birds," said Callow. "They'd talk if they could. They enjoyed their walk every evening, they enjoyed their splash in the pond. And they would no more think of leaving their master than Lee would think of leaving them. They always followed him willingly back to Lee's daughter's hut and laid eggs for the family as often as they could manage."

"Very dramatic, I must say!" someone piped up. "I've had enough of these wretched geese. Get on and tell us the story."

"What you must learn to enjoy is the lack of event, the silences of a tale." Callow paused, as if to emphasise the importance of what he was saying. The friends round the table took another drink; some lit up another cigarette. Some of Callow's listeners fidgetted – even when he continued on a different tack.

"There are as many kinds of story as there are kinds of reader. People can learn as much from inaction as action. And the humble life of this old man with his geese must be contrasted with another life: a life of great wealth, the life of a prince who lived nearby – a prince born in the same year, the Year of the Buffalo, as old man Lee."

"Hah, another protagonist at last!" The woman storyteller who had spoken clapped her hands. "So, Mr Callow, you do find it necessary to introduce a little character conflict into your dull village tale."

"Not at all." Callow shook his head. He spread his hands and, addressing the woman storyteller directly, said, "These two men, old Lee and the prince, had encountered one another only once, many years earlier, when the prince was on his way to his palace. The palace stood aloof at the end of the village. Lee got in the way of the prince's carriage. The prince shouted to him, kindly enough, perhaps rather mockingly, "Don't you value your life, man?" Lee never forgot those words, and often repeated them to his friends in the years of war. He marvelled at them, firstly because it was the only time he had been spoken to by a prince, and secondly because he had never thought that a peasant's life such as his could have value.

Don't you value your life?.... The question remained a puzzlement to him.

"This is all past tense stuff, you know," one of the men at the table reminded Callow with a sigh.

"Well, if there's tranquility anywhere, perhaps it resides in the past...." Callow responded. "When old Lee was standing by the pond while his geese had a drink and a swim, he could see the gates of the palace, quite nearby. Never once, during all the troubles and pestilences which beset the province, had those grand pretentious gates been opened. Until one day, this very day we are talking about, to Lee's amazement, he heard a gong resounding on the clear evening air – and witnessed the opening of the gates. What a creaking those unused hinges set up between them! And out came the prince himself.

"The prince stood in the roadway, looking about him, and Lee – at the distance of a hundred metres – bowed to him profoundly."

"So Lee gets his head chopped off?" suggested one of his more whimsical listeners.

"You must consider the situation. On the one hand, an old soldier, survivor of several campaigns, a man whose parents had been killed by bandits, whose wife, after bearing him children, had died in one of the epidemics which swept the country. He had been uprooted and now lived a thousand miles from the village where he had been born.

"And on the other hand, this grand person of privilege, born to reign over vast territories, who had known no hardship, who–unlike Lee–had been able to choose how he would live.

"Old Lee was a thin wasted man with a face brown and wrinkled as a walnut. His ribs showed under his thin shirt. Although his sight was not of the best, it was for another reason he would have failed to recognise the prince; failed – had it not been for the latter's elaborate garments, not grey homespun like Lee's, but of yellow silk, and tied with blue ribbons about the neck and knees.

"When Lee had seen the prince in his carriage, many years earlier, the prince had been a strikingly handsome young man, lean, athletic, known for his prowess at archery and blood sports. Now Lee was

staring at a bloated creature with a bald pate, who supported himself
with an ebony stick. The cut of his clothes could not conceal bow legs
and a sagging stomach. He had waddled rather than walked through
the palace gates...."

One of the storytellers at the table set down his glass and interupted. "Fine, fine, but enough of these comparisons, the rich and
the poor. What of it? Where's the drama in all this?"

"Simply this," said Callow. "I wished to tell you a story without
event. That I have done. Once the prince had regarded his ravaged
territories with disfavour, he turned and ambled back into his palace. He had not even deigned to notice the old peasant. The gates
closed behind him. Once more the gong sounded. Old Lee collected
his geese and returned to his sister's hut as usual. That night, lit by
a rush light, they ate for their supper a handful of rice with chopped
goose egg and chilli."

There were many complaints at the table when they realised Callow had finished his story.

"You mean to say this Lee and the prince never even shouted at
each other? Never even spoke?" exclaimed one of the disappointed
listeners. "Couldn't you have arranged it for the prince to recognise
your old chap, maybe invite him into the palace, to a banquet? Or
– your old man never even spat at the prince? That's what I call a dis-
appointing story...."

"It would have been out of character to have a peasant spit at a
prince, or a prince to recognise a peasant," Callow said. "I'm sorry
if you dislike my story. But don't you see that it's about the lack of
event? You believe tragedies are made from events, like Sophocles'
Oedipus Rex. But sometimes they are made from the vacuum created
by a failure of contact.

"You have to think about it. The prince abrogated his powers. Instead of exercising his traditional rights and duties, and maintaining
civic order, he had retreated into his private world and enjoyed his
concubines. He was too self-indulgent. His was a life without history.

For thirty years, he closed his eyes to the fate of his people and his bronze doors to life itself.

"Because of that idleness, that dereliction of duty, his province underwent far too much history. It became a theatre of events. Events ruled. The period was referred to later as The Age of the Seven Wars. Many volumes were written about it."

The storytellers looked at each other up and down the long table. One of them said, "Mr. Callow, couldn't you have made up a more interesting story about the wars themselves, and the people taking part in them? Or we could have had a nice erotic story about what went on in the prince's palace for all those years...."

Callow shook his head, saying nothing more. He felt he was not clever enough to make up the sort of story they all wanted to hear. He had imagined that to conjure up a portrait of a calm evening was enough to engage his listeners.

All he had had in mind was the picture of an old man walking as the day waned in a ruined village with his line of three white geese, an old man who had once been asked the question, "Don't you value your life?" He understood that the very poor could never answer such questions: just as the prince, in his eventless existence, had never valued the life even of a goose.

Total Environment

"WHAT'S THAT POEM about 'caverns measureless to man'?" Thomas Dixit asked. His voice echoed away among the caverns, the question unanswered. Peter Crawley, walking a pace or two behind him, said nothing, lost in a reverie of his own.

It was over a year since Dixit had been imprisoned here. He had taken time off from the resettlement area to come and have a last look round before everything was finally demolished. In these great concrete workings, men still moved – Indian technicians mostly, carrying instruments, often with their own headlights. Cables trailed everywhere; but the desolation was mainly an effect of the constant abrasion all surfaces had undergone. People had flowed here like water in a subterranean cave; and their corporate life had flowed similarly, hidden, forgotten.

Dixit was powerfully moved by the thought of all that life. He, almost alone, was the man who had plunged into it and survived.

Old angers stirring in him, he turned and spoke directly to his companion. "What a monument to human suffering! They should leave this place standing as an everlasting memorial to what happened."

The white man said, "The Delhi government refuses to entertain any such suggestion. I see their point of view, but I also see that it would make a great tourist attraction!"

109

"Tourist attraction, man! Is that all it means to you?"

Crawley laughed. "As ever, you're too touchy, Thomas. I take this whole matter much less lightly than you suppose. Tourism just happens to attract me more than human suffering."

They walked on side by side. They were never able to agree.

The battered faces of flats and houses – now empty, once choked with humanity – stood on either side, doors gaping open like old men's mouths in sleep. The spaces seemed enormous; the shadows and echoes that belonged to those spaces seemed to continue indefinitely. Yet before...there had scarcely been room to breathe here.

"I remember what your buddy, Senator Byrnes, said," Crawley remarked. "He showed how both East and West have learned from this experiment. Of course, the social scientists are still working over their findings: some startling formulae for social groups are emerging already. But the people who lived and died here were fighting their way towards control of the universe of the ultra-small, and that's where the biggest advances have come. They were already developing power over their own genetic material. Another generation, and they might have produced the ultimate in automatic human population control: anoestrus, where too close proximity to other members of the species leads to reabsorption of the embryonic material in the female. Our scientists have been able to help them there, and geneticists predict that in another decade – "

"Yes, yes, all that I grant you. Progress is wonderful." He knew he was being impolite. These things were important, of revolutionary importance to a crowded Earth. But he wished he walked these eroded passageways alone.

Undeniably, India had learned too, just as Peter Crawley claimed. For Hinduism had been put to the test here and had shown its terrifying strengths and weaknesses. In these mazes, people had not broken under deadly conditions – nor had they thought to break away from their destiny. *Dharma* – duty – had been stronger than humanity. And this revelation was already changing the thought and fate of one-sixth of the human race.

He said, "Progress is wonderful. But what took place here was essentially a religious experience."

Crawley's brief laugh drifted away into the shadows of a great gaunt stairwell. "I'll bet you didn't feel that way when we sent you in here a year ago!"

What had he felt then? He stopped and gazed up at the gloom of the stairs. All that came to him was the memory of that appalling flood of life and of the people who had been a part of it, whose brief years had evaporated in these caverns, whose feet had endlessly trodden these warren-ways, these lugubrious decks, these crumbling flights....

[II]

The concrete steps climbed up into darkness. The steps were wide, and countless children sat on them, listless, resting against each other. This was an hour when activity was low and even small children hushed their cries for a while. Yet there was no silence on the steps; silence was never complete there. Always, in the background, the noise of voices. Voices and more voices. Never silence.

Shamim was aged, so she preferred to run her errands at this time of day, when the crowds thronging Total Environment were less. She dawdled by a sleepy seller of life-objects at the bottom of the stairs, picking over the little artifacts and exclaiming now and again. The hawker knew her, knew she was too poor to buy, did not even press her to buy. Shamim's oldest daughter, Malti, waited for her mother by the bottom step.

Malti and her mother were watched from the top of the steps.

A light burned at the top of the steps. It had burned there for twenty-five years, safe from breakage behind a strong mesh. But dung and mud had recently been thrown at it, covering it almost entirely and so making the top of the stairway dark. A furtive man called Narayan Farhad crouched there and watched, a shadow in the shadows.

A month ago, Shamim had had an illegal operation in one of the pokey rooms off Grand Balcony on her deck. The effects of the operation were still with her; under her plain cotton sari, her thin dark old body was bent. Her share of life stood lower than it had been.

Malti, her oldest daughter, was a meek girl who had not been conceived when the Total Environment experiment began. Even meekness had its limits. Seeing her mother dawdle so needlessly, Malti muttered impatiently and went on ahead, climbing the infested steps, anxious to be home.

Extracts from Thomas Dixit's report to Senator Jacob Byrnes, back in America: *To lend variety to the habitat, the Environment has been divided into ten decks, each deck five stories high, which allows for an occasional pocket-sized open space. The architecture has been varied somewhat on each deck. On one deck, a sort of blown-up Indian village is presented; on another, the houses are large and appear separate, although sandwiched between decks – I need not add they are hopelessly overcrowded now. On most decks, the available space is packed solid with flats. Despite this attempt at variety, a general bowdlerization of both Eastern and Western architectural styles, and the fact that everything has been constructed out of concrete or a parastyrene for economy's sake, has led to a dreadful sameness. I cannot imagine anywhere more hostile to the spiritual values of life.*

The shadow in the shadows moved. He glanced anxiously up at the light, which also housed a spy-eye; there would be a warning out, and sprays would soon squirt away the muck he had thrown at the fitting; but for the moment, he could work unobserved.

Narayan bared his old teeth as Malti came up the steps towards him, treading among the sprawling children. She was too old to fetch a really good price on the slave market, but she was still strong; there would be no trouble in getting rid of her at once. Of course he knew something of her history, even though she lived on a different deck from him. Malti! He called her name at the last moment as he jumped out on her. Old though he was, Narayan was quick. He wore only his dhoti, arms flashing, interlocking round hers, one good powerful wrench to get her off her feet—now running fast, fearful, up the rest of the steps, moving even as he clamped one hand over her mouth to cut off her cry of fear. Clever old Narayan!

The stairs mount up and up in the four corners of the Total Environment, linking deck with deck. They are now crude things of concrete and metal, since the plastic covers have long been stripped from them.

These stairways are the weak points of the tiny empires, transient and brutal, that form on every deck. They are always guarded, though guards can be bribed. Sometimes gangs or "unions" take over a stairway, either by agreement or bloodshed.

Shamim screamed, responding to her daughter's cry. She began to hobble up the stairs as fast as she could, tripping over infant feet, drawing a dagger out from under her sari. It was a plastic dagger, shaped out of a piece of the Environment.

She called Malti, called for help as she went. When she reached the landing, she was on the top floor of her deck, the Ninth, where she lived. Many people were here, standing, squatting, thronging together. They looked away from Shamim, people with blind faces. She had so often acted similarly herself when others were in trouble.

Gasping, she stopped and stared up at the roof of the deck, blue-dyed to simulate sky, cracks running irregularly across it. The steps went on up there, up to the Top Deck. She saw legs, yellow soles of feet disappearing, faces staring down at her, hostile. As she ran toward the bottom of the stairs, the watchers above threw things at her. A shard hit Shamim's cheek and cut it open. With blood running down her face, she began to wail. Then she turned and ran through the crowds to her family room.

I've been a month just reading through the microfiles. Sometimes a whole deck becomes unified under a strong leader. On Deck Nine, for instance, unification was achieved under a man called Ullhas. He was a strong man, and a great show-off. That was a while ago, when conditions were not as desperate as they are now. Ullhas could never last the course today. Leaders become more despotic as Environment decays.

The dynamics of unity are such that it is always insufficient for a deck simply to stay unified; the young men always need to have their aggressions directed outwards. So the leader of a strong deck always sets out to tyrannize the deck below or above, whichever seems to be the weaker. It is a miserable state of affairs. The time generally comes when, in the midst of a raid, a counter-raid is launched by one of the other decks. Then the raiders return to carnage and defeat. And another paltry empire tumbles.

It is up to me to stop this continual degradation of human life.

As usual, the family room was crowded. Although none of Shamim's own children were here, there were grandchildren – including the lame granddaughter, Shirin – and six great-grandchildren, none of them more than three years old. Shamim's third husband, Gita, was not in. Safe in the homely squalor of the room, Shamim burst into tears, while Shirin comforted her and endeavored to keep the little ones off.

"Gita is getting food. I will go and fetch him," Shirin said.

When UHDRE – Ultra-High Density Research Establishment – became operative, twenty-five years ago, all the couples selected for living in the Total Environment had to be under twenty years of age. Before being sealed in, they were inoculated against all diseases. There was plenty of room for each couple then; they had whole suites to themselves, and the best of food; plus no means of birth control. That's always been the main pivot of the UHDRE experiment. Now that first generation has aged severely. They are old people pushing forty-five. The whole life cycle has speeded up – early puberty, early senescence. The second and third generations have shown remarkable powers of adaptation; a fourth generation is already toddling. Those toddlers will be reproducing before their years attain double figures, if present trends continue. Are allowed to continue.

Gita was younger than Shamim, a small wiry man who knew his way around. No hero, he nevertheless had a certain style about him. His life-object hung boldly round his neck on a chain, instead of being hidden, as were most people's life-objects. He stood in the line for food, chattering with friends. Gita was good at making alliances. With a bunch of his friends, he had formed a little union to see that they got their food back safely to their homes; so they generally met with no incident in the crowded walkways of Deck Nine.

The balance of power on the deck was very complex at the moment. As a result, comparative peace reigned, and might continue for several weeks if the strong man on Top Deck did not interfere.

Food delivery grills are fixed in the walls of every floor of every deck. Two gongs sound before each delivery. After the second one, hatches open and steaming food pours from the grills. Hills of rice tumble forward, flavored with meat and spices. Chappattis fall from a separate slot. As the men run forward with their containers, holy men are generally there to sanctify the food.

Great supply elevators roar up and down in the heart of the vast tower, tumbling out rations at all levels. Alcohol also was supplied in the early years. It was discontinued when it led to trouble; which is not to say that it is not secretly brewed inside the Environment. The UHDRE food ration has been generous from the start and has always been maintained at the same level per head of population although, as you know, the food is now ninety-five percent factory-made. Nobody would ever have starved, had it been shared out equally inside the tower. On some of the decks, some of the time, it is still shared out fairly.

One of Gita's sons, Jamsu, had seen the kidnapper Narayan making off to Top Deck with the struggling Malti. His eyes gleaming with excitement, he sidled his way into the queue where Gita stood and clasped his father's arm. Jamsu had something of his father in him, always lurked where numbers made him safe, rather than run off as his brothers and sisters had run off, to marry and struggle for a room or a space of their own.

He was telling his father what had happened when Shirin limped up and delivered her news.

Nodding grimly, Gita said, "Stay with us, Shirin, while I get the food."

He scooped his share into the family pail. Jamsu grabbed a handful of rice for himself.

"It was a dirty wizened man from Top Deck called Narayan Farhad," Jamsu said, gobbling. "He is one of the crooks who hangs about the shirttails of…" He let his voice die.

"You did not go to Malti's rescue, shame on you!" Shirin said.

"Jamsu might have been killed," Gita said, as they pushed through the crowd and moved towards the family room.

"They're getting so strong on Top Deck," Jamsu said. "I hear all about it! We mustn't provoke them or they may attack. They say a regular army is forming round…"

Shirin snorted impatiently. "You great babe! Go ahead and name the man! It's Prahlad Patel whose very name you dare not mention, isn't it? Is he a god or something, for Siva's sake? You're afraid of him even from this distance, eh, aren't you?"

"Don't bully the lad," Gita said. Keeping the peace in his huge mixed family was a great responsibility, almost more than he could manage. As he turned into the family room, he said quietly to Jamsu and Shirin, "Malti was a favorite daughter of Shamim's, and now is gone from her. We will get our revenge against this Narayan Farhad. You and I will go this evening, Jamsu, to the holy man Vazifdar. He will even up matters for us, and then perhaps the great Patel will also be warned."

He looked thoughtfully down at his life-object. Tonight, he told himself, I must venture forth alone, and put my life in jeopardy for Shamim's sake.

Prahlad Patel's union has flourished and grown until now he rules all the Top Deck. His name is known and dreaded, we believe, three or four decks down. He is the strongest—yet in some ways curiously the most moderate— ruler in Total Environment at present.

Although he can be brutal, Patel seems inclined for peace. Of course, the bugging does not reveal everything; he may have plans which he keeps secret, since he is fully aware that the bugging exists. But we believe his interests lie in other directions than conquest. He is only about nineteen, as we reckon years, but already gray-haired, and the sight of him is said to freeze the muscles to silence in the lips of his followers. I have watched him over the bugging for many hours since I agreed to undertake this task.

Patel has one great advantage in Total Environment. He lives on the Tenth Deck, at the top of the building. He can therefore be invaded only from below, and the Ninth Deck offers no strong threats at present, being mainly oriented round an influential body of holy men, of whom the most illustrious is one Vazifdar.

The staircases between decks are always trouble spots. No deck-ruler was ever strong enough to withstand attack from above and below. The staircases are also used by single troublemakers, thieves, political fugitives, prostitutes, escaping slaves, hostages. Guards can always be bribed, or favor their multitudinous relations, or join the enemy for one reason or another. Patel, being on the Top Deck, has only four weak points to watch for, rather than eight.

Vazifdar was amazingly holy and amazingly influential. It was whispered that his life-object was the most intricate in all Environment, but there was nobody who would lay claim to having set eyes upon it. Because of his reputation, many people on Gita's deck – yes, and from farther away – sought Vazifdar's help. A stream of men and women moved always through his room, even when he was locked in private meditation and far away from this world.

The holy man had a flat with a balcony that looked out onto mid-deck. Many relations and disciples lived there with him, so that the rooms had been elaborately and flimsily divided by screens. All day, the youngest disciples twittered like birds upon the balconies as Vazifdar held court, discussing among themselves the immense wisdom of his sayings.

All the disciples, all the relations, loved Vazifdar. There had been relations who did not love Vazifdar, but they had passed away in their sleep. Gita himself was a distant relation of Vazifdar's and came into the holy man's presence now with gifts of fresh water and a long piece of synthetic cloth, enough to make a robe.

Vazifdar's brow and cheeks were painted with white to denote his high caste. He received the gifts of cloth and water graciously, smiling at Gita in such a way that Gita – and, behind him, Jamsu – took heart.

Vazifdar was thirteen years old as the outside measured years. He was sleekly fat, from eating much and moving little. His brown body shone with oils; every morning, young women massaged and manipulated him.

He spoke very softly, husbanding his voice, so that he could scarcely be heard for the noise in the room.

"It is a sorrow to me that this woe has befallen your stepchild Malti," he said. "She was a good woman, although infertile."

"She was raped at a very early age, disrupting her womb, dear Vazifdar. You will know of the event. Her parents feared she would die. She could never bear issue. The evil shadowed her life. Now this second woe befalls her."

"I perceive that Malti's role in the world was merely to be a companion to her mother. Not all can afford to purchase who visit the bazaar."

There are bazaars on every floor, crowding down the corridors and balconies, and a chief one on every deck. The menfolk choose such places to meet and chatter even when they have nothing to trade. Like every-

where else, the bazaars are crowded with humanity, down to the smallest who can walk — and sometimes even those carry naked smaller brothers clamped tight to their backs.

The bazaars are great centers for scandal. Here also are our largest screens. They glow behind their safety grills, beaming in special programs from outside; our outside world that must seem to have but faint reality as it dashes against the thick securing walls of Environment and percolates through to the screens. Below the screens, uncheckable and fecund life goes teeming on, with all its injury.

Humbly, Gita on his knees said, "If you could restore Malti to her mother Shamim, who mourns her, you would reap all our gratitude, dear Vazifdar. Malti is too old for a man's bed, and on Top Deck all sorts of humiliations must await her."

Vazifdar shook his head with great dignity. "You know I cannot restore Malti, my kinsman. How many deeds can be ever undone? As long as we have slavery, so long must we bear to have the ones we love enslaved. You must cultivate a mystical and resigned view of life and beseech Shamim always to do the same."

"Shamim is more mystical in her ways than I, never asking much, always working, working, praying, praying. That is why she deserves better than this misery."

Nodding in approval of Shamim's behavior as thus revealed, Vazifdar said, "That is well. I know she is a good woman. In the future lie other events which may recompense her for this sad event."

Jamsu, who had managed to keep quiet behind his father until now, suddenly burst out, "Uncle Vazifdar, can you not punish Narayan Farhad for his sin in stealing poor Malti on the steps? Is he to be allowed to escape to Patel's deck, there to live with Malti and enjoy?"

"Sssh, son!" Gita looked in agitation to see if Jamsu's outburst had annoyed Vazifdar, but Vazifdar was smiling blandly.

"You must know, Jamsu, that we are all creatures of the Lord Siva, and without power. No, no, do not pout! I also am without power in his hands. To own one room is not to possess the whole mansion. But..."

It was a long, and heavy *but*. When Vazifdar's thick eyelids closed over his eyes, Gita trembled, for he recalled how, on previous occasions when he had visited his powerful kinsman, Vazifdar's eyelids had descended in this fashion while he deigned to think on a problem, as if he shut out all the external world with his own potent flesh.

"Narayan Farhad shall be troubled by more than his conscience." As he spoke, the pupils of his eyes appeared again, violet and black. They were looking beyond Gita, beyond the confines of his immediate surroundings. "Tonight he shall be troubled by evil dreams."

"The night-visions!" Gita and Jamsu exclaimed, in fear and excitement.

Now Vazifdar swiveled his magnificent head and looked directly at Gita, looked deep into his eyes. Gita was a small man; he saw himself as a small man within. He shrank still further under that irresistible scrutiny.

"Yes, the night-visions," the holy man said. "You know what that entails, Gita. You must go up to Top Deck and procure Narayan's life-object. Bring it back to me, and I promise Narayan shall suffer the night-visions tonight. Though he is sick, he shall be cured."

[III]

The women never cease their chatter as the lines of supplicants come and go before the holy men. Their marvelous resignation in that hateful prison! If they ever complain about more than the small circumstances of their lives, if they ever complain about the monstrous evil that has overtaken them all, I never heard of it. There is always the harmless talk, talk that relieves petty nervous anxieties, talk that relieves the almost unnoticed pressures on the brain. The women's talk practically drowns the noise of their children. But most of the time it is clear that Total Environ-

ment consists mainly of children. That's why I want to see the experiment closed down; the children would adapt to our world.

It is mainly on this fourth generation that the effects of the population glut show. Whoever rules the decks, it is the babes, the endless babes, tottering, laughing, staring, piddling, tumbling, running, the endless babes to whom the Environment really belongs. And their mothers, for the most part, are women who – at the same age and in a more favored part of the globe – would still be virginally at school, many only just entering their teens.

Narayan Farhad wrapped a blanket round himself and huddled in his corner of the crowded room. Since it was almost time to sleep, he had to take up his hired space before one of the loathed Dasguptas stole it. Narayan hated the Dasgupta family, its lickspittle men, its shrill women, its turbulent children – the endless babes who crawled, the bigger ones with nervous diseases who thieved and ran and jeered at him. It was the vilest family on Top Deck, according to Narayan's oft-repeated claims; he tolerated it only because he felt himself to be vile.

He succeeded at nothing to which he turned his hand. Only an hour ago, pushing through the crowds, he had lost his life-object from his pocket – or else it had been stolen; but he dared not even consider that possibility!

Even his desultory kidnapping business was a failure. This bitch he had caught this morning – Malti. He had intended to rape her before selling her, but had become too nervous once he had dragged her in here, with a pair of young Dasguptas laughing at him. Nor had he sold the woman well. Patel had beaten down his price, and Narayan had not the guts to argue. Maybe he should leave this deck and move down to one of the more chaotic ones. The middle decks were always more chaotic. Six was having a slow three-sided war even now, which should make Five a fruitful place with hordes of refugees to batten on.

...And what a fool to snatch so old a girl – practically an old woman!

Through narrowed eyes, Narayan squatted in his corner, acid flavors burning his mouth. Even if his mind would rest and allow him to sleep, the Dasgupta mob was still too lively for any real relaxation. That old Dasgupta, now – he was like a rat, totally without self-restraint, not a proper Hindu at all, doing the act openly with his own daughters. There were many men like that in Total Environment, men who had nothing else in life. Dirty swine! Lucky dogs! Narayan's daughters had thrown him out many months ago when he tried it!

Over and over, his mind ran over his grievances. But he sat collectedly, prodding off with one bare foot the nasty little brats who crawled at him, and staring at the screen flickering on the wall behind its protective mesh.

He liked the screens, enjoyed viewing the madness of outside. What a world it was out there! All that heat, and the necessity for work, and the complication of life! The sheer bigness of the world – he couldn't stand that, would not want it under any circumstances.

He did not understand half he saw. After all, he was born here. His father might have been born outside, whoever his father was; but no legends from outside had come down to him: only the distortions in the general gossip, and the stuff on the screens. Now that he came to reflect, people didn't pay much attention to the screens any more. Even he didn't.

But he could not sleep. Blearily, he looked at images of cattle ploughing fields, fields cut into dice by the dirty grills before the screens. He had already gathered vaguely that this feature was about changes in the world today.

"...are giving way to this..." said the commentator above the rumpus in the Dasgupta room. The children lived here like birds. Racks were stacked against the walls, and on these rickety contraptions the many little Dasguptas roosted.

"...food factories automated against danger of infection..." Yak yak yak, then.

"Beef-tissue culture growing straight into plastic distribution packs..." Shots of some great interior place somewhere, with meat growing out of pipes, extruding itself into square packs, dripping with liquid, looking rather ugly. Was that the shape of cows now or something? Outside must be a hell of a scaring place, then! "...as new factory food at last spells hope for India's future in the..." Yak yak yak from the kids. Once, their sleep racks had been built across the screen; but one night the whole shaky edifice collapsed, and three children were injured. None killed, worse luck!

Patel should have paid more for that girl. Nothing was as good as it had been. Why, once on a time, they used to show sex films on the screens – really filthy stuff that got even Narayan excited. He was younger then. Really filthy stuff, he remembered, and pretty girls doing it. But it must be – oh, a long time since that was stopped. The screens were dull now. People gave up watching. Uneasily, Narayan slept, propped in the corner under his scruffy blanket. Eventually, the whole scruffy room slept.

The documentaries and other features piped into Environment are no longer specially made by UHDRE *teams for internal consumption. When the* U.N. *made a major cut in* UHDRE's *annual subsidy, eight years ago, the private* TV *studio was one of the frills that had to be axed. Now we pipe in old programs bought off major networks. The hope is that they will keep the wretched prisoners in Environment in touch with the outside world, but this is clearly not happening. The degree of comprehension, between inside and outside grows markedly less on both sides, on an exponential curve. As I see it, a great gulf of isolation is widening between the two environments, just as if they were sailing away from each other into different space-time continua. I wish I could think that the people in charge here – Crawley especially – not only grasped this fact but understood that it should be rectified immediately.*

Shamim could not sleep for grief.

Gita could not sleep for apprehension.

Jamsu could not sleep for excitement.

Vazifdar did not sleep.

Vazifdar shut his sacred self away in a cupboard, brought his lids down over his eyes and began to construct, within the vast spaces of his mind, a thought pattern corresponding to the matrix represented by Narayan Farhad's stolen life-object. When it was fully conceived, Vazifdar began gently to insert a little evil into one edge of the thought-pattern....

Narayan slept. What roused him was the silence. It was the first time total silence had ever come to Total Environment.

At first, he thought he would enjoy total silence. But it took on such weight and substance....

Clutching his blanket, he sat up. The room was empty, the screen dark. Neither thing had ever happened before, could not happen! And the silence! Dear Siva, some terrible monkey god had hammered that silence out in darkness and thrown it out like a shield into the world, rolling over all things! There was a ringing quality in the silence – a gong! No, no, not a gong! Footsteps!

It was footsteps, O Lord Siva, do not let it be footsteps!

Total Environment was empty. The legend was fulfilled that said Total Environment would empty one day. All had departed except for poor Narayan. And this thing of the footsteps was coming to visit him in his defenseless corner....

It was climbing up through the cellars of his existence. Soon it would emerge.

Trembling convulsively, Narayan stood up, clutching the corner of the blanket to his throat. He did not wish to face the thing. Wildly, he thought, could he bear it best if it looked like a man or if it looked nothing like a man? It was Death for sure – but how would it look? Only Death – his heart fluttered! – only Death could arrive this way....

His helplessness... Nowhere to hide! He opened his mouth, could not scream, clutched the blanket, felt that he was wetting himself as if he were a child again. Swiftly came the image – the infantile, round-bellied, cringing, puny, his mother black with fury, her great white teeth gritting as she smacked his face with all her might, spitting.... It was gone, and he faced the gong-like death again, alone in the great dark tower. In the arid air, vibrations of its presence.

He was shouting to it, demanding that it did not come.

But it came. It came with majestic sloth, like the heartbeats of a foetid slumber, came in the door, pushing darkness before it. It was like a human, but too big to be human.

And it wore Malti's face, that sickening innocent smile with which she had run up the steps. No! No, that was not it – oh, he fell down onto the wet floor: it was nothing like that woman, nothing at all. Cease, impossibilities! It was a man, his ebony skull shining, terrible and magnificent, stretching out, grasping, confident. Narayan struck out of his extremity and fell forward. Death was another indelible smack in the face.

One of the roosting Dasguptas blubbered and moaned as the man kicked him, woke for a moment, saw the screen still flickering meaninglessly and reassuringly, saw Narayan tremble under his blanket, tumbled back into sleep.

It was not till morning that they found it had been Narayan's last tremble.

I know I am supposed to be a detached observer. No emotions, no feelings. But scientific detachment is the attitude that has led to much of the inhumanity inherent in Environment. How do we, for all the bugging devices, hope to know what ghastly secret nightmares they undergo in there? Anyhow, I am relieved to hear you are flying over.

It is tomorrow I am due to go into Environment myself.

[IV]

The central offices of UHDRE were large and repulsive. At the time when they and the Total Environment tower had been built, the Indian Government would not have stood for anything else. Poured cement and rough edges was what they wanted to see and what they got.

From a window in the office building, Thomas Dixit could see the indeterminate land in one direction, and the gigantic TE tower in the other, together with the shantytown that had grown between the foot of the tower and the other UHDRE buildings.

For a moment, he chose to ignore the Project Organizer behind him and gaze out at what he could see of the table-flat lands of the great Ganges delta.

He thought, It's as good a place as any for man to project his power fantasies. But you are a fool to get mixed up in all this, Thomas!

Even to himself, he was never just Tom.

I am being paid, well paid, to do a specific job. Now I am letting woolly humanitarian ideas get in the way of action. Essentially, I am a very empty man. No center. Father Bengali, mother English, and live all my life in the States. I have excuses... Other people accept them; why can't I?

Sighing, he dwelt on his own unsatisfactoriness. He did not really belong to the West, despite his long years there, and he certainly did not belong to India; in fact, he thought he rather disliked India. Maybe the best place for him was indeed the inside of the Environment tower.

He turned impatiently and said, "I'm ready to get going now, Peter."

Peter Crawley, the Special Project Organizer of UHDRE, was a rather austere Bostonian. He removed the horn-rimmed glasses from his nose and said, "Right! Although we have been through the drill many times, Thomas, I have to tell you this once again before we move. The entire – "

"Yes, yes, I know, Peter! You don't have to cover yourself. This entire organization might be closed down if I make a wrong move. Please take it as read."

Without indignation, Crawley said, "I was going to say that we are all rooting for you. We appreciate the risks you are taking. We shall be checking you everywhere you go in there through the bugging system."

"And whatever you see, you can't do a thing."

"Be fair; we have made arrangements to help!"

"I'm sorry, Peter." He liked Crawley and Crawley's decent reserve.

Crawley folded his spectacles with a snap, inserted them in a leather slipcase and stood up.

"The U.N., not to mention subsidiary organizations like the WHO and the Indian government, have their knife into us, Thomas. They want to close us down and empty Environment. They will do so unless you can provide evidence that forms of extrasensory perception are developing inside the Environment. Don't get yourself killed in there. The previous men we sent in behaved foolishly and never came out again." He raised an eyebrow and added dryly, "That sort of thing gets us a bad name, you know?

"Just as the blue movies did a while ago."

Crawley put his hands behind his back. "My predecessor here decided that immoral movies piped into Environment would help boost the birthrate there. Whether he was right or wrong, world opinion has changed since then as the specter of world famine has faded. We stopped the movies eight years ago, but they have long memories at the U.N., I fear. They allow emotionalism to impede scientific research."

"Do you never feel any sympathy for the thousands of people doomed to live out their brief lives in the tower?"

They looked speculatively at each other.

"You aren't on our side any more, Thomas, are you? You'd like your findings to be negative, wouldn't you, and have the u.n. close us down?"

Dixit uttered a laugh. "I'm not on anyone's *side,* Peter. I'm neutral. I'm going into Environment to look for the evidence of esp that only direct contact may turn up. What else direct contact will turn up, neither of us can say as yet."

"But you think it will be misery. And you will emphasize that at the inquiry after your return."

"Peter – let's get on with it, shall we?" Momentarily, Dixit was granted a clear picture of the two of them standing in this room; he saw how their bodily attitudes contrasted. His attitudes were rather slovenly; he held himself rather slump-shouldered, he gesticulated to some extent (too much?); he was dressed in threadbare tunic and shorts, ready to pass muster as an inhabitant of Environment. Crawley, on the other hand, was very upright, stiff and smart in his movements, hardly ever gestured as he spoke; his dress was faultless.

And there was no need to be awed by or envious of Crawley. Crawley was encased in inhibition, afraid to feel, signaling his aridity to anyone who cared to look out from his own self-preoccupation. Crawley, moreover, feared for his job.

"Let's get on with it, as you say." He came from behind his desk. "But I'd be grateful if you would remember, Thomas, that the people in the tower are volunteers, or the descendants of volunteers.

"When uhdre began, a quarter-century ago, back in the mid-nineteen-seventies, only volunteers were admitted to the Total Environment. Five hundred young married Indian couples were admitted, plus whatever children they had. The tower was a refuge then, free from famine, immune from all disease. They were glad, heartily glad, to get in, glad of all that Environment provided and still provides. Those who didn't qualify rioted. We have to remember that.

"India was a different place in 1975. It had lost hope. One crisis after another, one famine after another, crops dying, people starving, and yet the population spiraling up by a million every month.

"But today, thank God, that picture has largely changed. Synthetic foods have licked the problem; we don't need the grudging land any more. And at last the Hindus and Muslims have got the birth control idea into their heads. It's only *now*, when a little humanity is seeping back into this death-bowl of a subcontinent, that the u.n. dares complain about the inhumanity of uHDRE."

Dixit said nothing. He felt that this potted history was simply angled towards Crawley's self-justification; the ideas it represented were real enough, heaven knew, but they had meaning for Crawley only in terms of his own existence. Dixit felt pity and impatience as Crawley went on with his narration.

"Our aim here must be unswervingly the same as it was from the start. We have evidence that nervous disorders of a special kind produce extrasensory perceptions – telepathy and the rest, and maybe kinds of esp we do not yet recognize. High-density populations with reasonable nutritional standards develop particular nervous instabilities which may be akin to esp spectra.

"The Ultra-High Density Research Establishment was set up to intensify the likelihood of esp developing. Don't forget that. The people in Environment are supposed to have some esp; that's the whole point of the operation, right? Sure, it is not humanitarian. We know that. But that is not your concern. You have to go in and find evidence of esp, something that doesn't show over the bugging. Then uHDRE will be able to continue."

Dixit prepared to leave. "If it hasn't shown up in a quarter of a century – "

"It's in there! I know it's in there! The failure's in the bugging system. I feel it coming through the screens at me – some mystery we need to get our hands on! If only I could prove it! If only I could get in there myself!"

Interesting, Dixit thought. You'd have to be some sort of a voyeur to hold Crawley's job, forever spying on the wretched people.

"Too bad you have a white skin, eh?" he said lightly. He walked towards the door. It swung open, and he passed into the corridor.

Crawley ran after him and thrust out a hand. "I know how you feel, Thomas. I'm not just a stuffed shirt, you know, not entirely void of sympathy. Sorry if I was needling you. I didn't intend to do so."

Dixit dropped his gaze. "I should be the one to apologize, Peter. If there's anything unusual going on in the tower, I'll find it, never worry!"

They shook hands, without wholly being able to meet each other's eyes.

[v]

Leaving the office block, Dixit walked alone through the sunshine toward the looming tower that housed Total Environment. The concrete walk was hot and dusty underfoot. The sun was the one good thing that India had, he thought: that burning beautiful sun, the real ruler of India, whatever petty tyrants came and went.

The sun blazed down on the tower; only inside did it not shine.

The uncompromising outlines of the tower were blurred by pipes, ducts and shafts that ran up and down its exterior. It was a building built for looking into, not out of. Some time ago, in the bad years, the welter of visual records gleaned from Environment used to be edited and beamed out on global networks every evening; but all that had been stopped as conditions inside Environment deteriorated, and public opinion in the democracies, who were subsidizing the grandiose experiment, turned against the exploitation of human material.

A monitoring station stood by the tower walls. From here, a constant survey on the interior was kept. Facing the station were the jumbles of merchants' stalls, springing up to cater for tourists, who persisted even now that the tourist trade was discouraged. Two security guards stepped forward and escorted Dixit to the base of the tower. With ceremony, he entered the shade of the entry elevator. As he closed the door, germicides sprayed him, insuring that he entered Environment without harboring dangerous micro-organisms.

The elevator carried him up to the top deck; this plan had been settled some while ago. The elevator was equipped with double steel doors. As it came to rest, a circuit opened, and a screen showed him what was happening on the other side of the doors. He emerged from a dummy air-conditioning unit, behind a wide pillar. He was in Patel's domain.

The awful weight of human overcrowding hit Dixit with its full stink and noise. He sat down at the base of the pillar and let his senses adjust. *And he thought, I was the wrong one to send; I've always had this inner core of pity for the sufferings of humanity; I could never be impartial; I've got to see that this terrible experiment is stopped.*

He was at one end of a long balcony onto which many doors opened; a ramp led down at the other end. All the doorways gaped, although some were covered by rugs. Most of the doors had been taken off their hinges to serve as partitions along the balcony itself, partitioning off overspill families. Children ran everywhere, their tinkling voices and cries the dominant note in the hubbub. Glancing over the balcony, Dixit took in a dreadful scene of swarming multitudes, the anonymity of congestion; to sorrow for humanity was not to love its prodigality. Dixit had seen this panorama many times over the bugging system; he knew all the staggering figures – 1500 people in here to begin with, and by now some 75,000 people, a large proportion of them under four years of age. But pictures and figures were pale abstracts beside the reality they were intended to represent.

The kids drove him into action at last by playfully hurling dirt at him. Dixit moved slowly along, carrying himself tight and cringing in the manner of the crowd about him, features rigid, elbows tucked in to the ribs. *Mutatis mutandis,* it was Crawley's inhibited attitude. Even the children ran between the legs of their elders in that guarded way. As soon as he had left the shelter of his pillar, he was caught in a stream of chattering people, all jostling between the rooms and the stalls of the balcony. They moved very slowly.

Among the crowd were hawkers, and salesmen pressed their wares from the pitiful balcony hovels. Dixit tried to conceal his curiosity. Over the bugging he had had only distant views of the merchandise offered for sale. Here were the strange models that had caught his attention when he was first appointed to the UHDRE project. A man with orange goat-eyes, in fact probably no more than thirteen years of age, but here a hardened veteran, was at Dixit's elbow. As Dixit stared at him, momentarily suspicious he was being watched, the goat-eyed man merged into the crowd; and, to hide his face, Dixit turned to the nearest salesman.

In only a moment, he was eagerly examining the wares, forgetting how vulnerable was his situation.

All the strange models were extremely small. This Dixit attributed to shortage of materials – wrongly, as it later transpired. The biggest model the salesman possessed stood no more than two inches high. It was made, nevertheless, of a diversity of materials, in which many sorts of plastics featured. Some models were simple, and appeared to be little more than an elaborate *tughra* or monogram, which might have been intended for an elaborate piece of costume jewelry; others, as one peered among their interstices, seemed to afford a glimpse of another dimension; all possessed eye-teasing properties.

The merchant was pressing Dixit to buy. He referred to the elaborate models as "life-objects." Noticing that one in particular attracted his potential customer, he lifted it delicately and held it up, a miracle of craftsmanship, perplexing, *outré*, giving Dixit somehow as much pain as pleasure. He named the price.

Although Dixit was primed with money, he automatically shook his head. "Too expensive."

"See, master, I show you how this life-object works!" The man fished beneath his scrap of loincloth and produced a small perforated silver box. Flipping it open, he produced a live wood-louse and slipped it under a hinged part of the model. The insect, in its struggles, activated a tiny wheel; the interior of the model began to rotate, some sets of minute planes turning in counterpoint to others.

"This life-object belonged to a very religious man, master."

In his fascination, Dixit said, "Are they all powered?"

"No, master, only special ones. This was perfect model from Dalcush Bancholi, last generation master all the way from Third Deck, very very fine and masterful workmanship of first quality. I have also still better one worked by a body louse, if you care to see."

By reflex, Dixit said, "Your prices are too high."

He absolved himself from the argument that brewed, slipping away through the crowd with the merchant calling after him. Other merchants shouted to him, sensing his interest in their wares. He saw some beautiful work, all on the tiniest scale, and not only life-objects but amazing little watches with millisecond hands as well as second hands; in some cases, the millisecond was the largest hand; in some, the hour hand was missing or was supplemented by a day hand; and the watches took many extraordinary shapes, tetrakishexahedrons and other elaborate forms, until their format merged with that of the life-objects.

Dixit thought approvingly: the clock and watch industry fulfills a human need for exercising elaborate skill and accuracy, while at the same time requiring a minimum of materials. These people of Total Environment are the world's greatest craftsmen. Bent over one curious watch that involved a color change, he became suddenly aware of danger. Glancing over his shoulder, he saw the man with the unpleasant orange eyes about to strike him. Dixit dodged without being able to avoid the blow. As it caught him on the side of his neck, he stumbled and fell under the milling feet.

[VI]

Afterwards, Dixit could hardly say that he had been totally unconscious. He was aware of hands dragging him, of being partly carried, of the sound of many voices, of the name "Patel" repeated.... And when he came fully to his senses, he was lying in a cramped room, with a guard in a scruffy turban standing by the door. His first hazy thought was that the room was no more than a small ship's cabin; then he realized that, by indigenous standards, this was a large room for only one person.

He was a prisoner in Total Environment.

A kind of self-mocking fear entered him; he had almost expected the blow, he realized; and he looked eagerly about for the bug-eye that would reassure him his UHDRE friends outside were aware of his predicament. There was no sign of the bug-eye. He was not long in working out why; this room had been partitioned out of a larger one, and the bugging system was evidently shut in the other half – whether deliberately or accidentally, he had no way of knowing.

The guard had bobbed out of sight. Sounds of whispering came from beyond the doorway. Dixit felt the pressure of many people there. Then a woman came in and closed the door. She walked cringingly and carried a brass cup of water.

Although her face was lined, it was possible to see that she had once been beautiful and perhaps proud. Now her whole attitude expressed the defeat of her life. And this woman might be no more than eighteen! One of the terrifying features of Environment was the way, right from the start, confinement had speeded life-processes and abridged life.

Involuntarily, Dixit flinched away from the woman.

She almost smiled. "Do not fear me, sir. I am almost as much a prisoner as you are. Equally, do not think that by knocking me down you can escape. I promise you, there are fifty people outside the door, all eager to impress Prahlad Patel by catching you, should you try to get away."

So I'm in Patel's clutches, he thought. Aloud he said, "'I will offer you no harm. I want to see Patel. If you are captive, tell me your name, and perhaps I can help you."

As she offered him the cup and he drank, she said, shyly, "I do not complain, for my fate might have been much worse than it is. Please do not agitate Patel about me, or he may throw me out of his household. My name is Malti."

"Perhaps I may be able to help you, and all your tribe, soon. You are all in a form of captivity here, the great Patel included, and it is from him that I hope to deliver you."

Then he saw fear in her eyes.

"You really are a spy from outside!" she breathed. "But we do not want our poor little world invaded! You have so much – leave us our little!" She shrank away and slipped through the door, leaving Dixit with a melancholy impression of her eyes, so burdened in their shrunken gaze.

The babel continued outside the door. Although he still felt sick, he propped himself up and let his thoughts run on. "You have so much – leave us our little...." All their values had been perverted. Poor things, they could know neither the smallness of their own world nor the magnitude of the world outside. This – this dungheap had become to them all there was of beauty and value.

Two guards came for him, mere boys. He could have knocked their heads together, but compassion moved him. They led him through a room full of excited people; beyond their glaring faces, the screen flickered pallidly behind its mesh; Dixit saw how faint the image of outside was.

He was taken into another partitioned room. Two men were talking.

The scene struck Dixit with peculiar force, and not merely because he was at a disadvantage.

It was an alien scene. The impoverishment of even the richest furnishings, the clipped and bastardized variety of Hindi that was being talked, reinforced the impression of strangeness. And the charge of Patel's character filled the room.

There could be no doubt who was Patel. The plump cringing fellow, wringing his hands and protesting, was not Patel. Patel was the stocky white-haired man with the heavy lower lip and high forehead. Dixit had seen him in this very room over the bugging system. But to stand captive awaiting his attention was an experience of an entirely different order. Dixit tried to analyze the first fresh impact Patel had on him, but it was elusive.

It was difficult to realize that, as the outside measured years, Patel could not be much more than nineteen or twenty years of age. Time was impacted here, jellified under the psychic pressures of Total Environment. Like the hieroglyphics of that new relativity, detailed plans of the Environment hung large on one wall of this room, while figures and names were chalked over the others. The room was the nerve center of Top Deck.

He knew something about Patel from UHDRE records. Patel had come up here from the Seventh Deck. By guile as well as force, he had become ruler of Top Deck at an early age. He had surprised UHDRE observers by abstaining from the usual forays of conquest into other floors.

Patel was saying to the cringing man, "Be silent! You try to obscure the truth with argument. You have heard the witnesses against you. During your period of watch on the stairs, you were bribed by a man from Ninth Deck and you let him through here."

"Only for a mere seventeen minutes, Sir Patel!"

"I am aware that such things happen every day, wretched Raital. But this fellow you let through stole the life-object belonging to Narayan Farhad and, in consequence, Narayan Farhad died in his sleep last night. Narayan was no more important than you are, but he was useful to me, and it is in order that he be revenged."

"Anything that you say, Sir Patel!"

"Be silent, wretched Raital!" Patel watched Raital with interest as he spoke. And he spoke in a firm reflective voice that impressed Dixit more than shouting would have done.

"You shall revenge Narayan, Raital, because you caused his death. You will leave here now. You will not be punished. You will go, and you will steal the life-object belonging to that fellow from whom you accepted the bribe. You will bring that life-object to me. You have one day to do so. Otherwise, my assassins will find you wherever you hide, be it even down on Deck One."

"Oh, yes, indeed, Sir Patel, all men know –" Raital was bent almost double as he uttered some face-saving formula. He turned and scurried away as Patel dismissed him.

Strength, thought Dixit. Strength, and also cunning. That is what Patel radiates. An elaborate and cutting subtlety. The phrase pleased him, seeming to represent something actual that he had detected in Patel's makeup. An elaborate and cutting subtlety.

Clearly, it was part of Patel's design that Dixit should witness this demonstration of his methods.

Patel turned away, folded his arms, and contemplated a blank piece of wall at close range. He stood motionless. The guards held Dixit still, but not so still as Patel held himself.

This tableau was maintained for several minutes. Dixit found himself losing track of the normal passage of time. Patel's habit of turning to stare at the wall – and it did not belong to Patel alone – was an uncanny one that Dixit had watched several times over the bugging system. It was that habit, he thought, which might have given Crawley the notion that ESP was rampant in the tower.

It was curious to think of Crawley here. Although Crawley might at this moment be surveying Dixit's face on a monitor, Crawley was now no more than an hypothesis.

Malti broke the tableau. She entered the room with a damp cloth on a tray, to stand waiting patiently for Patel to notice her. He broke away at last from his motionless survey of the wall, gesturing abruptly to the guards to leave. He took no notice of Dixit, sitting in a chair, letting Malti drape the damp cloth round his neck; the cloth had a fragrant smell to it.

"The towel is not cool enough, Malti, or damp enough. You will attend me properly at my morning session, or you will lose this easy job."

He swung his gaze, which was suddenly black and searching, onto Dixit to say, "Well, spy, you know I am Lord here. Do you wonder why I tolerate old women like this about me when I could have girls young and lovely to fawn on me?"

Dixit said nothing, and the self-styled Lord continued, "Young girls would merely remind me by contrast of my advanced years. But this old bag – whom I bought only yesterday – this old bag is only just my junior and makes me look good in contrast. You see, we are masters of philosophy in here, in this prison-universe; we cannot be masters of material wealth like you people outside!"

Again Dixit said nothing, disgusted by the man's implied attitude to women.

A swinging blow caught him unprepared in the stomach. He cried and dropped suddenly to the floor.

"Get up, spy!" Patel said. He had moved extraordinarily fast. He sat back again in his chair, letting Malti massage his neck muscles.

[VII]

As Dixit staggered to his feet, Patel said, "You don't deny you are from outside?"

"I did not attempt to deny it. I came from outside to speak to you."

"You say nothing here until you are ordered to speak. Your people – you outsiders – you have sent in several spies to us the last few months. Why?"

Still feeling sick from the blow, Dixit said, "You should realize that we are your friends rather than your enemies, and our men emissaries rather than spies."

"Pah! You are a breed of spies! Don't you sit and spy on us from every room? You live in a funny little dull world out there, don't you? So interested in us that you can think of nothing else! Keep working, Malti! Little spy, you know what happened to all the other spies your spying people sent in?"

"They died," Dixit said.

"Exactly. They died. But you are the first to be sent to Patel's deck. What different thing from death do you expect here?"

"Another death will make my superiors very tired, Patel. You may have the power of life and death over me; they have the same over you, and over all in this world of yours. Do you want a demonstration?"

Rising, flinging the towel off, Patel said, "Give me your demonstration!"

Must do, Dixit thought. Staring in Patel's eyes, he raised his right hand above his head and gestured with his thumb. Pray they are watching – and thank God this bit of partitioned room is the bit with the bugging system!

Tensely, Patel stared, balanced on his toes. Behind his shoulder, Malti also stared. Nothing happened.

Then a sort of shudder ran through Environment. It became slowly audible as a mixture of groan and cry. Its cause became apparent in this less crowded room when the air began to grow hot and foul. So Dixit's signal had got through; Crawley had him under survey, and the air-conditioning plant was pumping in hot carbon-dioxide through the respiratory system.

"You see? We control the very air you breathe!" Dixit said. He dropped his arm, and slowly the air returned to normal, although it was at least an hour before the fright died down in the passages.

Whatever the demonstration had done to Patel, he showed nothing. Instead, he said, "You control the air. Very well. But you do not control the will to turn it off permanently – and so you do not control the air. Your threat is an empty one, spy! For some reason, you need us to live. We have a mystery, don't we?"

"There is no reason why I should be anything but honest with you, Patel. Your special environment must have bred special talents in you. We are interested in those talents; but no more than interested."

Patel came closer and inspected Dixit's face minutely, rather as he had recently inspected the blank wall. Strange angers churned inside him; his neck and throat turned a dark mottled color. Finally he spoke.

"We are the center of your outside world, aren't we? We know that you watch us all the time. We know that you are much more than 'interested'! For you, we here are somehow a matter of life and death, aren't we?"

This was more than Dixit had expected.

"Four generations, Patel, four generations have been incarcerated in Environment." His voice trembled. "Four generations, and, despite our best intentions, you are losing touch with reality. You live in one relatively small building on a sizeable planet. Clearly, you can only be of limited interest to the world at large."

"Malti!" Patel turned to the slave girl. "Which is the greater, the outer world or ours?"

She looked confused, hesitated by the door as if longing to escape. "The outside world was great, master, but then it gave birth to us, and we have grown and are growing and are gaining strength. The child now is almost the size of the father. So my stepfather's son Jamsu says, and he is a clever one."

Patel turned to stare at Dixit, a haughty expression on his face. He made no comment, as if the words of an ignorant girl were sufficient to prove his point.

"All that you and the girl say only emphasizes to me how much you need help, Patel. The world outside is a great and thriving place; you must allow it to give you assistance through me. We are not your enemies."

Again the choleric anger was there, powering Patel's every word.

"What else are you, spy? Your life is so vile and pointless out there, is it not? You envy us because we are superseding you! Our people – we may be poor, you may think of us as in your power, but we rule our own universe. And that universe is expanding and falling under our control more every day. Why, our explorers have gone into the world of the ultra-small. We discover new environments, new ways of living. By your terms, we are scientific peasants, perhaps, but I fancy we have ways of knowing the trade routes of the blood and the eternities of cell-change that you cannot comprehend. You think of us all as captives, eh? Yet you are captive to the necessity of supplying our air and our food and water; we are free. We are poor, yet you covet our riches. We are spied on all the time, yet we are secret. You need to understand us, yet we have no need to understand you. You are in *our* power, spy!"

"Certainly not in one vital respect, Patel. Both you and we are ruled by historical necessity. This Environment was set up twenty-five of our years ago. Changes have taken place not only in here but outside as well. The nations of the world are no longer prepared to finance this project. It is going to be closed down entirely, and you are going to have to live outside. Or, if you don't want that, you'd better cooperate with us and persuade the leaders of the other decks to cooperate."

Would threats work with Patel? His hooded and oblique gaze bit into Dixit like a hook.

After a deadly pause, he clapped his hands once. Two guards immediately appeared.

"Take the spy away," said Patel. Then he turned his back.

A clever man, Dixit thought. He sat alone in the cell and meditated.

It seemed as if a battle of wits might develop between him and Patel. Well, he was prepared. He trusted to his first impression, that Patel was a man of cutting subtlety. He could not be taken to mean all that he said.

Dixit's mind worked back over their conversation. The mystery of the life-objects had been dangled before him. And Patel had taken care to belittle the outside world: "funny dull little world," he had called it. He had made Malti advance her primitive view that Environment was growing, and that had fitted in very well with his brand of boasting. Which led to the deduction that he had known her views beforehand; yet he had bought her only yesterday. Why should a busy man, a leader, bother to question an ignorant slave about her views of the outside world unless he were starved for information of that world, obsessed with it.

Yes, Dixit nodded to himself. Patel was obsessed with outside and tried to hide that obsession; but several small contradictions in his talk had revealed it.

Of course, it might be that Malti was so generally representative of the thousands in Environment that her misinformed ideas could be taken for granted. It was as well, as yet, not to be too certain that he was beginning to understand Patel.

Part of Patel's speech made sense even superficially. These poor devils were exploring the world of the ultra-small. It was the only landscape left for them to map. They were human, and still burning inside them was that unquenchable human urge to open new frontiers.

So they knew some inward things. Quite possibly, as Crawley anticipated, they possessed a system of ESP upon which some reliance might be placed, unlike the wildly fluctuating telepathic radiations which circulated in the outside world.

He felt confident, fully engaged. There was much to understand here. The bugging system, elaborate and overused, was shown to be a complete failure; the watchers had stayed external to their problem; it remained their problem, not their life. What was needed was a whole team to come and live here, perhaps a team on every deck, anthropologists and so on. Since that was impossible, then clearly the people of Environment must be released from their captivity; those that were unwilling to go far afield should be settled in new villages on the Ganges plain, under the wide sky. And there, as they adapted to the real world, observers could live among them, learning with humility of the gifts that had been acquired at such cost within the thick walls of the Total Environment tower.

As Dixit sat in meditation, a guard brought a meal in to him.

He ate thankfully and renewed his thinking.

From the little he had already experienced – the ghastly pressures on living space, the slavery, the aberrant modes of thought into which the people were being forced, the harshness of the petty rulers – he was confirmed in his view that this experiment in anything like its present form must be closed down at once. The u.n. needed the excuse of his adverse report before they moved; they should have it when he got out. And if he worded the report carefully, stressing that these people had many talents to offer, then he might also satisfy Crawley and his like. He had it in his power to satisfy all parties, when he got out. All he had to do was get out.

The guard came back to collect his empty bowl.

"When is Patel going to speak with me again?"

The guard said, "When he sends for you to have you silenced for ever."

Dixit stopped composing his report and thought about that instead.

[VIII]

Much time elapsed before Dixit was visited again, and then it was only the self-effacing Malti who appeared, bringing him a cup of water.

"I want to talk to you," Dixit said urgently.

"No, no, I cannot talk! He will beat me. It is the time when we sleep, when the old die. You should sleep now, and Patel will see you in the morning."

He tried to touch her hand, but she withdrew.

"You are a kind girl, Malti. You suffer in Patel's household."

"He has many women, many servants. I am not alone."

"Can you not escape back to your family?"

She looked at the floor evasively. "It would bring trouble to my family. Slavery is the lot of many women. It is the way of the world."

"It is not the way of the world I come from!"

Her eyes flashed. "Your world is of no interest to us!"

Dixit thought after she had gone, She is afraid of our world. Rightly.

He slept little during the night. Even barricaded inside Patel's fortress, he could still hear the noises of Environment: not only the voices, almost never silent, but the gurgle and sob of pipes in the walls. In the morning, he was taken into a larger room where Patel was issuing commands for the day to a succession of subordinates.

Confined to a corner, Dixit followed everything with interest. His interest grew when the unfortunate guard Raital appeared. He bounded in and waited for Patel to strike him. Instead, Patel kicked him.

"You have performed as I ordered yesterday?"

Raital began at once to cry and wring his hands. "Sir Patel, I have performed as well as and better than you demanded, incurring great suffering and having myself beaten downstairs where the people of Ninth Deck discovered me marauding. You must invade them, Sir, and teach them a lesson that in their insolence they so dare to mock your faithful guards who only do those things – "

"Silence, you dog-devourer! Do you bring back that item which I demanded of you yesterday?"

The wretched guard brought from the pocket of his tattered tunic a small object, which he held out to Patel.

"Of course I obey, Sir Patel. To keep this object safe when the people caught me, I swallow it whole, sir, into the stomach for safekeeping, so that they would not know what I am about. Then my wife gives me sharp medicine so that I vomit it safely again to deliver to you."

"Put the filthy thing down on that shelf there! You think I wish to touch it when it has been in your worm-infested belly, slave?"

The guard did as he was bid and abased himself.

"You are sure it is the life-object of the man who stole Narayan Farhad's life-object, and nobody else's?"

"Oh, indeed, Sir Patel! It belongs to a man called Gita, the very same who stole Narayan's life-object, and tonight you will see he will die of night-visions!"

"Get out!" Patel managed to catch Raital's buttocks with a swift kick as the guard scampered from the room.

A queue of people stood waiting to speak with him, to supplicate and advise. Patel sat and interviewed them, in the main showing a better humor than he had shown his luckless guard. For Dixit, this scene had a curious interest; he had watched Patel's morning audience more than once, standing by Crawley's side in the UHDRE monitoring station; now he was a prisoner waiting uncomfortably in the corner of the room, and the whole atmosphere was changed. He felt the extraordinary intensity of these people's lives, the emotions compressed, everything vivid. Patel himself wept several times as some tale of hardship was unfolded to him. There was no privacy. Everyone stood round him, listening to everything. Short the lives might be; but those annihilating spaces that stretch through ordinary lives, the spaces through which one glimpses uncomfortable glooms and larger poverties, if not presences more sour and sinister, seemed here to have been eradicated. The Total Environment had brought its peoples total involvement. Whatever befell them, they were united, as were bees in a hive.

Finally, a break was called. The unfortunates who had not gained Patel's ear were turned away; Malti was summoned and administered the damp-towel treatment to Patel. Later, he sent her off and ate a frugal meal. Only when he had finished it, and sat momentarily in meditation, did he turn his brooding attention to Dixit.

He indicated that Dixit was to fetch down the object Raital had placed on a shelf. Dixit did so and put the object before Patel. Staring at it with interest, he saw it was an elaborate little model, similar to the ones for sale on the balcony.

"Observe it well," Patel said. "It is the life-object of a man. You have these" – he gestured vaguely – "outside?"

"No."

"You know what they are?"

"No."

"In this world of ours, Mr. Dixit, we have many holy men. I have a holy man here under my protection. On the deck below is one very famous holy man, Vazifdariji. These men have many powers. Tonight, I shall give my holy man this life-object, and with it he will be able to enter the being of the man to whom it belongs, for good or ill, and in this case for ill, to revenge a death with a death."

Dixit stared at the little object, a three-dimensional maze constructed of silver and plastic strands, trying to comprehend what Patel was saying.

"This is sort of key to its owner's mind?"

"No, no, not a key, and not to his mind. It is a – well, we do not have a scientific word for it, and our word would mean nothing to you, so I cannot say what. It is, let us say, a replica, a substitute for the man's being. Not his mind, his being. In this case, a man called Gita. You are very interested, aren't you?"

"Everyone here has one of these?"

"Down to the very poorest, and even the older children. A sage works in conjunction with a smith to produce each individual life-object."

"But they can be stolen and then an ill-intentioned holy man can use them to kill the owner. So why make them? I don't understand."

Smiling, Patel made a small movement of impatience. "What you discover of yourself, you record. That is how these things are made. They are not trinkets; they are a man's record of his discovery of himself."

Dixit shook his head. "If they are so personal, why are so many sold by street traders as trinkets?"

"Men die. Then their life-objects have no value, except as trinkets. They are also popularly believed to bestow... well, personality-value. There also exist large numbers of forgeries, which people buy because they like to have them, simply as decorations."

After a moment, Dixit said, "So they are innocent things, but you take them and use them for evil ends."

"I use them to keep a power balance. A man of mine called Nara-yan was silenced by Gita of Ninth Deck. Never mind why. So tonight I silence Gita to keep the balance."

He stopped and looked closely at Dixit, so that the latter received a blast of that enigmatic personality. He opened his hand and said, still observing Dixit, "Death sits in my palm, Mr. Dixit. Tonight I shall have you silenced also, by what you may consider more ordinary methods."

Clenching his hands tightly together, Dixit said, "You tell me about the life-objects, and yet you claim you are going to kill me."

Patel pointed up to one corner of his room. "There are eyes and ears there, while your ever-hungry spying friends suck up the facts of this world. You see, I can tell them – I can tell them so much and they can never comprehend our life. All the important things can never be said, so they can never learn. But they can see you die tonight, and that they will comprehend. Perhaps then they will cease to send spies in here."

He clapped his hands once for the guards. They came forward and led Dixit away. As he went back to his cell, he heard Patel shouting for Malti.

[IX]
The hours passed in steady gloom. The U.N., the UHDRE, would not rescue him; the Environment charter permitted intervention by only one outsider at a time. Dixit could hear, feel, the vast throbbing life of the place going on about him and was shaken by it.

He tried to think about the life-object. Presumably Crawley had overheard the last conversation, and would know that the holy men, as Patel called them, had the power to kill at a distance. There was the ESP evidence Crawley sought: telecide, or whatever you called it. And the knowledge helped nobody, as Patel himself observed. It had long been known that African witch doctors possessed similar talents, to lay a spell on a man and kill him at a distance; but how they did it had never been established; nor, indeed, had the fact ever been properly assimilated by the West, eager though the West was for new methods of killing. There were things one civilization could not learn from another; the whole business of life-objects, Dixit perceived, was going to be such a matter: endlessly fascinating, entirely insoluble....

His thoughts returned to his cell, and he told himself: Patel still puzzles me. But it is no use hanging about here being puzzled. Here I sit, waiting for a knife in the guts. It must be night now. I've got to get out of here.

There was no way out of the room. He paced restlessly up and down. They brought him no meal, which was ominous.

A long while later, the door was unlocked and opened.

It was Malti. She lifted one finger as a caution to silence, and closed the door behind her. "It's time for me...?" Dixit asked.

She came quickly over to him, not touching him, staring at him.

Though she was an ugly and despondent woman, beauty lay in her time-haunted eyes.

"I can help you escape, Dixit. Patel sleeps now, and I have an understanding with the guards here. Understandings have been reached to smuggle you down to my own deck, where perhaps you can get back to the outside where you belong. This place is full of arrangements. But you must be quick. Are you ready?"

"He'll kill you when he finds out!"

She shrugged. "He may not. I think perhaps he likes me. Prahlad Patel is not inhuman, whatever you think of him."

"No? But he plans to murder someone else tonight. He has acquired some poor fellow's life-object and plans to have his holy man kill him with night-visions, whatever they are."

She said, "People have to die. You are going to be lucky. You will not die, not this night."

"If you take that fatalistic view, why help me?"

He saw a flash of defiance in her eyes. "Because you must take a message outside for me."

"Outside? To whom?"

"To everyone there, everyone who greedily spies on us here and would spoil this world. Tell them to go away and leave us and let us make our own world. Forget us! That is my message! Take it! Deliver it with all the strength you have! This is our world – not yours!"

Her vehemence, her ignorance, silenced him. She led him from the room. There were guards on the outer door. They stood rigid with their eyes closed, seeing no evil, and she slid between them, leading Dixit and opening the door. They hurried outside, onto the balcony, which was still as crowded as ever, people sprawling everywhere in the disconsolate gestures of public sleep. With the noise and chaos and animation of daytime fled, Total Environment stood fully revealed for the echoing prison it was.

As Malti turned to go, Dixit grasped her wrist.

"I must return," she said. "Get quickly to the steps down to Ninth Deck, the near steps. That's three flights to go down, the inter-deck flight guarded. They will let you through; they expect you."

"Malti, I must try to help this other man who is to die. Do you happen to know someone called Gita?"

She gasped and clung to him. "Gita?"

"Gita of the Ninth Deck. Patel has Gita's life-object, and he is to die tonight."

"Gita is my stepfather, my mother's third husband. A good man! Oh, he must not die, for my mother's sake!"

"He's to die tonight. Malti, I can help you and Gita. I appreciate how you feel about outside, but you are mistaken. You would be free in a way you cannot understand! Take me to Gita, we'll all three get out together."

Conflicting emotions chased all over her face. "You are sure Gita is to die?"

"Come and check with him to see if his life-object has gone!"

Without waiting for her to make a decision – in fact she looked as if she were just about to bolt back into Patel's quarters – Dixit took hold of her and forced her along the balcony, picking his way through the piles of sleepers.

Ramps ran down from balcony to balcony in long zigzags. For all its multitudes of people – even the ramps had been taken up as dosses by whole swarms of urchins – Total Environment seemed much larger than it had when one looked in from the monitoring room. He kept peering back to see if they were being followed; it seemed to him unlikely that he would be able to get away.

But they had now reached the stairs leading down to Deck Nine. Oh, well, he thought, corruption he could believe in; it was the universal oriental system whereby the small man contrived to live under oppression. As soon as the guards saw him and Malti, they all stood and closed their eyes. Among them was the wretched Raital, who hurriedly clapped palms over eyes as they approached.

"I must go back to Patel," Malti gasped.

"Why? You know he will kill you," Dixit said. He kept tight hold of her thin wrist. "All these witnesses to the way you led me to safety – you can't believe he will not discover what you are doing. Let's get to Gita quickly."

He hustled her down the stairs. There were Deck Nine guards at the bottom. They smiled and saluted Malti and let her by. As if resigned now to doing what Dixit wished, she led him forward, and they picked their way down a ramp to a lower floor. The squalor and confusion were greater here than they had been above, the slumbers more broken. This was a deck without a strong leader, and it showed.

He must have seen just such a picture as this over the bugging, in the air-conditioned comfort of the UHDRE offices, and remained comparatively unmoved. You had to be among it to feel it. Then you caught also the aroma of Environment. It was pungent in the extreme.

As they moved slowly down among the huddled figures abased by fatigue, he saw that a corpse burned slowly on a wood pile. It was the corpse of a child. Smoke rose from it in a leisurely coil until it was sucked into a wall vent. A mother squatted by the body, her face shielded by one skeletal hand. "It is the time when the old die," Malti had said of the previous night; and the young had to answer that same call.

This was the Indian way of facing the inhumanity of Environment: with their age-old acceptance of suffering. Had one of the white races been shut in here to breed to intolerable numbers, they would have met the situation with a general massacre. Dixit, a half-caste, would not permit himself to judge which response he most respected.

Malti kept her gaze fixed on the worn concrete underfoot as they moved down the ramp past the corpse. At the bottom, she led him forward again without a word.

They pushed through the sleazy ways, arriving at last at a battered doorway. With a glance at Dixit, Malti slipped in and rejoined her family. Her mother, not sleeping, crouched over a washbowl, gave a cry and fell into Malti's arms. Brothers and sisters and half-brothers and half-sisters and cousins and nephews woke up, squealing. Dixit was utterly brushed aside. He stood nervously, waiting, hoping, in the corridor.

It was many minutes before Malti came out and led him to the crowded little cabin. She introduced him to Shamim, her mother, who curtsied and rapidly disappeared, and to her stepfather, Gita.

The little wiry man shooed everyone out of one corner of the room and moved Dixit into it. A cup of wine was produced and offered politely to the visitor. As he sipped it, he said, "If your stepdaughter has explained the situation, Gita, I'd like to get you and Malti out of here, because otherwise your lives are worth very little. I can guarantee you will be extremely kindly treated outside."

With dignity, Gita said, "Sir, all this very unpleasant business has been explained to me by my stepdaughter. You are most good to take this trouble, but we cannot help you."

"You, or rather Malti, have helped me. Now it is my turn to help you. I want to take you out of here to a safe place. You realize you are both under the threat of death? You hardly need telling that Prahlad Patel is a ruthless man."

"He is very very ruthless, sir," Gita said unhappily. "But we cannot leave here. I cannot leave here – look at all these little people who are dependent on me! Who would look after them if I left?"

"But if your hours are numbered?"

"If I have only one minute to go before I die, still I cannot desert those who depend on me."

Dixit turned to Malti. "You, Malti – you have less responsibility. Patel will have his revenge on you. Come with me and be safe!"

She shook her head. "If I came, I would sicken with worry for what was happening here and so I would die that way."

He looked about him hopelessly. The blind interdependence bred by this crowded environment had beaten him – almost. He still had one card to play.

"When I go out of here, as go I must, I have to report to my superiors. They are the people who – the people who really order everything that happens here. They supply your light, your food, your air. They are like gods to you, with the power of death over every one on every deck – which perhaps is why you can hardly believe in them. They already feel that Total Environment is wrong, a crime against your humanity. I have to take my verdict to them. My verdict, I can tell you now, is that the lives of all you people are as precious as lives outside these walls. The experiment must be stopped; you all must go free.

"You may not understand entirely what I mean, but perhaps the wall screens have helped you grasp something. You will all be looked after and rehabilitated. Everyone will be released from the decks very soon. So, you can both come with me and save your lives; and then, in perhaps only a week, you will be reunited with your family. Patel will have no power then. Now, think over your decision again, for the good of your dependents, and come with me to life and freedom."

Malti and Gita looked anxiously at each other and went into a huddle. Shamim joined in, and Jamsu, and lame Shirin, and more and more of the tribe, and a great jangle of excited talk swelled up. Dixit fretted nervously.

Finally, silence fell. Gita said, "Sir, your intentions are plainly kind. But you have forgotten that Malti charged you to take a message to outside. Her message was to tell the people there to go away and let us make our own world. Perhaps you do not understand such a message and so cannot deliver it. Then I will give you my message, and you can take it to your superiors."

Dixit bowed his head.

"Tell them, your superiors and everyone outside who insists on watching us and meddling in our affairs, tell them that we are shaping our own lives. We know what is to come, and the many problems of having such a plenty of young people. But we have faith in our next generation. We believe they will have many new talents we do not possess, as we have talents our fathers did not possess.

"We know you will continue to send in food and air, because that is something you cannot escape from. We also know that in your hidden minds you wish to see us all fail and die. You wish to see us break, to see what will happen when we do. You do not have love for us. You have fear and puzzlement and hate. We shall not break. We are building a new sort of world, we are getting clever. We would die if you took us out of here. Go and tell that to your superiors and to everyone who spies on us. Please leave us to our own lives, over which we have our own commands."

There seemed nothing Dixit could say in answer. He looked at Malti, but could see she was unyielding, frail and pale and unyielding. This was what UHDRE had bred: complete lack of understanding. He turned and went.

He had his key. He knew the secret place on each deck where he could slip away into one of the escape elevators. As he pushed through the grimy crowds, he could hardly see his way for tears.

[X]

It was all very informal. Dixit made his report to a board of six members of the UHDRE administration, including the Special Project Organizer, Peter Crawley. Two observers were allowed to sit in, a grand lady who represented the Indian Government, and Dixit's old friend, Senator Jacob Byrnes, representing the United Nations.

Dixit delivered his report on what he had found and added a recommendation that a rehabilitation village be set up immediately and the Environment wound down.

Crawley rose to his feet and stood rigid as he said, "By your own words, you admit that these people of Environment cling desperately to what little they have. However terrible, however miserable that little may seem to you. They are acclimated to what they have. They have turned their backs to the outside world and don't *want* to come out."

Dixit said, "We shall rehabilitate them, reeducate them, find them local homes where the intricate family patterns to which they are used can still be maintained, where they can be helped back to normality."

"But by what you say, they would receive a paralyzing shock if confronted with the outside world and its gigantic scale."

"Not if Patel still led them."

A mutter ran along the board; its members clearly thought this an absurd statement. Crawley gestured despairingly, as if his case were made, and sat down saying, "He's the sort of tyrant who causes the misery in Environment."

"The one thing they need when they emerge to freedom is a strong leader they know. Gentlemen, Patel is our good hope. His great asset is that he is oriented towards outside already."

"Just what does that mean?" one of the board asked.

"It means this. Patel is a clever man. My belief is that he arranged that Malti should help me escape from his cell. He never had any intention of killing me; that was a bluff to get me on my way. Little, oppressed Malti was just not the woman to take any initiative. What Patel probably did not bargain for was that I should mention Gita by name to her, or that Gita should be closely related to her. But because of their fatalism, his plan was in no way upset."

"Why should Patel want you to escape?"

"Implicit in much that he did and said, though he tried to hide it, was a burning curiosity about outside. He exhibited facets of his culture to me to ascertain my reactions – testing for approval or disapproval, I'd guess, like a child. Nor does he attempt to attack other decks – the time-honored sport of Environment tyrants; his attention is directed inwardly on us.

"Patel is intelligent enough to know that we have real power. He has never lost the true picture of reality, unlike his minions. So *he wants to get out*.

"He calculated that if I got back to you, seemingly having escaped death, I would report strongly enough to persuade you to start demolishing Total Environment immediately."

"Which you are doing," Crawley said.

"Which I am doing. Not for Patel's reasons, but for human reasons. And for utilitarian reasons also – which will perhaps appeal more to Mr. Crawley. Gentlemen, you were right. There are mental disciplines in Environment the world could use, of which perhaps the least attractive is telecide. UHDRE has cost the public millions on millions of dollars. We have to recoup by these new advances. We can only use these new advances by studying them in an atmosphere not laden with hatred and envy of us – in other words, by opening that black tower."

The meeting broke up. Of course, he could not expect anything more decisive than that for a day or two.

Senator Byrnes came over.

"Not only did you make out a good case, Thomas; history is with you. The world's emerging from a bad period and that dark tower, as you call it, is a symbol of the bad times, and so it has to go."

Inwardly, Dixit had his qualifications to that remark. But they walked together to the window of the boardroom and looked across at the great rough bulk of the Environment building.

"It's more than a symbol. It's as full of suffering and hope as our own world. But it's a man-made monster – it must go."

Byrnes nodded. "Don't worry. It'll go. I feel sure that the historical process, that blind evolutionary thing, has already decided that UH-DRE's day is done. Stick around. In a few weeks, you'll be able to help Malti's family rehabilitate. And now I'm off to put in my two cents' worth with the chairman of that board."

He clapped Dixit on the back and walked off. Inside he knew lights would be burning and those thronging feet padding across the only world they knew. Inside there, babies would be born this night and men die of old age and night-visions....

Outside, monsoon rain began to fall on the wide Indian land.

A Chinese Perspective

[ONE]

THE TANKS WERE OF GLASS, a metre deep and almost as generous in their other dimensions. Each table contained eight tanks, and the laboratory contained ten tables. A constant temperature of 18.5 degrees Centigrade was maintained in every tank. And in every tank, oxygenators blew a chain of bubbles up their sides.

The water was of a different green in each of the tanks on a table, ranging from a pale stramineous yellow to a deep mid viridian. The tanks were lit in such a way that watery reflections moved across the ceiling of the lab.

This perpetual underwater movement was lethargic. It lent the room a drowned and drowsy aspect in contrast with the dance taking place in all eighty tanks, where marine creatures of graded size underwent the capers of growth, performing such antics as their limited gene-patterns allowed.

Among this incarcerated activity went the Chinese girl who was known here as Felicity Amber Jones, neat in her orange lab coat, content because at present absorbed completely in her work.

The laboratory of which Felicity Amber Jones had charge was a part of the great institution of Fragrance Fish-Food Farms Amalgamated. The FFFA, whose premises, buried deep into the plastic core of Fragrance II, produced one of the chief exports of the planetoid – a range of marine food-products famed all round the Zodiacal

Planets. Those exports, packed in glass, plastic, or palloy, circulated in their various forms throughout the artificial worlds much as the free-swimming forms of oysters travelled through Felicity's ranged algae tanks on their way to maturity.

When it was time to go off duty, she registered the event on the computer-terminal in her office. Although she had plenty of other interests, Felicity always left this, her Main Job, with some regret. There was more peace here than at home in her cramped pile-apt. She switched off the overhead lights. The tanks, vats, and separators still glowed, spreading a languid jade reflection through the room.

At the changing-lockers, she removed her coat, standing naked for a moment before assuming a saffron overall, sokdals, and flesh mask. She called farewell to some passing colleagues as she made for the nearest exit.

Outside, someone had scrawled "Banish Impermanence" on the wall. Felicity made a moue at it and caught a petulent. In the moments of travel, she tried some astro-organic thought, but was too highly strung. It was almost time for her weekly assignation with Edward Maine, the great inventor.

[TWO]

In a homapt near the heart of Fragrance 11, Fabrina Maine and her friend Anna Kavan stood before a small mock-fire. Its patterns cast themselves upon the legs of the two women in scarlet and gold, although they were overshadowed by the gleaming wall-screen which Fabrina was now addressing.

Fabrina was a small plump lady whose wispy fair hair stood out unfashionably round her head; but she had a certain dignity. In an effort to improve that dignity, or otherwise express herself, she was currently studying Tease Structure, the psycho-dynamics of altered body-image. She adopted a vernal sacrifice position and said to the reporter on the screen, "Yes, of course I can provide referents of my brother Edward's behavioural drives – none better than I – but that may not be convenient. First, you should introduce yourself. Which zeepee are you from?"

The reporter, looming easily on the screen and dwarfing the apartment she shared with her brother, said, "My name's Sheikh Raschid el Gheleb, and I represent the *UAS Daily Modesty*. I've come up from Earth to investigate new technophilosophical developments in the zeepees. So of course your brother ranks highly on the list of those people whom I hope to interview for my scatter."

She frowned. Edward's increasing success brought increasing interruptions to their snugly predictable lives.

"Your Main Job?" she asked the reporter.

"On Earth, we don't have that same concept, although the World State Employment Council is studying its possibilities. I'm just the Modesty's technophilosophical correspondent, though I do also lecture in Predestination at Cairo University. I hope you don't feel xenophobic about me just because I'm from Earth; we're very interested in the zeepees, you know."

She sniffed. "We manage very well without outside interference. Edward will be back later. Ring another time. You'd better speak to him direct. In any case, he has an Internal booked as soon as he gets home."

She switched off and turned to Anna Kavan, leaning slightly toward the defile stance to show contrition. "Perhaps I shouldn't have been sharp with him, but I'm uneasy about the thought of the World State meddling in our affairs, and so is Edward."

"It's at least five years before the World State comes into being officially," Anna said, extending her hands to the fake flames. "Besides, the Chinese are very scrupulous."

"Why should I care about the World State or the state of the world when I have my little lin with me?" Fabrina asked. She turned and petted the animated ornament by her side. "Tell me something funny, Lin."

"We are all radioactive particles in the mind of God," said the lin. The women laughed.

"Now tell me a new story," Fabrina said.

And the lin said, "Here's one called 'High Courts.' There were high ideals in the courts upon the mountains. Photographers were scarce under the towering apple trees. No snails any longer laid their eggs among the eyes of the goats in the market. The Lady Cortara, that dinosaur of royal line, said, 'Life is like death by drowning: it feels good when you cease to struggle.' So worldly regiments failed to close the entanglement of minds."

"You'll be able to afford a better model lin now, Fabrina," Anna said. "Edward will be rich from now on."

"I happen to like mad old stories," said Fabrina. "And my little linikin's tales have the advantage of being original and sounding familiar."

[THREE]

In the boardroom of Smics Callibrastics, high in the Fragrance 11 urbstak, they were celebrating Maine's achievement. Wine flowed, as well as the more customary aphrocoza, mitrovits, pam-and-lime, and other good things. The prototype of Maine's prediction machine stood at one end of the chamber; Edward Maine stood meekly by it, allowing the press to photograph him, and his colleagues to congratulate him.

"... and furthermore, I'd like to say, Edward, what a pleasure it has been to have you under our wing here at Smics for all these years," Marvin Stein-Presteign told him. Stein-Presteign was Managing Director, and built for the job, with plenty of meat separating him from the rest of the world, topped by a florid enough countenance to remind that world that blood pressure and work pressure often run in alliance. "Everyone enjoys working with you, Edward."

"You're very kind, sir," Maine said, smiling so energetically that his untidy fair hair, which stood out wispily all round his head, trembled in response. He was a small, plump man in his early thirties – clever but not very good at talking. Certainly not very good at talking to his meaty managing director.

Having shaken hands with Maine, Stein-Presteign moved away and said to Sheila Wu Tun, the Personnel Manager, "There's no cynicism about Edward – he surely is a thoroughly admirable little man."

"It's kind of funny the way everyone calls him Edward," Sheila said. "Never an Ed or a Ted or a Teddy.... It's a factor of his rather remote personality, I suppose."

"What's his private life like? Lives with his sister, doesn't he?"

"Yes. He's diffident with women, bless him. Although he has established a tentative relationship with a young woman who goes to his homapt once a week for an Internal."

"Well, we have your little treat in store for him. Perhaps we can step up his fun-level there."

"That's a thought – but Maine's entitled to be remote," Curmodgely from Statistics said. "After all, the man is undeniably a genius." He was rarely so bold with the Managing Director, but he disliked the patronising way Stein-Presteign and Wu Tun spoke. He added with a note of apology, "I mean, his damned machine works. The future is now foreseeable, more or less. It's going to change the history of mankind."

Stein-Presteign said to Sheila, ignoring Curmodgely, "I'll see Edward in my office tomorrow." He moved on, leaving the lower echelons, who pressed admiringly if unavailingly round Sheila Wu Tun, to carry on the conversation.

Gryastairs of Kakobillis, who was heavy and eager, said, "Luckily it was our organisation which employed Maine and not the opposition. I suppose you all know that Gondwana of Turpitude have a patent on a destimeter which gives reliable predictions for up to thirty-six hours ahead?"

"It won't work as efficiently as our PM, Mr. Gryastairs," said a minor technician who had just joined the group. "Our chance theories are much more sophisticated than theirs, for a start. The destimeter uses only superficial biochemical and physiological manifestations. There's no hormonal printout. It was Maine's genius that he accepted right from the start that alpha-wave intensity is the key to reliable prediction, and for that you need constantly updated information-flow regarding hormonal activity and related data such as glucose breakdown. The destimeter doesn't even take account of blood sugar levels, which to my way of thinking – "

"Quite so, quite so," said Gryastairs heavily. "Given the Chinese proof that Predestination can be the basis of an exact science, obviously you are going to get a number of approaches to the problem. Machines follow theory, as I always say. My point is simply that it was Smics Callibrastics who had the good sense to employ Edward Maine when everyone else regarded him as a crank. Now, we should have a marketable PM at least two years before the opposition. There's no ceiling to our potential selling platform."

"I must talk to you about that," said little Hayes of Marketing. "It is going to be hellishly more difficult to promote and sell the product when the World State is established on Earth, and all their piddling new regulations and tariffs come into force – "

"Let's leave the World State out of the conversation just for tonight," Curmodgely said. While his confrères were talking shop, Edward Maine shook all the extended hands and smiled his simple smile. Occasionally he brushed his hair from his face, which was pink from several glasses of wine. With all the compliments ringing in his ears, he was very much the picture of a successful inventor; a slightly complacent smile hovered round his lips, while his manner was a little abstracted, as if even now he was elaborating his theory of non-randomness which lay behind the prototype PM.

The prototype resembled one of de Chirico's metaphysical figures mated with a small battery car. Maine was gazing not at it but at an immense painting which hung on the wall behind it.

The painting was the sole ornament on the walls of the Smics boardroom. It showed a strange feast taking place in the market square in a terrestrial country which might be Mexico or South America or Spain. A drunken peasant girl lay sprawled on a crude wooden table among the dishes; several men were feeling her while they ate and drank. Other people, men and women, stood round the table, laughing as they fed. Some of the men wore old raincoats. A skeleton was present, dressed as a monk.

Maine was interested in this central tableau. He also liked the way in which the picture was crowded with barrels and bright costumes and pots. The cobbles of the market square were vividly depicted. At the corners were further perspectives, a white-walled lane leading downhill, a cobbled stair leading up. The houses had tiles on their roofs. Maine supposed that such places must still exist on Earth, or else why paint them? Real things were amazing enough without inventing any more.

Out of habit, he began visualising all the possible parameters of action implicit in the situation depicted on the canvas. The skeleton might signify that plague was about and that all present would soon die. Or further indignities might be heaped upon the drunken girl. Or the men might fight. Graphs of non-randomness flowed in his mind; where they intersected lay points of maximum possibility.

"It would be wonderful to visit Earth again...."

He felt the scale of the sundial under his wrist-skin. Seventeen-thirty. Soon time to get home for his Internal. Oh, that lovely girl! – If only he knew her externally! Well, at least there was that to look forward to.

Sighing, he turned and shook another extended hand.

[FOUR]

The last hand had come and gone. Maine caught the mainline home as usual, changing on to a graft and so to his own particular warren, deep among the braces of Fragrance. He hardly thought about the celebratory party which had been held in honour of his research team; his mind was on the pleasures to come.

"How did it go, Edward?" Fabrina asked. "The party?"

"They were all very kind. It was a nice party. They are a pleasant firm to work with."

"Mr. Marvin Stein-Presteign?"

"Oh, yes, even Mr. Marvin was there. He had quite a conversation, as the PM forecast."

"Edward, did he – did he make you any kind of a *donation?*"

"Well, Fabrina, he made a speech. A eulogistic speech. Said that Western Civilisation was not dead yet, and that we could still show China and the coming World State a thing or two." He broke off, using his sister's visitor as an excuse to evade his sister's interrogation. "Hello, Anna, how are you?"

"I'm just a radioactive particle in the mind of God," Anna Kavan said, smiling, as she came forward and kissed Edward's cheek. "At least, so your lin tells me. Why do you keep such an old-fashioned model, a man of your standing? You could afford some of the really intelligent ones, with up-to-date religious phobias and everything."

"Like Fabrina, I enjoy our old lin. It's our pet. Anything too intelligent can't remain a pet. And the original idea of lins was to act as pet-substitutes, since live pets are not allowed in the zeepees."

"You're both very eccentric," Anna said. "And I am going back to Earth very soon, where I shall purchase a Persian cat."

"Some might think that was eccentric, Anna," said Edward mildly.

Putting on her sentient extra face, she moved to the door. "Edward, your innocence protects you from perceiving how eccentric I am. Stick to prediction and leave the squalor of human relationships to others."

She blew them a kiss and left.

"What exactly did she imply?" Edward asked his sister. "It's fashionable to talk in epigrams nowadays," said Fabrina, who did not know either.

"Pretending she's about to go to Earth... People are always saying that, and they never go."

Edward marched through into his own room, calling to the lin to follow him. The lin, an antique of the twentieth century, came in and stood against the wall until wanted, its plastic curlicues gleaming in the mock firelight.

Among all the clutter of Edward Maine's hobby, which was also his Main Job, stood his one extravagance. Most homapts, at least in the Superior group of zeepees, were equipped with funfaxes, for the reception of all media, including Internals. But Edward's was a two-way funfax. He could have his partner here with him.

Only in this vital respect had his shyness not entirely triumphed.

When the Intern-girl entered, shown in by Fabrina with proper courtesy and just a whiff of instinctive jealousy, she wore as usual a molycomp flesh mask, so that he had few visual clues to her real personality. She was dressed in a saffron tunic, with turn-up sokdals on her feet. There were white gloves on her hands. She bowed to him.

"You are well this week, Zenith?" he asked. Zenith was the code name they had agreed between them.

"Perfectly, thank you. As I hope you are."

"Yes. And you still find happiness in your Main Job? With what is it connected?"

"My happiness is connected with artificial seas, thank you." Of course she assumed the Mandarin etiquette which was currently the rage on more progressive zeepees; so that she could only take her refusal to deliver a direct answer to a direct question – itself a breach of the Anonymous Internaliser contract – as far as a riddle. But the finesse she showed made him suspect that she was true Oriental.

As to her voice, it was low, but that meant nothing, for the moly-comps often spread into pseudopods around the maxillae and sometimes down into the throat, altering the pitch of the voice in an attempt to baffle concealed voice-printers, just as her gloves baffled finger-printers.

"May I offer you an aphrohale before we go Internal?" he asked in a trembling voice. There she stood before him. He had but to reach out.

"It is better that we both defer to the terms of the contract binding us both, don't you think?"

"Of course, Zenith. As you wish. Apologies."

Formal as a sarabande, they stepped one to one side of the fun-fax, one to the other. Edward pressed his face to the viewer, checking that the controls were set for his stipulated ride and the automap clued to the contracted region of her anatomy. He scarcely felt the hypodermic sting his ear lobe, or the hallucinogen course to the plea-sure-centres of his hypothalamus. He had paid for a full twelve-week course with Zenith; this was week eleven; he was to venture into un-known, unvisited sectors of the girl he so terribly thought he loved only twice more.

[FIVE]

Her thorax was a complex geography moving toward Edward through a syrup of ultraviolet. A great epidermal plain travelled be-neath his view, its pitted inclines seemingly bereft of life, although the plain itself shuddered and vibrated like a wheat-field in storm. Gleaming, it rose to take in the universe; but the universe was illu-sion C at point of impact, the vertiginous plain melted and folded, revealing blue craters through which Edward's viewpoint – Edward himself – penetrated.

As he sank through her internscape, both magnification and rate of progress accelerated. The subcutaneous constellations of her sweat glands and adipose tissues fell upwards, entangled in path-ways of vein and nerve fibre. Beyond them, barely glimpsed, were colossal geodesic structures which he recognised from previous jour-neys as an edifice of costal cartilage and rib – structural supports of the energy jungle he now invaded.

The wavelength was decreasing. As if the distant superstructure was a radio telescope trained on the violence of a far nebula, he was conscious of varying densities and materials working round him. Much of this material was as hostile to him as any pulsar emitting gamma rays. Immune, he sank further down into her unknown galaxies, at once penetrator and penetrated.

He passed unaware into the races of her thoracic aorta. There was no sensation of travelling down a tube, so congested was it, so packed with racing amorphous things – and every object packed with semi-autonomous intent. The intense ultraviolet magnification enabled him to see through the walls to vivid pulsations of energy beyond. They were at once like lightning and spaghetti. Everywhere, the disturbed and anonymous life of energy. He was merging with it. As the depth, the drug, took hold, he was no more than a rhythm in this tide of rhythmic impulses.

The predestined course wafted him timeless through galaxies of pancreas, duodenum, kidney, where renal syphonings registered on his senses like ever-falling cascades of fire. From the boiling vat came a flood of grand spectral beings, lymphocytes and leucocytes, and the more meagre erythrocytes, pulsing yellow and mauve in colour, accompanying him down along the Amazon of the abdominal aorta and its deltaic offshoots.

Now the light was more subdued, the pace slower, the vanquishment of time and dimension more extensive. Now he was himself astro-organic – at once estranged from himself and coextensive with all being. Inarticulate outpourings of truth and life bathed him and radiated from him.

Beside him among the mute arterial ways was another presence: Hers, and yet something much more enduring than Her, a calm centre, which radiated back to him in dialogue the comforts he was involuntarily pouring out. It assured him of something for which his ordinary state of being had no vocabulary – something to the effect that this microcosm of body had no more to do with the whole human being than had the macrocosm of the starry universe, yet that both microcosm and macrocosm were intimately, intricately, nonrandomly, related to the human... and there was a word there like psyche or soul... a non-existent word which possibly implied "conundrum."

And the Anima which teased him in a way that seemed lucid at the time – that Anima was as much of him as of her, a common spirit which perhaps, in similar circumstances, he might equally well have found in a leopard or a reindeer, a spirit born of all the mindless energy, yet itself calm, mindful.

It led him to one of the cable-like branches of the nervous system, where obscure messages rattled past him like lighted express-trains at night, carrying news of who-knows-what to who-knows-where. In the hypogastric system, lights were as jarring as sound, until he slipped away into a less frenetic area, resting in a rococo region of ligament and ramus patterned like a feather. The impetus of his voyage was dying. He floated there in stasis, knowing that soon tides over which he had no control would bear him back again to whatever condition he had relinquished.

At that, a sense of desolation seized him, but he threw it off in wonder at the splendid pelvic landscape surrounding him. The solemn structures among which he moved, bathed in low X-ray, had no macrocosmic equivalent, being at once gaseous formations, jungle growths, architecture. He became enclosed in a cathedral-like galactic lagoon, where nerve fibres stood out to meet him like roots of mangroves, welcoming him to the infinite confines of her vesico-uterine fold. There he stayed while a state much brighter than darkness fell, brooding like God over the measureless waters.

[SIX]

When Edward found himself back to ordinary consciousness again, he was touched with disappointment. It was under the cloak of such characteristic melancholy that the girls who hired themselves out for Internals generally managed to vanish away, avoiding meeting their clients face to face.

As he sank into a chair, soaked and exhausted, Edward saw that his hired Zenith was going.

"One week more," he said. He held his face with trembling hands.

"I will return next week."

"Zenith – whatever your name is – stay a moment until I recover. Touch me!"

"You know the Contract."

He looked at her desperately, and his gaze lit on the lin, standing silent against the wall.

"For courtesy's sake – for kindness – let my lin amuse you with a short tale! Lin, tell Zenith one of your stories." Before Zenith could say anything, the lin spoke.

"This story is called 'Pacific Squalor.' New taxation caused squalor in a Pacific town. 'Weaving mills require a pretty sponsor,' cried the citizens atrabiliously. But an airport was built and a sparkling bucolic comedy performed. All denied attempting to pervert justice. 'Let fate no longer lead to loneliness,' whispered the oldest lady. So patterned windows were built."

"You have an old-fashioned lin," said Zenith.

Edward wiped the damp hair from his forehead. "You must know more about me than I about you. I am not rich."

"I apologise for implied criticism. The story your lin has told pleases me."

Every time, he had coaxed a little conversation from her. In pleasure now, he said eagerly, "It really amused you?"

She stood before him, the molycomp mask smiling but expressionless.

"Didn't Anton Chekhov say that stories should not be about life as it is or as it ought to be but as it appears in dreams? Your lin's story is of that kind."

"You know Chekhov's writings?"

"I make a close and interested study of European writing... I mean, that is one of my Side Jobs... Now please excuse me – I have overstayed my time."

In her tunic, her robe, her gloves, her mask, she went. Edward sat on his chair.

"Would you like a story or a joke?" asked the lin.

"No."

"She had made a slip there, definitely a slip. 'European writing'... that was not a phrase anyone of American or European stock would use about a Russian writer. Despite his French influences, Chekhov would be regarded as a European writer only by someone completely outside the European community. An Asiatic, for instance." He was more certain than ever that Zenith was Chinese. And after next week, he would never see her again. Contracts were non-renewable. The damage that Internals did to anyone submitting to them – damage that could ultimately result in death – shrouded the transactions in mystery and restriction. The Japanese, Edward recalled, had invented this ritual, investing it with all the formality of a tea-drinking ceremony.

Much as he might dislike that formality, he saw its point. The intimacy of a person-to-person Internal was such that it had to be guarded by formula. Otherwise he, at least, would have been too shy to face the confrontation.

"The Contract!" he said aloud. Always, he was bound by contracts, written or unwritten, whether to his firm or his sister, his landlord or his Internal-girl. With a flash of insight, Edward perceived that all men were similarly bound, whether they recognised it or not. Otherwise, his predestination machine would have no hope of working. The illusion of free will was simply a lubricant to keep the machine working smoothly.

He couldn't face it. Getting up, he staggered over to the aphrocoza bottle.

[SEVEN]

The computer controlling the gyroscopes at the heart of Fragrance 11 kept the planetoid riding precisely in its orbit. That orbit was elliptical, with the planet Earth at one of its nodes, set at an angle of 83.45 degrees to the plane of the ecliptic, so that the sun's energy washed ceaselessly like an ocean about the speeding body.

In its eternal morning, Edward Maine woke to another manmade morning, accepted coffee from Fabrina (who offered it in the classical auspices stance), and staggered over to do his daily horoscope seated at the PM.

The analytics went into action, reading his basic physiological functions, such as pulse rate, hormone level, encephalic activity, tension index, and so on, and immediately the transmitter began a printout.

The very first symbol on the paper caught Edward's attention. It showed that this was to be a day of prime magnitude. He had never received that signal before, except once – on the day they had been expecting it at Callibrastics, when the breakthrough came with the application of chance laws to personal data banks.

For a second time the analytics went into action, feeding Edward's response level into the computer, where it would be matched against all the background data plus the new data on all local events arriving during the artificial night of Fragrance. This double-check on response levels ensured that, by gauging Edward's current reaction to challenge, the day's reading of event-flow would be as accurate as possible.

The event-flow began to appear. The further ahead in the day, the less reliable the prediction. Possibility percentages were attached to each nodal event. All items were listed in likeliest chronological order, related in the PM's usual cryptic style.

**Key day. Surprise gift from corp mixed with contempt 95
View provides revelation on which future hinges 89

Do not attach too much importance to self
HL (Hormone Level) indicates sudden mind-change 91
Unsettling news. Fogginess. Presumption leads to quarrel
    with sister 85.5
Concealed beauty leads to religious argument 78
Lack of lobster recognition interests 77
Make simpler daily the beating of man's heart
Priestly contact aids welfare approach 69
Search yields nil result 79

Summary: day of interest, many new possibilities

Edward sat looking at the printout for a long while. Every line seemed to pose a fresh mystery, although that was the way with the PM prototype, even on a quiet day. The problem was often a simple semantic one: that to predict an event accurately, the terms had to be imprecise; conversely, when the terms were precise, the accuracy quota was forced down. Heisenberg's uncertainty principle ruled.

All the same, some of the factors were mildly staggering. "Quarrel with sister." Precise enough, but he never quarrelled with Fabrina. Then, "Do not attach too much importance to self." This contrasted with the machine's favourite homily, which was that Edward should attach more importance to himself. Advice instead of straight prediction generally indicated fuzzy set thinking, where the computer was unable to make any either-or evaluation, or else concealed a surprise factor determined by event-currents (in the jargon of Callibrastics) on which the computer had insufficient data. The final line sounded horribly downbeat, whereas the summary held ambiguous promise.

One thing at least was clear. He had a challenging day ahead. He took a timid shot of aphrocoza before heading for the elevator.

[EIGHT]

Edward spent the first hour of the morning with a calculator, trying to work out applicable Laplace formulations for human action. Once they developed a suitable tool for handling the equilibrium and motion of human life-flow, they would have a convenient way of making the PM smaller and more marketable. Edward believed that in a non-intermeshing event world, perturbations of behaviour would be periodic rather than cumulative; if Callibrastics could achieve a field-equation to cover this reaction, an all-applicable calculus of chance would do away with most of the tedious process of physiological function-reading which at present inaugurated every day's prediction.

Edward was deep in the work, and enjoying it, when Sheila Wu Ton poked her elegant face up on his screen and said, "Edward, dear, would you mind going to see Mr. Marvin Stein-Presteign, please?"

"Of course, Sheila." He jumped up. Making sure that none of his assistants had their eye on him, he licked his hands and tried to straighten out his untidy hair. He adjusted his collar as he made his way to managerial level.

Surprise gift from company. Surely that could only be good.

Stein-Presteign was all smiles. He was a genial green colour. His office, as befitted the managing director of Smics Callibrastics, was set on the outside of the Fragrance Light Industrial pyramid. His window looked out over the edge of Fragrance before it fell away in sheer cliff, and the sun, blazing through the planetoid's dome, was toned down by chlorophylter shutters, whose output went to feed the riotous blooms of Stein-Presteign's indoor garden.

For a world that practised the formalities, Stein-Presteign was remarkably informal. He bowed as deeply as his solid bulk would allow and motioned his visitor to a chair.

Awed as ever in the presence of his boss, Edward sat meekly down to listen to a general preamble.

"The scatters are always telling us that we are through creatively,"

Stein-Presteign said. "The argument goes that the Renaissance was the period when Western man set his targets toward the next few hundred years. In Italy in the fifteenth century, rich middle-class families in Milan, Venice, and Florence and such cities suddenly came out with dynamic ideas of humanism, individualism, and speculation about the material world. You could say that the Borgias and the rest of them were the early founders of those goals that led us to space travel.

"Then the movement spread outwards through Europe and so, eventually, to the Americas. Particularly to North America, although Brazil is now having her turn. But the general impression seems to have gotten around that, with the rise of China to world dominance and the dwindling of mineral and fossil oil deposits, the spirit of the Renaissance is dead."

He put his fist down heavily on the desk, leaning forward and looking hard at Edward. "I do not believe that the Renaissance is dead, Edward. I have never believed it. We have in you and your team here in Callibrastics proof positive that the old inventive enquiring spirit of Leonardo and the other guys lives on. The scatter-pundits fail to see that the general retreat of the brains of much of the Western world to the zeepees in search of free energy has caused a revolutionary regrouping. My firm belief is – I have stated this before and shall state it again, in defiance of defeatist thinking – that the zeepees duplicate in many essential ways the conditions of the Italian Renaissance cities. My belief is that Fragrance and the Ingratitudes – even Turpitude, for God's sake – are so many little Florences and Milans. Of course, the Italians didn't have the goddamned Chinese to deal with...."

The managing director followed up this last remark with a moody silence. Feeling something was required of him, Edward said, "Of course, an argument by analogy –" but Stein-Presteign swept the puny sentence away with a new flood of talk.

"Well, I've been reviewing things in that light since I returned home from the party last night. Among the matters I reviewed was your pay structure, Edward, and it did occur to me that for a man as distinguished in his way as Leonardo da Vinci, you have not been treated entirely with the generosity for which Smics Callibrastics is rightly renowned, right? That is to say, not on a scale commensurate with the generosity of the merchant princes toward the painters, architects, and scientists they patronised. So I determined to make a gesture – a grand gesture that will perhaps fire you to greater things."

"Really, sir, you're very kind, but –"

"Edward, the company is going to send you on vacation to Earth for a whole month. You need a vacation, and travel will broaden the mind. You have no damned personal life here worth speaking of. Well, we're going to send you down there –" he gestured eloquently toward the window "– to relax and refresh the springs of your mind, work up some more psychic energy. We pick up all the tabs, OK?"

Edward hesitated, and Stein-Presteign added, "What's more, the vacation, including the space travel involved, is for two. So you can take that sister of yours along for company."

Confused though he was, Edward registered the note of contempt in the director's voice. Unable to sit still, he got up and went to the window to hide the workings of his face. Taken at face value, the offer was terribly generous; but could he take it at face value? Stein-Presteign despised him. Were they trying to sack him?

Between elation and dismay, he stared out at the panorama of urbstaks marching toward the edge of Fragrance's disc. Maybe the planetoid was too small for him, although that was also one of its attractions; yet how wonderful to see the oceans again, as he had when a boy.

From where he stood he could see the far-ranging boxes of the administration of FFFFA, whose industrial levels went down into the core of Fragrance. Most of the planetoid's food was produced there – whereas on Earth he would be able to eat natural food again. A phrase floated to his mind: "My happiness lies in artificial oceans..."

He turned about.

"I accept your kind offer. I'd love to be Earthside and stand on a shoreline watching the ocean again. I'll go."

Pulling a solemn face, Stein-Presteign came round the desk and shook Edward's hand without speaking, looming over him as he did so. He laid a hand on his employee's shoulder and said, "There's one point to take into consideration, Edward. We – you, I, Callibrastics, the whole of Fragrance – stand to get very rich from our PMs. We can sell 'em by the thousand among the zeepees and break even very comfortably, as I suppose you realise.

"But our real target must be Earth. We must be able to sell PMs on Earth. That's where the real market lies."

"That shouldn't be hard," Edward said. "The Chinese have long believed in predestination –"

"You're being politically naive, Edward." He took a step forward, almost as if determined to crush Edward under his great prow. "What the Chinese believe on that score is neither here nor there. What they do believe in is selling their own wares just as we do, come to that. They're getting this World State into constitutional order, and there's no doubt they can set up destructive tariffs against us out here. Many of my friends believe that is one of the chief objects of World State. I don't myself. My belief is – I have stated this before and shall state it again – that the Chinese are good horse-traders. And that's where you come in."

"I hardly know what a horse looks like," said Edward, aghast.

"Holy gravities!" Stein-Presteign exclaimed, clutching his forehead. "I'm speaking metaphorically, son, metaphorically! Does the name Li Kwang See mean anything to you?"

"Apart from the fact that it's a Chinese name, no."

"Li Kwang See is a very distinguished bureaucrat. He's served his time in the Peking government and now he's just been appointed Minister for External Trade, a post he takes up when the World State becomes reality. He has the usual prejudice of his kind against Western science. When you're on holiday, Edward, the company wants you to go round and call on Mr. Li Kwang, and persuade him to like our PM."

"You want me to –?" He was overcome by excitement.

"Callibrastics *trusts* you, Eddy." Again the hand on the shoulder. "*I* couldn't be trusted to chat up Li Kwang. I'd be too heavy-handed. But your nice quiet little way of going about things..."

"All right. Of course I'll go and see him," Edward said, breaking free of what threatened to be an embrace. "I believe in the virtues of the PM probably even more than you do, sir. I certainly know more about its working. Some of these Chinese statesmen are very civilised men. If I can't sell it, nobody can, sister or no sister."

He blushed, seeing himself in the diplomatic role. "People were good enough to say last night what a pleasure it was to work with me – well, I will impress Mr. Li Kwang favourably. We can get in before Gondwana and our other rivals. I can persuade him to order some machines. He'll know someone in the Internal Trade department – I'll come back with a big order, rely on me."

"Of course, I have always admired your enthusiasm, Edward." Stein-Presteign retired round the desk and gestured curtly to Edward's chair. "It is best that we all know our capabilities and limitations. Frankly, you alarm me. You must understand that all we want you to do is to establish a friendly contact with Li Kwang, nothing more. When the time comes to sell, believe me, Edward, Callibrastics will send out its prime sales force on the job. Professionals, not amateurs. We certainly shall not rely on anyone in Research for such a delicate task..."

Seeing that he had been too crushing, he added, "But yours will be the perfect touch to convince the Minister that our slice of Western science is fully in accord with Chinese principles, non-exploitive, non-imperialist, and so on. You're so obviously a non-imperialist character that you are our first choice for such a mission, right? OK, get Sheila Wu Tun to assist you with any little problems. She has been briefed."

Edward rose. "You're extremely – I'm extremely –" He held out his hand, then he scratched his head with it. Then he left.

[NINE]

He went back and stared at the flowers growing under the falsie in his office so much less prolifically than the flowers below the managing director's real window. He decided that he was trembling too much to do any creative work and might as well go home for the day.

Pleasant odours wafted through the carriage on the way home – someone had slipped their card in the Perfume slot – but he was restless and curiously upset. On the one hand, the corporation had been generous; on the other hand, they had tied a condition to the vacation and had been insulting. Of course, he deserved all he got, both the good and the bad. "You're too damned self-effacing for your own good," he told himself. "And at the same time you think too much about yourself."

He attached too much importance to self – at a time when predestination brought the whole nature of self into question. That was something they'd never had to bother about in ancient Venice, or wherever it was.

To his relief, the homapt was empty when he returned. At this time of day, Fabrina was at her job in the Fire Department. The lin was activated by his presence; it unplugged itself from its charge socket and came to him. Its simulated wrought-iron framework gleamed. It had dusted itself this morning.

"Your pleasure levels are low, Edward. Would you care for a story?"

"No."

He tramped past it into his room and poured himself a large aphrocoza. The mixture of liquid and heavy gas rolled into his beaker like a slow wave. He poured it into mouth and nostrils, quaffing it back till all was gone. Then he felt slightly better.

The lin was standing meekly beside him.

"All right, all right!" Edward said. "For g's sake, do your thing!"

"Here's a story called 'Volcano Obliteration.' Lorna put her hands conversationally round an old grey falcon," the lin told Edward. "In the town, a silver band played, but she had heard too many promises. She cried, 'I must return with honour to my father.' But a volcano obliterated the valley. Now she lives with incredible leopards while a harlot plays 'Flower Patterns' in her head. She attempts to mind the animals courteously."

"Good, now go and plug yourself in again."

"You have tired of my stories."

"Emotional blackmail is something you weren't programmed for."

Edward sat silent and glum, pouring more aphrocoza into himself and finally falling asleep in his chair, to undergo curious waking dreams which were dispelled when Fabrina entered the homapt.

He went through and said to her, "I've just dreamed up the final proof of why God can't exist. Everything is predetermined; our more fortunate ancestors were able to believe in free will only because they did not understand that random factors are themselves governed by immutable laws."

"You're home early, Edward. I've bought us a halibut steak for supper."

"Everything was always predetermined. How could anyone big-minded enough to be God enjoy sitting back for countless aeons of years and watching what was to him a foregone conclusion working itself out?... Of course, I suppose what seems such an incredibly long time to us may be just a flash to him. Maybe he has a lot of pinball machine universes like ours all spinning at once."

"You've been at the aphrocoza, Edward. It always gets you on to ontology."

"Maybe we could develop a computer which would prove conclusively whether or not God exists. No, that would hardly be possible, just as Karl Popper proved that no computer can predict a future that includes itself, although it can predict personal futures. Perhaps there are personal gods. Or maybe fully developed PMs will turn into personal gods...."

"Father used to say that God was much more dirty-minded than was generally allowed for."

"There are limits to the possible. There must be a formula for those limits. It might be possible to compute those limits. But then, again, if we knew what the limits were, and how near we were to them, that would make the universe even more boring than it is now. Think how tired I am of my *own* limitations. I'm just a souped-up version of lin."

She settled into a bending reed position and said dismissively, "You know you like lin's stories when you're sober."

"Ah, ah, ha –" He waved a finger at her. "But why do I like them? I enjoy their limitations. I enjoy the sense of being able to determine the limits of lin's brain, of being able to encompass easily the farthest distance its story-patterns can reach. You don't mean to tell me God is as petty-minded as to enjoy our little patterns of circumstance in a similar way?"

"Has something happened to upset you?"

"There are those who might say that 'orbitally-perturbed' was a better phrase than 'upset,' my dear, but – in a word, yes. I was up before Wine Stain this morning, and he has given me a month's vacation on Earth, to go wherever fancy takes me, to wander in the Rockies, to march to the sea... Thalassa! Thalassa!" There it was out!

Fabrina's pose collapsed. "You shouldn't say such things, whether you're high or not. I try never to think or speak about Earth."

He was startled at this. "You don't hate Earth? Just because we hear how much it's changing!"

She looked up at him and then covered her eyes. "Hate? I never said anything about hate. It's just that we've been on Fragrance for so long that I've ceased... I've ceased to believe anywhere else really exists. Fields, ordinary skies, irregular ground, wide horizons, trees – I can't imagine them any more. There's just these walls and the fake view out of the falsies and the caverns and trafficways. Anything else is like – a Greek myth, I guess. I can't even believe in Death any more, Edward, you know that? I think we're doomed to go on here forever, unchanging."

Edward went rigid, defending himself against what she was saying."Time goes too fast..."

"You only add to the imprisonment, Edward. Father always said you lacked humanity.... You spend your life trying to drag in the future to be more like the past, to make everything all the damned same...."

He moved over to her, leant over her, only to find himself unable to touch her, to do more than stare at her carefully turned shoulder.

"Fabrina, why are you talking this nonsense? What's the matter with you? Things are changing all the time! Are you really afraid of change? Didn't you hear what I just said? – Callibrastics has given me a vacation for two on Earth. That's good! You act like it was something awful."

She looked up at him. He took a step back.

"You're not just fogged with aphrocoza? It's true? Oh, Edward, a whole month on Earth for the two of us." She jumped up and threw her arms round him. "I just thought you were lying, and I couldn't bear it. It reminded me how I hate this place. When do we go?"

"You don't hate this place. You have your friends here, every comfort."

She laughed bitterly. "OK, you like it so much, you stay and I'll go. I'll take Anna – she's dying to get back!"

"Listen, Fabrina, you aren't invited yet."

"I'm coming with you – you said so."

Suddenly he was furious. His hair came quivering down about his eyes; he dashed it away. "All I said was it was a vacation for two. I didn't say who I was taking with me. Why should it be you? Why do I have to have you round my neck all the time? If I want a holiday, then I'll take someone else. You're only my damned sister, not my wife, you know!"

They stood facing each other, slightly crouched, their hands rigid and not quite clenched, as if they were about to attack each other.

"I know I'm not your wife. I'm more like your servant. All these years I've looked after you! If you're going to Earth then you'll take me and nobody else."

"I'll take whom I please." But he weakened, recalling Stein-Presteign's contemptuous assumption that he would go with his sister because he had nobody else. Assumptions such as Stein-Presteign's and his sister's carried terrible power.

"You'll have to take me, Edward. What would people think if you didn't?"

This unexpected feebleness on her part strengthened him. "I don't care what people think – this is something I've earned and I'm going to enjoy it. I'm going to take a woman with me. I'm going to enjoy myself. Just for once, I'm going to live. That's something you've never thought of."

"What woman would have you? They'd laugh!"

"Little you know about women! Father always said you should have been a boy."

"Don't bring that up! Let's not go into the past. The things our parents did to us are all over and done with. Father wanted me to be a boy, didn't he, because you were so flaming inadequate in the role, but that's not my fault. You were always his little pet, weren't you, and what went on between the pair of you was none of my business."

"You tried to make it your business, just as you still try to interfere in all my relationships now. Besides, who was mother's little pet, eh?"

"Well, come on then, give – who was mother's little pet? It wasn't me, that's for sure. It was Alice, wasn't it, your favourite sister!"

"Leave Alice out of this, you bitch. She's dead too, and we both know what killed her."

She hit him across the face.

He stepped back, raising his hand to his cheek, resting his knuckle on his lip and glaring at her across the edge of his palm. "You're still lousy with guilt," he said. "It shows in everything you do. It settles like a blight on everything you touch."

"If you're trying to blame your blighted life on me, think again. You may recall that it was you who persuaded me to come and live up on this miserable pseudoplanet."

"More fool me!"

"Right, more fool you! You always were a fool."

"I'm going out," he said. "I can't take any more of you!"

"And you're a coward, too!"

"Relax, I know you'd love to have me strike you and pummel you into a pulp. That's really what you want, isn't it? Not just from me, from any man!"

"You talk so big to me. You creep to all the real men in your precious Callibrastics, don't you?"

He went through into his room and sat on a chair to pull his sokdals on. As he came back through the main room to reach the outer door, she said, "Don't forget Anna will be here at five." He left without answering. Unfortunately it was impossible to slam their airtight door.

[TEN]

Fragrance Fish-Food Farms Amalgamated presented a clear profile only where their administrative levels rose above mean city-level. Below that, successive storeys down mingled with the surrounding establishments and were interpenetrated by the mainlines and tunnels of the public transport system, so that they merged into the complex web of the city capsule. Most storeys nevertheless had a formal entrance as well as many functional ones, perhaps as a fossil of ancient two-dimensional approaches to urban planning, and it was at one of these formal entrances that Edward Maine presented himself.

Edward had a Brazilian friend in FFFFA called José Manuela do

Ferraro, who worked in the Genetic Research department of the giant corporation. A neat little Japanese assistant came to meet Edward and escorted him to José's floor. She led among huge vats milling with young prawns and deposited him at the door of José's office.

The Brazilian was a big man, who jumped up and shook Edward's hand, clapping him on the back and smiling broadly.

"You're very successful nowadays, Edward – I saw a report of your celebratory party on the scatter. It makes you too busy to attend Tui-either-nor meetings, I guess?"

"Afraid so. Are you still a priest in your Side Job?"

"Can't afford to give up Main Job – besides, it fascinates me so. Come and see what we are doing in the Homarus division."

"That's very kind, José but –"

"Come on, we can talk as we go. I miss our arguments at Tui meetings, Edward. You were so good – you sharpened my wits. Now I suppose you work too much with computers to have any religious feelings."

Edward had other matters than religion on his mind, so all he said, reluctantly, was, "We need computers."

"Agreed, we need computers at this stage of man's progress," José said, opening a swing door for his friend. "But progress should be toward the sciences of self-knowledge not toward technology slanted sciences. That's a dead end. Even I have to work with computers in Main Job, while denouncing them in Side Job. We must think in fuzzy sets, not the old either-or pattern so basic to Western ideology."

"I know, I know," Edward muttered. "But either-orness has brought us a long way."

"Now we are being defeated by alien Chinese ways of thought. You must believe in my sub-thought. Sub-thought exists and is measurable – we are getting proof. Sub-t is much more random and instinctive than ordinary logical thought; it must not be structured like thought. Sub-t is related to will, and will, as we know, can modify neural patterns in the brain. If we believe in Freud, then we have Freudian dreams, and so on. If we believe in computer-human analogies, then we will come to think and sub-t like our machines. So we will be totally dominated by either-orness. Then all creativity will be lost."

"Creativity always breaks out anew, every generation."

"Yes, but unpredictably – even in your worlds of predestination, old friend! With Tui-either-nor, we can nourish it, make barren logic subject to creativity, rather than the other way round as at present."

"That's putting it too strongly," Edward said, with a feeble smile.

"No, it's not, not while the Western world is in recession generally. Tui is the old Mandarin symbol for water – a lake, for instance, signifying pleasure and fluidity. That's what we need, fluidity. Among all the religions of the zeepees, Tui is the only fructifying one, the only one that genuinely offers redemption – the redemption not just of one's self but of others!"

"I must try and get round to meetings again," Edward said. "Do you still make those ringing priestly addresses to God about Tui?"

"Of course."

"And does God answer?"

José laughed good-naturedly. "When you speak to God, that's just prayer. When he starts speaking to you–that's just schizophrenia."

They were walking among gigantic three-layered tanks in which large lobsters sprawled. The tanks were dimly lit, while the laboratory itself remained unlit. Yet it looked as if many of the lobsters could see the men, so quickly did they turn to the glass walls of their prisons and signal with antennae and claws, as if asking to be released.

"We are just beginning to realise how many kinds of thinking there are," José said. "Predestination works only for those who believe in it."

"I feel bound to challenge that statement!" Edward exclaimed. "After all – "

"Don't challenge it, remember it. Feel it fertilise you. I will show you how a little Tui thinking worked for us here." They had come to a fresh series of tanks in which more lobsters sat. José changed the subject as smoothly as if he imagined he was still talking about the same thing. "These lobsters that you see here are not much different from the ancestral lobster, *homarus-vulgaris*. You can see they're a sort of dull reddy yellow, spotted with little bluish-black patches. The only difference is that these chaps are bigger; they weigh up to six kilos. We have to breed 'em big, which we do in the traditional way of mixing inbred lines with genetic mutations for hybrid vigour. By applying ideal temperatures, we can persuade them to grow to mature market size in two years rather than three."

"Do you import sea water from Earth?" Edward asked.

"Genes, no – far too expensive, *and* sea water is not pure enough for our purposes. This is all artificial sea water – in fact, synthetic water in the first place, hydrolized out of hydrocarbons and oxides floating in space."

He rapped against the glass. "But you see the trouble with ordinary lobsters. They're nasty pugnacious creatures, so aggressive that they have to live in solitary confinement throughout life, or they'd eat each other. Which puts up *per capita* costs greatly, when you consider that on Fragrance alone some twenty-three million kilos of lobster meat are consumed per annum – which means a lot of lobsters, and a lot of tanks."

"I mustn't take up any more of your time," Edward commented.

José took his elbow and led him back along the way they had come, where the rows of tanks were more brightly lit. Here, lobsters jostled together in apparent *bonhomie*, armour notwithstanding.

"These certainly are highly-coloured," Edward said. "I didn't recognise them as lobsters at first."

"They don't recognise *each other* as lobsters," José said. He beamed, and made embracing gestures at the crustacea. The latter were certainly a remarkable sight, being in all cases bicoloured, the two colours contrasted and arranged in stripes and jagged lines, rather like the camouflaged dreadnoughts of World War I. There were many colours in the tanks: lobsters yellow and black, lobsters white and cerise, lobsters scarlet and orange, lobsters viridian and grey, lobsters sky blue and sienna brown, lobsters carmine and paint-box purple. There were scarcely two lobsters of the same pattern.

"What we have done is simple," said José, rapping on the plate glass with one creative knuckle. "Firstly, we have altered their genetic coding so as to transform their original vague colouration until we hit on strains which are the eccentric hues you see now. Then we bred them true, using cloning methods. Next, taking a clue from the coloration, we made use of research into orientation anistropy in acuity."

"Whatever's orientation anistrophy in acuity?

"Not anistrophy. Anistropy. It's an anomaly of vision. Permit nothing but horizontal lines in the environment of an infant mammal, and ever after it will have no neural detectors for vertical ones, becoming completely orientated on the horizontals. We found that the immature visual cortex of the lobster responds in the same way. See what I mean? The effect is on the brain, not the vision, but what happens is that, after the treatment we give the larvae in their visual environment, no striped lobster can see another striped lobster. Although they basically have the same nasty pugnacious natures as their terrestrial ancestors, they live together peacefully. For them as for us, it all depends how you look at things."

"Very interesting," said Edward politely. Then he added, "Yes, that really is very interesting...."

"You get the implications for human conduct, eh?" said José. "You see where my Tui thought came in? I believe that the culture matrix of our civilisation – of any civilisation – imprints us from birth so that we can only see horizontal lines or, in other words, only think along channels deemed correct by long-established custom."

Genuinely interested now, Edward said as they walked back to José do Ferraro's office, "I wonder if all the slightly differing environments of the zeepees will eventually give rise to a generation who are oriented to verticals or – to an entirely new way of thought."

"My guess would be that we're seeing some such phenomenon already. It would account for all the cults springing up daily. I believe that Tui is one of the true new directions."

They settled down in the office and José got them two pam-and-limes from the machine. As they were sucking, he said, "So, what can I do for you, my lapsed friend?"

"Don't call me that, José. I still believe, but I've been so busy."

"Ha, you're killing your spiritual life with work – you'll become a robot. The sad thing is, you know what you're doing.... Well, how can I help you?"

Now that his moment had come, Edward was embarrassed. "It's about a girl, José."

"Good. I didn't think you were interested. Women are full of Tui-either-norness. Do I know her?"

"You may do. I believe she works here in FFFFA."

"But you aren't sure?"

"It's an Internal girl, José. She comes personally to my place, but in disguise, of course. She has dropped clues about her real identity. For instance, once she said to me, 'My happiness lies in artificial oceans.' I made nothing of it at the time. This morning, it suddenly hit me that it could be the remark of a girl who worked in FFFFA. A reference to your sea water tanks. Then again, a remark she made about Chekhov convinced me she must be Asiatic."

"Who's Chekhov?"

"How pleased you make me that I know some things you don't! He's a writer. Never mind him. You have a lot of Chinese staff here, haven't you?"

"You probably know that Four F A's fifty-five per cent Chinese-owned. Eighty per cent or more of the work staff are Chinese or North Korean. If your girl's here, she's one of probably two thousand. You'd have no way of identifying her, not if you've never seen her externally."

Edward paused, then he said, "Yes, I have a means. I think I have. I think I could identify her internally."

"How can you do that? I've never heard of such a thing!"

"Nobody has. It's my own idea. And it's not unlike your variable lobster idea. José, I've studied my Internal-girl through the eyes of the electron microscope plus the eyes of love. I've been down into her with magnifications in the millions, and I've seen something in her which no other human being has – her print, as individual as – no, far more individual than any lobster."

"You mean – you don't mean a disease?"

"No, no, I mean her histocompatibility antigens."

"Oh, the substances that set up immune reactions in tissue transplants."

"Exactly. They insure that we are all immunologically foreign to each other, unless we happen to have an identical twin. They're sort of chemical badges of personal identity. There's a sufficient diversity of them to insure that everyone's antigen kit is different. It's the most basic form of identification there is."

"And you know what your girl's kit looks like?"

"I have stills of her antigens. They're beautiful. I know them by heart. What's the matter? You're wearing your priest face!"

José do Ferraro was looking at him with a peculiar creased face, its expression seeming to alternate between mockery and affection.

"Oh, Edward, 'Make simpler daily the beating of Man's heart...' Every day love reveals itself in a new form, as fluid and vigorous as Tui itself. Here you stand, enraptured by the girl with the beautiful antigens..."

Edward was touched by this speech, since he had not thought of himself as capable of rapture. "You don't believe I'm being silly?"

"I didn't say that, did I?"

Edward laughed. "OK. Do an idiot a favour. Your welfare department must have records of all the girls employed here. Can we run their medical data through a scanner? Under suitable magnifications, I know I could identify my Zenith."

"Such records exist, of course. But it's illegal for anyone but the qualified Welfare staff to see them. So we'd better go and see Dr. Shang Tsae, who works in Welfare – happily, his Side Job is acolyte to Priest Ferraro..."

[ELEVEN]

"I was worried about you. Wherever have you been?" Fabrina asked. No sign of the quarrel.

"Oh, engaged in a little private research of my own," Maine said. "I'm exhausted. Let me rest." He walked over to the mirror and tried to pat his hair into order.

"Of course, my dear. Lin, come over here and tell your master a story. Make it a nice restful one."

"All my stories are adapted to the mood of the moment," said the lin, humbly yet smugly. "This one is called 'Dinosaur Inspector.' 'Taste the squalor of old obliterated airports,' cried the dinosaur inspector. The people and incredible harlots were lusty upon the mountains. The dunes knew no spring. No animal eggs slept among the entanglements. But one strong man changed everything. Now bucolic perverts no longer lead the market. Falcons fly and magnesium bands play atrabiliously."

"Not very cheerful," Fabrina complained.

"I'm going to take a shower," Maine said.

José do Ferraro had secured Edward access to the medical files of FFFFA, thanks to the illegal aid of Dr. Shang Tsae. Then Edward had had to attempt his task of antigen identification without the aid of computer – something for which he had scarcely bargained. He allowed himself twenty-five seconds to flip up each internscape in turn and scrutinize it. Even so, it was going to take him fourteen hours to get through the whole batch of two thousand, and sometimes he had to shuffle through several internscapes of one woman to get a clear view of the antigens. He tried to speed up his viewing; then fatigue slowed him again. The day had been fruitless, as predicted by his PM. He told the sober little Chinese doctor that he would return the next day.

[TWELVE]

Early on the following morning, Edward Maine heaved himself from bed and padded over to the PM, letting it gather all his physiological data while he was still half-asleep. On depressing the read-out bar, he became fully awake.

** Key day. Persistence needed at start. Do not yield to
   impatience
Antigen quest rewarded 96
Oysters yield great beauty 94.5
Increased heart-rate leads to precipitate action 94
Visit to the ever-punctual fly 79.5
Conversation delights 87
More initiative needed
Outburst of invective can be avoided 77.5

Summary: happy day, partly enjoyed in attractive company

The second key day running. His life was certainly changing. One of the constant troubles he had had while developing the PM was that nothing ever happened in his life, so that in consequence the machine had nothing to predict, which made it difficult to tell whether it was working or not.

Now it seemed to be working full blast.

Just for a moment, as he dressed, Edward wondered how much the PM really told him. He could have guessed without its aid that this would be a key day. From the line "Antigen quest rewarded" on-wards, it looked as if he would trace his longed-for Zenith; but that also was expected. On the other hand, it was difficult to tell from the read-outs where the unexpected lay. There were displeasing implications in that last line, "Invective can be avoided." With whom? The machine could not tell him, or Chaos Theory would be violated; it predicted the unexpected in such a way that it remained unexpected.

As soon as he could, he returned to the file-room of the FFFFA.

It was over halfway through the morning before he thought he had what he wanted. Before him glowed a remarkably clear shot of antigens in body tissue; they resembled strange deep-ocean sponges, and were brightly coloured. His heart beat at an increased rate. He felt his mouth go dry. In colour, in shape, they matched with Zenith's. He forgot that he was regarding a complex defence system designed to protect the human body from invasion by cells from another body; instead, he was gazing at a part of a world with its own perspectives, atmosphere, and laws which had no exact counterpart anywhere in the cosmos – an alien territory of beauty and proportion almost completely overlooked by man in his quest for new environments. By a paradox, this most personal view of his love was totally impersonal.

He turned to the file and read the name there : Felicity Amber Jones. Main Job: Marine Larvologist; speciality, Bivalves.

Felicity Amber Jones. Beautiful name. Of course, it was probably not her real name. The fashion was to adopt a name on arrival at the zeepees.

Whatever her name, it was Felicity Amber Jones herself he wanted...

An information board told him that Bivalves were in Level Yellow Two.

At Level Yellow Two, a preoccupied lady at a console told him that he would find Felicity Amber Jones along to his right.

Edward could hardly walk, so weak did his legs feel. His popliteal muscles trembled. He made his way along, clutching at a bench for support, face close to a range of tanks in which little agitated blobs of life flitted. Each successive tank contained water of a slightly different hue from the previous one. And in each, the blobs became larger and less agitated. In the last tank of the series, the blobs had come to rest on plastic trays inserted vertically into the water, and were recognisable as minute oysters. There stood a young Chinese lady in an orange lab coat, doing complicated things at a trolley involving small oysters and full beakers. She looked up at his approach and smiled questioningly.

He had never been in love before – not properly. "Are you Felicity Amber Jones?" he asked.

She was in her twenties, a neat little figure with a slender neck on which was balanced one of the most elegantly modelled heads Edward had ever seen. The lines of this exquisite head were emphasised by a short crop of hair which curled round the back of the skull to end provokingly as two upturning horns. These seductive dark locks pointed to two dimples nestling under slanting cheekbones. Her eyes, slightly set back in her eye-sockets, were round and moist, being sheltered by dark eyelashes.

Didn't those pupils widen involuntarily, despite lack of any other sign of recognition, as she answered, "Yes, I am Miss Jones."

"Look, I'm Edward Maine." He stammered his address.

"Oh, I see. Are you interested in our oyster-breeding? From pin-head to adult, it takes only fifteen months under our accelerated growth scheme. Here you see the algae tanks, each with a different algae table for different stages of larval growth, with temperature – "

"Miss Jones, you recognise me, don't you?"

She put a finger – the smallest finger of her right hand curling it like a little prawn – into her mouth – receiving it between dainty white teeth – which were embedded in the clearest of pink gums – and said, "Have we met before, Mr. Maine?"

"Oh yes," he said. "You're the girl with the most beautiful antigens in the world. I knew them instantly. You're the – well, you come to visit me at home once a week...."

Her gaze evaded him. Turning one shoulder – the gesture itself poetry – the shoulder itself a miracle – she made a little fluttering noise.

Standing on tiptoe in order to see her cheek over her shoulder, he said in a rush, "Look, please – I know it's a terrible breach of etiquette – I know I shouldn't be here – but I've got a vacation on Earth – a whole month, courtesy of my corporation – and I can take along anyone I like – please, will you come with me? – I mean, it has to be you – you can name your own terms, of course – but please don't tell me I am mistaken – because you're too beautiful to be anyone but Zenith!"

She turned back. With an effort, she raised her head – despair of any sculptor – and looked into his eyes – beauty of a Medusa – and said, "Well, I may as well say it. You're right, I am Zenith. They'll sack me from the Internscan Union for admitting it."

To his extreme pleasure and embarrassment, he found that he was clasping her hands. Even worse, lit by artificial sea water, he was kissing her on the mouth.

Felicity Amber Jones proved to have just the shape and flavour of mouth of which he had always dreamed.

"I should be more formal," she said, drawing back. "Internal girls are not meant to behave so freely. Please do not try to kiss me again!"

"I'll do my best," he said. He was not on oath. "I feel I know you so well, Miss Jones, Felicity – Miss Jones. Now we must get to know each other in more traditional ways. You – you are so delightful on the microscopic level that I long to discover all the other ways in which you are delightful."

"Please speak more formally to me during my Main Job."

"Are you afraid the oysters will overhear?"

She laughed. "Your average oyster is a very unreliable creature. It can't be trusted to keep its trap shut."

"Then we must go elsewhere to talk."

He was not sure exactly what to do with the girl when he had found her; her presence added to his usual confusion. But she was pliant and docile and readily agreed to any suggestion he made.

Despite which, it happened to be at her instigation rather than his that they found themselves in the Inarguable Paradise, the biggest of Fragrance's three fun-centres. The Inarguable Paradise had, as one of its chief attractions, The Ever Punctual Fly. This Fly was a small satellite which orbited the planetoid once every fifty minutes. Unlike its parent body it had no artificial gravity; one of its chief attractions was the free-fall restaurant, in which delectable dishes were enjoyed while watching agoraphobic views in absurd postures.

There were some other Chinese-Western couples here; such liaisons were common enough – at least on this zeepee – not to excite comment; but Felicity Amber Jones declared that this was the first time she had been out informally with a Westerner.

"We call you 'foreign devils,'" she told Edward. "The Chinese are at least as conscious of race and nationality as you Americans are."

He found her mixture of directness and modesty both exciting and paradoxical. She was so perfect, her outline, her every contour, so clearly placed, that he was in awe of her. He wondered what her real name was – it was the custom with many people to take up a new name on arrival in the zeepees. His own terrestrial name had been Oscar Pythagoras Rix.

"Will you really come to Earth with me? I won't ask anything of you but your company." His crossed fingers kept his real desires at bay.

"Oh, that's quite all right."

It was not exactly the answer that he had expected; yet he wondered if its seeming complaisance was more than he had hoped for. A premature gratitude flowed into the lagoons of his being.

He pressed her hand – opportunely, as it happened, for at that moment a quartet of Voivodina gypsies, specially imported from Earth, began a passionate lament to love, springtime, swordplay, Smederevo, the tide, innocence, moonlit nights, deserted churches, and a pair of forgotten lace gloves.

Edward did not tell Felicity Amber Jones that he had a commission to carry out on Earth. That might, he considered, make her less keen to join him. Instead, he concentrated on the pleasure aspect, unwilling to believe she could wish to come along for his company alone.

"What would you most like to see when we reach Earth? The glaciers of Alaska? Smederevo?" The wild music was still provoking his blood.

"Oh, I would love to see the reindeer herds of the Chinese Arctic, grazing by the East Siberian Sea. I have never seen a reindeer, and they're so guilty and luxurious creatures."

"I've never seen a penguin. How about a trip to the Ross Ice Shelf in the Antarctic, to see the Adele penguins? You know they reproduce in subzero temperatures?"

"We mustn't concentrate only on cold regions. What about the warm regions? How marvellous to see Kilimanjaro rising from the zebra-trampled veldt and floating in the crumpled air."

"How marvellous to swim in the Red Sea and wave to passing dahabeeyahs!"

"To take a trip to the Iguazu Falls, where Brazil, Uruguay, and Argentina meet."

"To jump into the chain of volcanoes along the spine of Sumatra."

"To dive down to the new underwater city off Ceylon."

"To surf off Honolulu."

"Do you really know how to surf?" she asked.

"No. But I've seen guys do it on the scatter..."

[THIRTEEN]

When he returned home, the twenty-hour Fragrancian day was almost spent and a new one only half an hour away. Edward had held her hand on parting. They smiled at each other and promised to meet another day.

Now, like any callow youth, he cursed himself for not showing more initiative and kissing Felicity Amber Jones goodnight. Surely she would have allowed – wanted – it after such a splendid evening.

Fabrina was home with Anna Kavan. They were practising altered body images together, and becoming rather entangled. Fabrina stood up, blowing her hair from her eyes.

"We wondered what had happened to you. That reporter from Cairo is trying to get in touch with you again."

"Only good things happened," Edward replied, moving with nonchalance toward his room.

"So you are going to Earth, Edward," Anna said. "Aren't you fiendishly fortunate? You wouldn't like to take me with you, I suppose? I hear you have a spare ticket."

He turned and confronted them both, drawing in his stomach and standing his full height.

"Not any more! You might both like to know that I'm taking a girl friend to Earth with me. It's all fixed, and I don't want any arguments."

Fabrina threw herself at him. "You fool, Edward, you fool! I can guess who it is – it's that little Internal-girl of yours, isn't it? You know nothing about her. She'll make your life a misery, you'll see."

"Hope what you like," he said, and escaped into his room. As the PM said, outbursts of invective could be avoided.

[FOURTEEN]

Next morning, relationships between Edward Maine and his sister were strained.

"What will you do while I'm on holiday, my dear?" he asked.

"I'd rather not talk about it. I'm too hurt. You don't care a bit about me."

That killed that conversation.

The lin said, "Neither of you is very happy. Let me tell you a story."

"I'm perfectly happy, and I do not want a story," Fabrina said, sniffing into a tissue.

"This one's called 'Floating Airports,'" said the machine, temptingly.

"No."

"It is full of atmosphere and there is action on a metaphysical level. Also it features a strong tax inspector, together with some animals such as you like."

"Oh, for god's sake, let him tell his story!" Edward said.

"Thank you. 'Floating Airports.' All over the old grey oceans airports floated. The towering sponsors walked drowning under deserted windows. And the tax inspector claimed, 'Now all can sleep who cease to guard the leopards.' So the strong officer went to the weak ruler and applied modesty. 'Large export markets lead to decayed temples,' one stated. So the animals laid eggs among the worldly."

"Very nice," said Edward politely. His sister did not speak. The lin bowed and retreated to stand itself against a wall.

For Edward, it was a busy morning, and one on which he embarked with some apprehension, since the PM's read-out forecast two embarrassing encounters. He went to Smics Callibrastics to sort out unfinished work, and was besieged by callers from other departments, among whom the most persistent were Sheila Wu Tun from Personnel and Greg Gryastairs from Kakobillis, who wanted errands run or messages delivered when he was on Earth. Edward was glad to escape at noon and go down to the travel agency, On the Scent, at Main Plaza East, to make his arrangements for the flight.

On the Scent were very helpful. He was booked aboard the *Ether Breather* in two days' time. The manager was somewhat awed by meek little Edward Maine, for the firm had given him a very generous luggage allowance. Kilo-costs for freight were so much steeper for the Fragrance-Earth run than for inter-zeepee trips, that anyone who travelled to Earth with more than two kilos of personal baggage was marked out as someone special; Maine, with his massive allowance, was a being apart.

The being apart was not content with his corporation's generosity, however. As usual, it had an ulterior motive. Callibrastics had prevailed upon him to take the prototype PM along, in order to do a field test in the more random conditions which prevailed upon the mother planet. Slightly dazed by a pile of documents and brochures, Edward made his way from the travel agency to the nearest aphrohale parlour and got gassed on a nitojoy-pip.

As the heavy fumes poured into his nostrils, he heard the sound of musical instruments. A small religious parade was approaching, charmed on by pipe and drum.

It was a cheerful sight, bright even in the Plaza, which had been decorated for striking colour effects. Most of the people in the parade wore brightly coloured dominoes, complete with cloak and half-hood, and many of the hoods mimicked animal heads. Edward recognised the style. These were followers of Tui-either-nor and, if he had continued with one of his Side Jobs he would now be among them, complete with mouse-mask and a lust to convert.

Feeling guilty, he slipped back to a table at the rear of the parlour; which was a simple matter, since most of the patrons had moved forward to see what was going on. Religious belief was a participator sport in the Zodiacal Planets.

When the procession stopped near the parlour, one of its number, a well-built man in giraffe-mask and priest's insignia began to speak.

"Friends, would-be friends, wouldn't-be friends, greetings all! Let me tell you what you're thinking right now. To some extent, you are aware of this procession. But you'll soon dismiss it; your mind's on trivial personal matters. It will be no part of you. Why not make it a part of you? You'll be richer. We're here to make you and Fragrance and the world a richer place." The haughty giraffe face surveyed the denizens of the square.

"Do you know what sub-t or sub-thought is? It's a random pattern of thought which we all enjoy. It exists and is a measurable quantity.

It has been denied in Western thought because it has no logic to it. That is why we have sunk into materialism. Sub-t can give you a rich spiritual life, with all alternatives open. This little procession can be your procession toward Tui-either-nor, the full thinking and spiritual existence. Espouse alternatives, or you will find yourself in one of life's cul-de-sacs, living in cul-de-sackcloth and ashes.

"Only yesterday, my friends, I had an old acquaintance come to me in my Main Job – yes, like you I have to work for my living – I'm not a fake priest – and this old friend was in search of something. Once he was a member of this movement, but he reneged. He hadn't the persistence, the initiative required to follow what he believed in his heart. He had become a hollow man."

Edward began to look about him, feeling warmth creep round his cheeks and ears. Eyes of frog, cat, leopard, hippo, marmoset, he sensed were on him.

"Yet that old acquaintance, my friend," said the giraffe remorselessly, "deluded as he was, he was in search of love, and love in a new form. He knew without knowing – he knew by sub-t – that his own spiritual life was dead, and he was driven to exercise fantastic ingenuity to look for a means whereby that dead life might be made alive again. There was a force in him greater than himself. You and I might think him a poor shrivelled creature, but all the while his life was being lived secretly for him.

"My word to you is – "

Putting two F-tallies on the table, Edward crept blushingly away without waiting for the word. He felt indeed a poor shrivelled creature as he hurried toward the nearest trafficway. As he scrambled into the first carriage, his attention was caught by a message scrawled on the nearest wall: AMBIGUITY CLARIFIES.

Suddenly, he hated Tui. Life was difficult enough without emphasising its difficulties. He was inadequate enough without anyone emphasising his inadequacies. He could see why an earlier generation had turned away from religion and the spiritual life. It was too much for them.

What they really needed were fixed co-ordinates. A predictable path through life.

No nasty surprises from sub-t or the collective unconscious or the endocrine system.

Just the dark glasses and white stick of certainty.

His immediate impulse was to go home, but he could not face his sister. Feelings still ruffled, he headed for Felicity Amber Jones's con-apt, right in the heart of the urbstak.

Section Coty was a crowded place. Lower rates went with higher densities. He remembered that Felicity had said he should not come to her home. He pressed her signal all the same, and in a moment she appeared at the door, wearing a knee-length gown of cerulean blue chased with an embroidered electric design in silver. She wore a matching blue ribbon in her hair, which gave her an incongruously childish look.

Smiling, he waved the wad of documents at her.

"I've got our tickets! We catch a flight the day after tomorrow, Felicity. Can you be ready in time?"

She looked anguished. "I live in a poor way here, Edward. You will despise me when you see how dreadfully I exist."

"I'm not a bloated capitalist. Why should I despise you for being poor?"

"You know I had to take to being an Internal-girl. That's to support my brother, Shi Tok, who is an artist. He's here now. He lives with me."

"I'll be glad to meet him. You didn't tell me that you live with your brother, as I live with my sister."

She let him in reluctantly. "He is very prejudiced against Americans, worse luck."

Sharply, he said, "Have you told him we are going to Earth together?"

Felicity covered her nose and mouth with a narrow hand and bowed her head. As she did so, a man appeared from an inner room, wearing a paint-stained shirt and smoking an absurdly small pipe.

His hair was cut square, his face painted in stripes.

"What do you want?" he asked.

"This man is my friend, Shi Tok. His name is Edward. Edward this is my brother, Shi Tok. He is a great artist."

"You probably don't care much for art, do you?" Shi Tok asked.

"Why, yes, I have a great respect for works of art – and for artists."

"I see. The usual crappy worthless lip service. Why don't you get honest and say that you hate and fear art and artists?"

"Because he does not wish to be as rude as you," Felicity said. "Give Edward a pam-and-lime or something."

"No, I'd better be going, Zenith. I can see I'm not welcome here."

"Why's he calling you Zenith, Felicity? Say, Edward, while you're here, why don't you come and see what I'm currently working on? With all that enthusiasm for art, you might get a buzz."

Despite himself, Edward found himself being pushed into a small room where the three of them formed a crowd – perhaps because of the way in which brother and sister jostled and gestured, continually getting in each other's way – she trying to produce beverages, he to produce artworks.

The table was piled with boxes full of plaques. Another plaque stood in a vice attached to the edge of the table. Shi Tok spun the vice open and held the plaque out to Edward, who accepted it reluctantly. The plaque was a rectangle about the size of an envelope and not much thicker. It was cream in colour.

"I haven't finished that one yet. Know what it is?"

"Is it ivory?"

Shi Tok laughed harshly. "I didn't mean what is it made of I mean what does it represent. But no, of course it is not ivory. It's just a block of garsh, one of the new palloys. Ivory! Stars above! Don't you know that all the tariffs and duties stacked against the zodiacal planets by Earth make it almost prohibitive to import ivory to Fragrance? Not that I could afford ivory even at Mother Earth prices. I'm a poor artist, Edward, a creator, not a civil servant, or whatever secure dull little job you hold down – no, don't tell me. That sort of information makes me feel bad, puts me off my work... This is only a block of garsh, manufactured just a light-second away on one of the Ingratitudes. You know what it is?"

Since there seemed to be no answer to this question, Edward took with some gratitude the glass which Felicity offered and said, "I'm not against art, although it's true I have a secure job. I'm a sort of artist myself, in a way – although perhaps not in a way you might recognise. What form does your art take?"

Felicity's brother looked upwards at the low ceiling and made grunting noises of despair. "This is my art-form." He waved the garsh under Edward's nose. "And these boxes are stacked with more of them, masterpieces every one. Look!"

He stirred up the boxes, pulling out rectangular plaques at random. Each block had a band incised and painted across it. The bands varied slightly in width, colour, and positioning, but there was never more than one band to a plaque.

"They're all named on the back, and signed by me," Shi Tok explained. "Here you are: *A Clutch of Underground Cathedrals, The Last Bite of an Unseen Shrapnel, Legs Trapped in an Embroidered Sea, Suntans of an Inoffensive Moon, The Spirit of the Male Climacteric Regards Narcissus, Friction Between Skull and Prisoner Brain...*Take your pick."

"Um...do you sell these?" Edward asked.

"Of course I sell them...when I can. They go to rich dolts in your country or mine with more cash than brains. I rook 'em for what I can get. Like you, they hate and fear art but they think it impresses other people, so I turn out this real junk for the pleasure of making fools of them."

Edward sipped his pam and looked at the floor. "Is it pleasurable to make fools of people?"

"They were fools long before I got to them. Why give them the real thing when they can't appreciate it? Art's as dead in China as it is in America. The artists helped kill it – they don't know what the hell they're doing either. The stupid oafs worked themselves into a dead end."

Edward gnawed his lip and scratched his leg.

Felicity said, "Edward is going to visit Earth soon," and was ignored.

"Well," Shi Tok said, throwing the plaques back in the box, "why don't you say something? Don't you like my works of art?"

"It's not for me to say," Edward muttered.

"Why not? I'm asking you, aren't I? You did come here uninvited, didn't you? What do you think of them, you a sort of artist and all that?"

Edward looked at him and felt a blush steal round his ears and cheeks. "I think nothing of them, if you want the truth. Which appears to be exactly what you think of them. I'm sorry that you can claim to be an artist and yet know that what you produce is worthless, however much you get paid for it. You must be aware of the contradiction there. Perhaps it's that which makes you so angry all the time."

The stripes rippled on Shi Tok's face. He raised a clenched fist, as much for emphasis as attack. "I sell these for what I can get. No one respects the real artist these days. Even the lousy critics – "

"I'd better be going, Felicity," Edward said, setting his glass down on the table close to the vice. "Thank you both for the drink."

"It's all very well for you to be superior, you don't suffer – "

She followed Edward to the door, despite the roaring of her brother. At the door, she stood on tiptoe and kissed him on the cheek.

"You're just wonderful," she said. "A real man."

[FIFTEEN]

Despite all the efforts to glamorise it, getting to Earth was just hell.

It started being hell at Fragport, where passengers for Earth had to go through long examinations in Customs, Medical, Expatriation, and Ecology, as well as the space line's Check In – where great exception was taken to Edward's PM, although he had all the requisite documents, and some small exception to his lin, which was only allowed through because it was an obsolete model (and he had only brought it to spite his sister).

Several people had come to interview Edward before he left Fragrance.

He was cornered by a plump shiny young man with a sharp-bladed nose, who shook Edward's hand and said he was proud to meet him.

"My name is Sheikh Raschid el Gheleb, and I lecture in Predestination at Cairo University. That's Cairo, Earth, of course. I've been trying to catch up with you for some while. Of course I am personally interested in your attempts to build a Predestination Machine."

"Kind of successful attempts," Edward said.

"So I understand. Spare me a moment of talk, please. What interests me is that Predestination is a pretty new thing in the West. Perhaps it is merely because I am Arab that I equate the outgoing capitalism of the West over the last few centuries with a firm belief in free will. The religion of the West, Christianity, lays heavy emphasis on choice."

"Ah, the either-orness of Heaven and Hell," Edward murmured, remembering the teaching of his Tui-either-norness phase.

"Now that Christianity is dying out and the West, faced with Chinese supremacy and the World State, has fewer alternatives, the peoples of the West – in the United States in particular – are turning more and more to predestination. This seems to me interesting, because the Chinese, in a sense, have always believed in predestination. So both sides of the world are becoming philosophically more ready for union. Do you see it that way?"

Edward hesitated. He liked discussions; they made him feel important; but he also wanted to board the *Ether Breather* and be alone with Felicity. "No, Sheikh, I don't quite see it that way. The impetus that moves the West toward predestination is mainly scientific and technological. It's the running down of ready sources of energy which has given the average man fewer alternatives. Better scientific knowledge of the workings of the brain and the genetic system has simply ruled out the old notion of free will. We really are programmed – it is that knowledge which makes a PM possible."

"I see, a diametrically opposed approach to the Chinese, in a way. I wonder if the Chinese will object to your turning what they have regarded as a philosophical outlook into a mechanistic one. May I ask you if your PM takes coincidences into account?"

"We are still in the prototype stage, you understand. But of course predictions can be thrown badly wrong by coincidence until such time as we fully understand the working of chance; there will then be no random factors, and coincidence will cease to exist, just like free will."

"Do you personally believe in coincidence, Mr. Maine?"

"Not in its old sense of a freak and rather unsettling concurrence of events, no. It is only under an Aristotelian system of logic that coincidences appear unaccountable."

"Mr. Maine, thank you. May we ask which ship you are taking to Earth?"

"We shall be on the *Ether Breather*. If you will excuse me."

"I see, a real-life case of ether-or eh,..."

[SIXTEEN]

The *Ether Breather* had come in from the Tolerances, and was already crowded. Edward and Felicity found adjacent couches in the Soft Class lounge and strapped themselves in. There was a fifty-minute wait till blastoff; no foggers or sniffers were permitted.

"Shall I tell you a story?" asked the lin, ever-solicitous, from under Edward's couch. "I have one called 'Familiar Struggle.'"

"At least the title sounds appropriate at the moment," Felicity said.

" 'Familiar Struggle.' Bishop Cortara stood on heavy stone. 'Struggle is as sure as death or spring: so be leopards while the high valleys flower.' But the squalid photographers had heard too many promises. Musical weaving-mills burned. Pacific courts decayed. The pretty regiments came. He put his arms round a returning falcon and floated above the familiar windows of the Pacific."

Edward fell asleep. When he woke, they were nosing out of the hangar in a mild cuddle of acceleration.

Passengers had the option of listening to music or of using the small screen-table before them either to watch a current film, generally Chinese or Japanese, or to view the panorama beyond the ship as seen from the captain's monitor. Most people opted for the film – *Confessions of the Love Computer* – but Edward and Felicity switched over to the spectacle of space.

Flying among the Zodiacal Planets provided a superb visual experience. The planetoids glittered all about, like a galaxy built of poker chips, their palloy hulls and domes giving them a high albedo. They circled Earth like a swarm of floodlit mosquitoes. There were hundreds of them, given life by the thermonuclear ardours of the sun.

Most of them had been constructed three and four decades earlier, in ambitious response to the Great Power Crisis. Energy was here for the taking – but energy always at a price. Many of the zeepees had been built under private enterprise, by large corporations of all kinds. At first, when enthusiasm was high and expertise rare, the failure rate was formidable. There were romantic tales of half-finished zeepees, of ruined zeepees, of zeepees unregistered at Lloyd's, of zeepees filled with water or poisonous gases, in which renegades and pirates lived; such things were the standard fare of scatter shows. Eventually, governments had stepped in when death tolls grew high enough to rouse public opinion. Later, groups of zeepees had formed alliances, often slightly altering their orbit to do so, and now governed themselves like so many city states.

Independent zeepees still existed; but they were mainly the poorer ones. Even the alliances fell increasingly into the hands of terrestrial nations as tariffs nibbled away their profitability. All came more and more under the Chinese hegemony. The Chinese owned – if only at second – or third hand – the essential space routes and most of the space lines. Chinese artefacts and fashions ruled increasingly on even the most strenuously independent zeepees.

There were pessimists who claimed that the great days of the Zodiacal Planets were already over. Optimists claimed that the great days had hardly begun, and that the time would come when zeepees equipped themselves with their own fleets – a nucleus existed already – and towed themselves to new orbits round Venus, away from terrestrial interference. Nonsense, said the pessimists (who as usual in these cases called themselves realists); in a cytherean orbit, solar emissions would prove lethal and, in any case, the zeepees were only economically viable as it was because they were not too far from Earth. We don't need Earth any more, cried the optimists. The day will come, said the realists, when all our beautiful new worlds will float silent and deserted about the mother planet, stripped of their luxury and machineries – and that in our lifetime. Never, said the optimists, upping their insurance.

"We're lucky to be the generation that enjoys all this beauty," Edward said. "But I'm looking forward to the sight of an Earth landscape again. To gazing at distant horizons. Myopia has become such a fashionable zeepee complaint. Of course, much will have altered since I was there last, because of the energy shortage. It's fifteen years in my case."

"Only five in mine, but things will have changed," Felicity said. "Do you know what they have now? Sailing ships again! Big ones!"

"So I heard."

"They are so short of horsepower. One horsepower will shift only one kilo in the air or nine kilos on land, but over five thousand kilos by water. So now all cargoes go by the oceans, just as in earlier centuries. In Shanghai and Canton, the ship yards have built huge windjammers with five masts which travel at seventeen knots–as fast as the old mammoth tankers."

"They must need huge crews. The profession of sailor has returned."

"No, it hasn't, Edward. These windjammers are quite solitary, with no crew aboard except just one technician. The constant sail-changing is now fully automated and controlled by computer in response to weather-readings taken on-ship and from weathersats. Isn't that romantic – those great white ships sailing the oceans all alone, each managing its own lonely course?"

"Marvellous!" he said. "Like albatrosses...." He sat relishing the picture she conjured up in his mind, thinking how much of life he had missed by his concentration on work for Callibrastics. And he thought too of a model yacht he had had as a boy. He launched it on a pond near home and it sailed to the far bank, with a brave wooden sailor standing by its mast.

"I'd really like to see one of those ships," he said. Oh, the early days of life, before the machineries of the brain took charge. The dragon-haunted seas of Earth and youth.... A wave of poignance cut through him, so that he could have wept. In his early teens, he had once loved a girl whose father was a seaman in the navy. She had e'd him a mad twelve page letter describing Montevideo, exorcism, the secret parts of her body, and many other interesting things, and then had disappeared from his life. The oceans of the world were beyond all prediction.

Finally, he turned to Felicity, fragile in her couch, and gazed into her deep, dark eyes.

"We know such different things about each other. I know about you internally, but nothing about your circumstances, although I had the pleasure of meeting your brother –"

She burst into laughter, hiding her pleasant mouth with a hand.

"You hated my brother, just as he hated you! Why are you always so polite?"

"I was taught that one should be polite to Chinese ladies." He smiled.

She clutched his hand, giggling. "Don't be polite much longer, Edward."

He thought he caught her meaning. Turning to her hungrily, he said, "Tell me more about yourself, where you've come from, what you want from life, what you think about, what happened to you when you were surrounded by real seas, not artificial ones!"

Felicity told him of a life lived mainly in the Province of Chekiang, of their holidays by the sea, of camping in the mountains, of her father's rise in the civil service, and of his promotion to Peking. She was most happy in Peking when she joined a girls' Whole Diet Circle, which was established in a small rural township that was wholly self-supporting; there she had learnt fish-farming and other ecological arts. During those happy days, catastrophe overtook the family. Their mother became increasingly difficult, family quarrels an every day occurrence. A favourite younger daughter was run over through the mother's neglect. The family polarised, Shi Tok siding with his mother, Felicity with her father. They felt scandal close about them. The father was given a post in the city of Hangchow but, in a fit of rage, he sent Shi Tok off to the zeepees to work for his living.

"And it was all predictable," Felicity said. "My mother was suffering from a brain tumor, as we should have diagnosed. She died suddenly, only a few weeks after Shi Tok had left home. My father became a very sad man, particularly when Shi Tok would not communicate with him, believing that mother's death came through his neglect. I volunteered to go and see Shi Tok, but it is expensive to travel in space and, with having to support Shi Tok, I might never have saved enough money to return if you had not come along..."

He tried to hold her story in mind, but his sense of injury won.

"You only came with me because you wanted to get back to your father!"

"That is not so, and I am very grateful to you. You know that; I have shown you."

He remained uneasy.

Ether Breather was not designed for high stress. Its structure was built from various of the metal-plastic alloys. To get down to Earth, at the bottom of its steep gravity well, passengers had to change into a much stouter ferry.

Accordingly, they disembarked when they were 5,700 kilometres from Earth, alighting for a couple of hours at a duty free way-station called Roche's Limit.

As they stood at one of the great windows of the way-station, looking out on the tremendous bowl of Earth below them, Edward said suddenly, "I will take you to China. We'll go together. First, I must visit Cleveland, Ohio, to see my only surviving relations. You can come with me, and then we will visit your country. I have an errand for the corporation, after which we shall be free to do what we like."

"Lovely, Edward! I will show you the ocean, and you shall watch the new breed of clipper ships sailing the China Seas!"

He clutched her and she did not draw away. "That will be marvellous. First, I have to talk to a Minister in Peking, a man called Li Kwang See. It is important to get his approval of the PM unofficially."

She gave a little squeak in the region of his right shoulder and buried her face in his chest.

"Do you know the minister's name?" he asked.

Felicity covered her mouth and nose with a narrow hand, shaking her head. "Go on," she said indistinctly. "Why do you need Chinese approval?"

"We must secure Earth markets for full expansion. The World State will be in operation soon. Everything is getting very Chinese these days..."

"Only American things! Meanwhile, Chinese things are getting Westernised."

Her voice was strained; he attributed it to the fantastic view before them.

"Even my little old lin is Chinese in origin."

"I know – the very name Lin is Mandarin, meaning a fabulous creature like a unicorn, whose voice coincides with all the notes of music – melodious, you'd say!"

"My lin isn't much like a unicorn."

"Maybe not. *But* it is symmetrical and beautifully proportioned, *and* it only appears when benevolent kings are on the throne. And those are legendary characteristics of our unicorns."

"Aha! Then I like my lin a great deal, and will never part with it."

They crowded into the ferry when it came, together with a flock of other passengers, happy that theirs was not a longer wait – unlike the zeepees, Roche's Limit worked by the twenty-four-hour terrestrial clock, and there were only four ferries a terrestrial day to and from Earth.

The nightmare of sinking down to the planetary surface. The choking moment of landing. The nausea of full gravity. The rank smell of natural atmosphere, full of millions of years of impurities. The horror of finding that they had arrived during that antiquated and inconvenient hiatus, night. The boredom of getting through Check Out, with its interminable examinations. The contempt at the antique forms of transport. The excitement of being together in this irrational, random world...

[SEVENTEEN]

A week in Cleveland, Ohio, was like a cycle of Cathay. They left after only five days. It was true that Edward's old uncle was kind to them, and took them pedal-boating on the Cuyahoga River. "You'd never believe that this waterway was once notorious," he told them. "It was the first body of water ever to be insured as a fire-hazard. Now you catch big fish in it, and the duck-shooting's great, in season."

But Cleveland itself was a relic when it was not entirely a slum. Its industries had died for lack of nourishment. Like most of the great industrial cities of the West, its inhabitants were villagers again, painfully feeling their way back to a rooted way of life.

There was no private transport. They caught an infrequent coach to the West Coast, waiting in San Francisco until they could get a passage to one of the distant Chinese ports. Eventually, they boarded a steam-assisted schooner, *The Caliph*, bound for Hangchow.

Edward Maine was anxious. A veil had come between him and Felicity. He did not understand, and feared that he had somehow offended her, so maladroit was he with women.

They had a fair-sized cabin opening on the promenade deck. After long arguments with their steward, Maine managed to get both the PM and the lin brought up from the hold and installed in the cabin. The familiar objects brought with them a sense of security.

"That makes it more like home," he said. "Lin, can you tell us a cheerful story?"

"America is disappearing," said the lin, which was perfectly true. Already land was a mere blue line on the horizon. "I have a story called 'Deserted Dunes.'"

"Would you like to hear it, Felicity?"

"I suppose so."

"Leopards burned atrabiliously among the magnesium fountains. Musical girls walked among sand dunes because heavy increases in taxation were demanded. One old man said, 'The ocean will return next year.' Spring brought rain. Stone decayed. And again bells sounded along the deserted temples."

She forced a laugh. "Very cheering. 'The ocean will return next year...' I wonder what exactly that means!" She looked a little green, as if the pitching of the schooner was having its effect.

With an effort, he went over to her and took her in his arms. "I know Cleveland wasn't too successful. This is the first time we have been alone together since Fragrance. The world distracts us... What the lin says means nothing – and nothing will return unless we seize it now. Oh, dear Felicity, I don't know what you really think of me – I know you really only came along for the ride – you really want to be

with your father and never go back to Fragrance, isn't that it? – but
I care greatly for you, and I want to know what you feel about me.
Please, please, speak out to me!"

She gave him a look of – he took it for despair and something
more. Then she broke from him and ran from the cabin. He followed,
watching her run along the deck, her coat flapping in the breeze, a
vivid figure against the tumbled drama of ocean. Then he went back
into the cabin and shut the door.

For a long while, he sat on the edge of his bunk. Then with an
effort, he rose again, beginning to unpack the parts of the PM and
assemble them. *The Caliph* had its own wind-assisted generators,
and passenger electricity was on at this hour of day. When the
machine was assembled, he plugged it in at the power point and
switched on.

The PM was not programmed with supplementary terrestrial data
as yet. Edward realised more clearly than ever how far ahead lay the
first generation of portable PMs. Nevertheless, the prototype should
still be reliable as far as his and Felicity's personal situation was con-
cerned. He was determined that they must disentangle that situation
as soon as possible; the sudden lapse in their easy relationship was
more than he could bear.

As the machine began to read him, he became aware of a queasi-
ness in the stomach, a light film of perspiration on his forehead, the
symptoms of incipient *mal de mer*. He tried to relax as the PM absorbed the levels of his physiological functions.

He set the machine to print out for the next twelve hours only. It
began to deliver, its print finger moving with an irascible, jerky action common to machines and tyrannosauri.

> Persist in your mission
> Anxiety precipitates crisis 76
> Fragrance faces imminent destruction 99

Shock endangers love 47
Maintain contact with girl
Further study of chance laws needed 99.5

Summary: multiple crisis in attractive company

Edward switched the machine off, pulled the plug from the power socket, and began to dismantle the machine, making a long face as he did so.

The PM was programmed for the confined world of Fragrance II. It had been fed no routine data since leaving the zeepee. Its prediction of catastrophe was a phantom, based purely on his current physiological state which, on Fragrance, would indeed have presaged some phenomenal disaster: here it presaged only possible seasickness.

"Maintain contact with the girl" was another plain nonsense, since on shipboard it was impossible to do anything else.

Unless – the thought came like a shot – Felicity fell overboard.

But it was a miserable little read-out, with crazy probabilities. And the "Further study of chance laws needed" was irrelevant, since he had stressed such needs at every stage of research. The PM could not be expected to work in transposed environments without elaborate preparation.

He ought to dismiss the read-out, knowing how out of touch with reality it was. He was listening to a blind oracle, he told himself. Then he remembered that oracles were traditionally blind.

Searching the ship for Felicity in a state of anxiety, he found her eventually in the stern, leaning against a covered winch, staring at the horizon below which the last of America had disappeared.

"Don't stand here, my dear Felicity. It's too cold. Come into the cabin."

The sails drummed above them. He put an arm tightly round her waist, taken again by her beauty, for all her present pallor.

She gave him a tortured look, then followed meekly. He kept one hand on her arm and the other on the rail. Noise was all about them, in sails and boat and sea, while his lungs rejoiced in the wild air. He was not going to be seasick. There were minor victories of which no one knew.

Even in the cabin, with the door closed, they could still hear the gallant sound of sails and rigging. Felicity stood looking so helpless that he became angry.

"You've fooled me, haven't you? You came with me simply to get to Earth. I was mad to expect anything else. You don't want anything further to do with me, do you?" He ran his hands through his wild hair.

"Don't try to drive me away, Edward. What you say is not true."

"Then tell me, for god's sake. Something's the matter. What is it?" He was shaking her angrily.

"All right, all right, you bastard! I'm not afraid of telling you – I'm afraid of your being unable to understand. You are going to visit Li Kwang See, is that so?" Her face was set. She scowled at him.

"I told you it was so."

"Edward, Li Kwang See is my respected father."

"Your father?" They stared at each other meaninglessly. "Your father?" He did not know what to say. He went and gazed out of the small window at the hammering waves until he regained his voice.

"The minister is your father? Are you a member of the Chinese secret police, the Khang?" He turned to examine her. "You were put on to me when my holiday on Earth was first on the cards. Your agents probably heard about it before I did. I was tricked into choosing you."

"Edward, no, please don't think that. I'm nothing to do with the Khang, of course I'm not!"

"No? Wait – I know. It was that sneering thing Stein-Presteign said, moving me subtly toward you. This was all engineered by Callibrastics, so that someone would come along with me and see how

I performed. Typical of them! You're paid by Callibrastics, aren't you?"

"No, Edward. I don't know anyone connected with your firm. It's just coincidence, nothing more. When you mentioned my father's name on the ferry to Earth, I could have died with astonishment. Literally, I could have died!"

"Yes? Then why didn't you say something then?" The tears in her eyes only made him more savage.

"I was just so amazed... I couldn't speak. I had to have time to think it over. But it really is just a coincidence. I cannot come to terms with it myself."

He shook his head. "You ask me to believe that? How many Chinese are there? Eight hundred billion? And I pick on you by accident? I'd be mad ever to believe that."

"You must believe it. I have to believe it. Or else I have to believe that you sought me out just because you thought I would help you speak to my father and win his favour."

"Nonsense, I hired you by accident, through the Intern Agency! I didn't even ask for a Chinese girl."

"Well, then, and you came to seek me out by devious means at FFFFA. I didn't seek you out. The advantage is with you, not me, and for me it's just as much of a coincidence as for you."

"An eight hundred billion to one coincidence? It's a trick." Another thought struck him. "You're lying, aren't you? Li Kwang See *can't* be your father."

"He is, he is! Why are you so horrid? Your little scientific world's turned upside down."

They continued to argue. They ate no meal that evening. Finally they fell into their separate bunks exhausted, and slept. The morning made no difference. Still they argued.

For a whole sea-week they argued. Seasickness never touched them, so busy were they with the problem.

"This is ridiculous," Edward said at last. "After all, I know a great deal more about the laws of probability than you do, Felicity. I cannot believe that this is a coincidence; the odds are just too long against it. It runs counter to everything in my theory of non-randomness – I'd be mad to believe it."

"I'm fed up with your stupid little mathematical arguments," she said wearily. She was pale and fatigued, huddled in the cabin's only armchair. "You're mad to let a coincidence, however big, get in the way of our love."

So exhausted were they that for a moment neither of them seemed to realise what she said. Then he looked at her again.

He began to smile. A great burden fell from him. She smiled back, concealing her nose and mouth with one small hand.

"Felicity, Zenith..." he said. He took her into his embrace, feeling her arms move about his neck as he kissed her, feeling her lips open and her slender body press against his.

"Oh, Felicity..." he whispered. They scrambled into the lower bunk, weeping and laughing and kissing.

[EIGHTEEN]

Edward never accepted the coincidence. By the end of the voyage, when they were adepts at love, he had come to live with it. But his mind still rejected it whenever the thought of it arose. It was as if he opened a familiar door and found that it led, not into the kitchen, but to the summit of Everest. It would always be there. He could not assimilate it.

Felicity adjusted more easily. As she explained, her view of life was in any case more random than Edward's. She positively skipped on to the Chinese shore at Hangchow.

The stinks and perfumes of the place amazed Edward, as well as its bustling life – private lives lived much more publicly than he was used to. He viewed it all with fascination and a little dread, realising again how much of his urge to create a working PM stemmed from his own timidity, his suspicion of the new, the exotic. But with Felicity for guide, he felt entirely safe.

They spent that night in a small hotel overlooking the Grand Canal and next morning boarded a train for Peking. The train was pulled by an enormous solar engine and was spotlessly clean. As they waited in Hangchow station, little old ladies with faces wrinkled like contour maps of the Pyrenees sprang out of the ground and rubbed down windows and brass-work until everything gleamed. Then the express set off again through the great tamed tawny countryside.

To Edward Maine's eyes, Peking looked formidable, grim, and bleak, even in the fresh spring sunshine. At first it seemed like one more big monolithic capital, with its enormous squares, factories, and barrack-like buildings. As they crossed Chang-an Square in a blue trolley-car, the wide spaces made him feel dizzy; but Felicity effected a partial cure by showing him slogans set in coloured tiles into the series of grey paving stones. She translated for him, squeezing his hand.

"You young people, full of vigour and vitality, are in the bloom of life, like the sun at eight or nine in the morning. The world belongs to you. China's future belongs to you. Mao Tse-Tung."

He liked the sentiment. It was still only nine-thirty, he thought.

The trolley-car took them past one of the great grey old watchtowers which had overlooked the city for a thousand years, to an older part of the town.

Felicity guided them to a small hotel in a side street where tourists rarely went, where the human scale was more to their taste.

"Oh, you will grow to love Peking, Edward. You see it was never a motorcar city, like the big cities of America and even Europe; so now that the motor car has gone, the city remains as it always was, without malformations. Wait till you get used to it!"

"I don't want to get used to it. I like it all as it is now – novel in every stone."

It proved difficult to visit Li Kwang See officially. The Ministry for External Trade and Exotic Invisible Earnings was a gaunt grey building near the Tou Na Ting Park, its flanks patched by large-letter posters. It was eight storeys high, with dysfunctional elevators. Edward, clutching his letter of introduction from Stein-Presteign of Smics Callibrastics, took a whole day to work through junior officials on the ground floor up to senior officials on the top floor. The officials, dressed in grey or blue, were always smiling. One of them, greatly courteous – this was on the fifth floor, when Edward showed signs of impatience – said, "Naturally, we realise that Smics Callibrastics is very important, both to you and to the planetoid Fragrance II. Unfortunately, in our ignorance, we fail to have heard of the company, and so must remedy that error by applying to a better-informed department. You must try to excuse the delay."

He smiled back. The whole exercise, he thought, was beautifully designed to make him see matters in perspective. A Chinese perspective. He admired it, admired both the courtesy and the slight mystery, just as he admired those qualities in Felicity.

During his second day in the waiting-rooms and staircases of the Ministry of External Trade, it was revealed to him in a mobile phone call that the Minister himself was at present negotiating a trading agreement elsewhere, and that consequently the Ministry was unable to help him this week. They hoped that he would enjoy the pleasures of Peking, and that they might be able to assist him on another occasion. They presented him with a free ticket to a concert in the Park of Workers, Financiers, and Soldiers.

"Oh, my father is so elusive!" Felicity exclaimed, when all this was reported to her. To relieve her feelings, she tore up the free ticket and scattered the pieces equably about the room. "All these bureaucrats are the same. While you were languishing in that horrible building, I was calling some relations who live near here. They will try to trace my father. Meanwhile, tonight they invite us both to a feast."

The feast was a glory in itself and successful as a social occasion. Among the multitudinous courses, many a toast was drunk to matters of mutual esteem, such as good health, longevity, wisdom, freedom from indigestion, prosperity, and the success of trading enterprises. Edward blundered home afterwards, holding Felicity's hand down narrow lanes, sharing his new knowledge of China with her.

"You see, this part of the world is better off than anywhere else on Earth. This is China's century, as one of your uncles said. I suppose the same claim could be made back in history. But now China has come out from behind her wall. She's been well-organised and peaceful for millennia – that excellent Shantung wine must have helped in that respect. Even during the purges in Mao's time, there was a tradition of forgiving and even welcoming back those who confessed the error of their ways. And no other country so swiftly modernised on China's scale. Solar and tidal powers support us. So now that fossil fuels and metals are as rare as rubies, China is not faced with the massive need to adjust which confronts the West. Why, take that gorgeous roast sucking pig we had – it never needed an internal combustion machine! That lobster in prawn and ginger sauce – it had never been near a nuclear fusion plant! You can't tell me that that stuffed goat's udder ever drew up at a filling station and found it closed for lack of gasoline!..."

They climbed laughing into their hard broad bed. He fell asleep with his head on her soft narrow breast.

[NINETEEN]

A smiling, reserved uncle on a mobile phone call brought them word that Brother See was in committee at No. 35 Flowering Maidenhood Lane.

Edward went there. The lane managed to look almost as rustic as its name, although new concrete houses had been slotted in an ugly way behind the walls which sheltered traditional mansions of artisans.

It was evidently still necessary for him to get global matters into proper perspective. He sat out another session of waiting in a small upstairs room, looking out over concrete, grey-tiled eaves, dangling cables, a wooden house where two children played with a transistorised doll, and a pigsty which contained five small porkers and a flowering cherry. He liked it.

His read-out that morning had told him he would sight his quarry today; but he remained sceptical of anything the PM said until he could feed it up-to-date programming. However, at three-thirty, a small procession of men in pallid business suits walked in dignity through the waiting-room. One of them had a face like a squeezed lemon and looked at Edward with a marked gaze as he passed; that would be the minister, Felicity's father.

"My father-in-law?" he asked himself. That would depend on how the interview went, among other things.

Mindful of his manners, he followed respectfully down the stairs. A limo like a hearse waited outside on the cobbles. A lackey sprang to open doors and the company climbed in. The hearse drove off.

As Edward stood watching it go, preparing to be at least a little angry, the lackey came up and offered him a small yellow envelope. He tore it open. Inside was a square of card. On it, printed, the legend: Minister for External Trade and Exotic Invisible Earnings. Beneath it in a perfect script were the words, "Happy prognostications show that we shall meet soon in more harmonious surroundings."

"He must have a better PM than I have, then," Edward said, stuffing the envelope into his pocket. But the message pleased him, nevertheless.

When he showed the card to Felicity, she chewed the edge of it and puckered her brow in thought. To please Edward, she had gone out and bought a cheongsam, although she protested that the garment was wildly old-fashioned and, in any case, not true Chinese but invented in Manchester, England, for the benefit of the cotton trade. In this garment, as she lounged in a cane chair, she looked perfectly provocative. He went over and stroked her thigh.

"My father is a wily old fox," she said. "This is what I think. He did not expect that you would grasp all the implications of this message. But he guessed that you would bring it to me, and that I would understand it. The message shows that he is inharmonious here, therefore he wishes to get away for a while. You see, he prefers philosophy to trade. So he will go to our coastal house in Chin Hsiang, in the

Chekiang Province. He has learned from the uncle whom you met that we are together, so he expects us both to join him informally."

"It must have been more than coincidence that we came together. Otherwise how should I manage?"

"If you are grateful, then never, never tell my honoured father that I was once Internal-girl and had men peering at the inside of my magnified private organs!"

"Shall I ever see those delicious organs again?"

"You have seen the traditional entrances to them. So, let's pack up and go to Chin Hsiang."

"It should be good there at this time of year. How far is it?"

"Only two and a half thousand kilometres by rail. A full day's journey on the train. Or we can fly. Lin, you are very idle while in China, so you may tell us a story while we pack up.

"I have a story called 'Justice Performed,'" said the lin.

"It sounds like a good omen for Edward. Let us have it in an alto voice this time. Proceed." She gave the machine a mock formal bow.

"Flight was impossible where perverted justice ruled. 'Let us return with honour to the volcano,' cried the lusty silver band of oldest harlots. 'Let us build the weaving mills among the mountains.' Next year, musical patterns led to familiarity. Falcons brought spring. Towering photographers performed before the strong ruler. Sleep came."

"That's very sweet," Felicity said. "You know, Edward, it would be both politic and polite if you give a present to my father when you meet. Why don't you donate this antiquated lin to him?"

"It's worth nothing. I'd be ashamed to present him with something so limited."

She smiled and said, "Of the lin as of humans, the attraction lies in the limitations and in the maximum that can be achieved within those limitations. I hate my brother's toy paintings because he cowers within his limitations, but this lin is bold and imaginative within his, and my father would surely appreciate such a gift."

Edward clapped his hands together. "Then it shall be done. Lin, you are to have a more appreciative master."

"We are all in the fiery hands of God," said the lin.

[TWENTY]

Chin Hsiang was a quiet agricultural town, built where two canals met. There were inviting hills to the south, their lower slopes sculpted into paddy terraces which flowed like living contour lines. The town itself was set partly on a hill. The modest house of the Li Kwang family was halfway up this rising ground, its wooden gate opening on a square. Blossom trees were flowering everywhere. Lying to the east, and tiny in the distance, was a bay of the sea.

"It's one of the loveliest places I've ever seen," Edward exclaimed. He went and walked in the square under the midday sun. There were a few stalls in the centre of the square, tended by stalwart peasant women, who offered gay paper toys, pocket computers, picture books, chillis and blue-shelled eggs and toads in baskets, pallid lettuce and withered tomatoes, huge radishes, bright green peppers, and little fish speared on reeds. Beside them were barrels and pots and colourful animals dangling on strings.

The whole picture pleased him. An ochre-walled lane led down from the square, a cobbled stair led up. The houses had tiled roofs. It reminded him of something, but of precisely what he could not recollect. He felt at home here.

That afternoon, they went to meet Felicity's father, the Minister. His bungalow overlooked a secluded courtyard shared by the main house. Felicity led Maine to a bare room at the rear of the bungalow, where a small fire burned. The fire was of sticks and peat; real flames played there, real ash fell. Maine, long accustomed to the mock-fire in his homapt on Fragrance 11, gazed at it with astonishment; he had lived too much of his life between fireproof doors.

The delicate noises of the fire emphasised the quiet of the room. There was one window, which looked out at the courtyard. The wall

TV screen was blank. Beneath the window was a large desk of polished wood. Behind the desk stood a small man dressed in a smart grey suit. He made a small bow as Maine stepped forward. It was the official Maine had seen in the ministry in Peking, his face wrinkled like a lemon, his eyes guilty and gentle like a reindeer's.

When the ceremony of greeting was over, Felicity brought them some wine and the men sat down facing one another.

"There is something eternal about China," Edward said, embarking with verve upon a flattering speech. "I am very pleased to be here. Of all civilisations, yours weathers the ages best. You have accepted time as a natural element. In the West, time is a challenge. We've treated it that way ever since the Renaissance. The Renaissance has provided our great fund of ideas over the past few centuries. I mean the dynamic ideas of humanism, individualism, and speculations about the external world. You could say that the impulse which sprang from the prosperous families of Italy in the fifteenth century led us eventually to space travel, and so to the Zodiacal Planets, which are like little city states.

"But we're in trouble now that that questing spirit has brought about the exhaustion of fossil oil and mineral deposits. Some say that America and the West are played out. I don't believe so. But I do believe the times are temporarily against us, and that we are having to weather a storm of our own creating. Whereas China sails grandly on as if time does not exist."

He paused several times during this speech, inserting gaps and "ums," as he tried to remember what he wanted to say. He was not good at big theories, and had to recall what the eloquent Stein-Presteign would have said in similar circumstances.

"You are generous in your comments," Li Kwang See replied. "The strength of China lies in her land, and in the people who inhabit it. There is nothing else. Possibly in the West you have been too arrogant with your land, and have not understood its meaning and importance. The big businessman has possibly been more revered than the small farmer, if I may so comment. However, as to time, let me relate to you an amusing incident which illustrates that time can stand still even in your ever-moving country.

"Whenever I am in Houston, Texas, I visit the elegant museum there to look at one thing and one thing only. That object is an eighth-century vase of the T'ang dynasty. When I regard that vase, the material and the spiritual come together and I am restored. The last time I was there, standing by the vase, a guide came along with a bunch of tourists, and he said to them, 'This beautiful vase is thirteen hundred years old.' Now, when I was there fifteen years earlier, that same guide announced to another bunch of tourists, 'This beautiful vase is thirteen hundred years old.' So, you see, time has been standing absolutely still in the Houston Museum for at least fifteen years."

Edward wondered if he cared for the humour of foreigners, but professed to enjoy the story. He then produced the lin with due formality.

Li Kwang admired the curlicues of its plasticwork and Edward asked the machine if it had a suitable story for its new master.

"New master, I have an exciting story for you," said the lin. "It is called 'Old Regiments.' The regiments with goat eyes came among the valleys. Lonely old officers cried among the royal courts because taxation returned. 'The export market is a dinosaur; it increases the flight from towering ideals,' one said. But the magnesium airports changed towns. Volcanoes were built. Promises were obliterated. Girls put their arms demandingly round old fathers."

"Very pretty – although we hope that exports are not necessarily in conflict with towering ideals," said Li Kwang, smiling politely and hiding his mouth behind his hand.

"At least we can make part of the story come true," said Felicity, going over to hug her parent. "You see, girls put their arms demandingly round old fathers. Daddy, you must listen to what Edward has to say about his invention, the prediction machine, because it is very important for him that you approve of it. Tell him, Edward."

So Edward embarked on an explanation of the principles of the PM. He described how the prototype worked. He put it frankly that the PM represented a large financial investment and that his corporation would be greatly assisted if they knew in advance that they would be able to export and sell the machine on Earth as well as among the zeepees – a matter on which he understood Li Kwang's word to be all-important.

For most of this speech, Li Kwang listened while gazing out at the courtyard, where a shower of rain was falling.

When Edward had finished, he gestured to his daughter to pour more wine.

"My word is a poor thing," he said. "You must not set too much store by it. Your invention sets great store by words. We are all aware of the power of words and must bow to them, but we should seek escape from their demands when we can. It is mistaken to fall even more into their power. Words must be staunched with silence."

"Daddy, let us talk philosophy later. First, you must say yes to Edward."

He smiled at her reproof, his face wrinkling into an even closer resemblance to a lemon, a humorous lemon. "It is precisely because this is a philosophical matter that I am not able to say yes to our guest, vexing though that is for me." He leaned forward and said to Edward, "Mr. Maine, you probably know that in China we already have a method of guidance for every day of the year. I will not call it prediction, but prediction is possibly a misnomer also for your prototype, seeing that it interpolates advice among its percentages. Our method of divination is based on one of the great books of the Orient, the *I Ching* – or *Book of Changes*, as it is known in the West. The *I Ching* is almost four thousand years old and still regularly consulted. It is a permanent source of wisdom, as well as a daily guide."

"Oh, I know about the *I Ching*, sir, and I assure you we wouldn't want to put it out of business," said Edward hastily.

"That is kind of you. Most considerate. However, the problem lies elsewhere. You see, your invention dramatically embodies a basic conflict between East and West, whether you realise it or not."

Taking alarm at this, Edward said, "I certainly do not realise it, sir. With the ability to see ahead a little, men should be less in conflict."

"Allow me to make myself clear. Your machine is very elaborate in itself. It has complex diagnostic elements, and of course it relies on a power input. Then, it is not really effective unless its data is kept current by daily bulletins from a computer system, thus encouraging centralism. All told, it is most ingenious and will for that reason always be expensive and cumbersome; even more pertinently, it will merely intensify the self generating nature of Western technology – technology demands more technology."

"But –"

"On the other hand, here is my modest divination machine." Li Kwang rose, turned to the north-facing wall behind him, and lifted a black package from a shelf set at shoulder height. He set this on his desk. From the same shelf, he took a container of carved cherry-wood, and placed it beside the package.

He opened the package, which was a book wrapped in a square of black silk. "This is my copy of the *I Ching*," he said.

He opened the container. A number of polished sticks lay inside. "These are fifty twigs of the common yarrow, which I gathered myself in a Chin Hsiang hedgerow. They and the book constitute the world's best-tried method of divination.

"I need only these. Oh, I also need a little time and thought, and maybe a little interpretation from Confucius. But that's all."

Maine laughed. "Without wishing to sound scornful, Minister, when our PM is perfected, it will cause you to wrap your book up and put it back on its shelf for good. A four-thousand-year-old book can't take much account of today's hormone levels, can it now?"

"Nor will your machine ever be advanced enough to enable us to grasp something of the sensuous cycles and rhythms of nature which shape our inner being, or help us to live in harmony with our surroundings, as does the *I Ching*."

As he said this, Li Kwang slowly folded up the book and closed the box of yarrow sticks. He replaced them on their appointed shelf.

Maine told himself that this was merely a discussion, and he must not grow angry. He glanced at Felicity, but she had moved tactfully to the window and was staring out at the rain.

"Maybe our PM is a bit more accurate than your yarrow sticks," he said. "At least it works on a scientific principle. It's rational, it doesn't grow in hedgerows. Once we fully grasp the laws of chance and can predict coincidences, then we'll be almost one hundred per cent accurate."

"And of course you see that as important. Yet in part you work on something called the Uncertainty Principle! Now that is very much how the *I Ching* works. The uncertainty is essential, forcing us to learn; otherwise we would all be robots, utterly predictable in a universe where every event is as foreseeable as a railway line."

"You are making excuses for the inaccuracy of the *I Ching* by saying that. We do not excuse our inaccuracy; we aim to eradicate it. We want accuracy – and we're getting it. What's more, we have only been working on this project for a decade, whereas you've had four thousand years!"

"Frankly, accuracy is one of the most destructive targets of the West. Also, you must realise that to work with devotion on something for four thousand years is very instructive, whether it is a rice field or an item of philosophical debate."

"Yes, but if the concept is all wrong... I mean, I don't want to knock the *I Ching*, but I do know that the Chinese have claimed that it has predicted all the great Western inventions, like electricity and nuclear energy. That seems nonsense to me."

"Forgive me, but it seems to me nonsense to say that the West invented electricity and nuclear energy. Both natural forces have always been around, and were around even four thousand years ago."

"A slip of the tongue. I meant that we harnessed them. What I was going to say was, if you believe that the *I Ching* is true, that it functions effectively, then you should not mind the PM being sold on Earth, because it will not supersede your system. We maintain that millions of people who will live under the World State will be unable to use or believe in the *I Ching*, and so will turn to the PM for guidance. Besides, we are not in competition. If we make a little money, you do not lose it, because nobody makes any money from *I Ching*, as you yourself admit."

"That is one great attraction of our ancient system. It is diffusive and not profit-cumulative."

Maine gave up for a moment, and took a deep swig of the wine.

"May I ask if you got a prediction on our little meeting and how it turned out, Mr. Maine?" Li Kwang asked.

"Well, you know this prototype is rather cumbersome; we didn't want to bring it on the train, so we've left it in Peking for the time being. Eventually, we hope to get the production model down to the size of a small radio. But I'm sure it would have said, 'Persistence needed, do not yield to impatience.'"

Both men laughed.

"In the circumstances, I consulted the sticks to see how I ought to conduct our discussion," said Li Kwang. "My six sticks which I drew gave me the two trigrams of the Khien hexagram. Let me show you with match sticks."

He drew a box of matches from his gown and from it extracted six purple matches with yellow heads. He lined them up neatly together, parallel and not touching.

"There you are, the Khien hexagram. Six long sticks. No need to break a single match."

"What does it mean?"

"It symbolises a lot of things. This undivided stick being lowest represents a dragon hidden. That is to say, it is not a time for activity. Maybe that signifies my coming to Chin Hsiang for a bit of a rest."

"Go on."

"I should also say that the whole hexagram represents some great originating power from heaven. That surely indicates that *you* are being considered, having arrived from space. Dragons also represent great men, and this second line shows there is an advantage in our meeting. The third line is difficult and vague. It could indicate that much talk goes on over the day and that by evening apprehension remains. Taken in conjunction with what follows, it indicates that I should avoid what is error in my eyes. And so on... The dragon goes beyond the proper limits."

"Is that dragon you or me?"

"It could be me. If I behave properly in respect to the demands made on me, then a proper state of equipoise and fortune will be reached. That is a reference to your request to sell your machine here, of course."

Maine clenched his fists together. He longed to sweep the feeble little sticks away. But at that moment, a servant entered the room and announced that a light meal was served.

Li Kwang would talk only on general topics during the meal. He was smiling and polite, and received without emotion the toned-down version Felicity gave him of Shi Tok's behaviour on Fragrance.

"He sent you one of his paintings, father," Felicity said. She produced it. It was one of the oblongs of garsh; a band of an intermediate brown had been painted across it. "Shi Tok says it is called *The Benefits of a Fast-Paced Sleep.*"

For a long moment, Li Kwang studied the plaque. "I shall look at it later and derive benefit from it," he said. Then he went on placidly eating his rice.

When they reassembled after lunch, Maine was feeling desperate.

"May I say, sir, that I was asked to come and speak to you because naturally my corporation wants to know the size of their market before investing their capital. I was not happy to represent them in such a matter. My strong feeling is that we should now shelve this discussion, because it is premature. If you will permit, I should like to come back in, say, a couple of years, when we have a PM model which will impress you more than anything I can say."

"Since you are frank with me, I will be frank with you. I will speak as your friend and as Felicity's father. It is not your machine to which there is a fundamental objection, but to the thinking behind it."

"But you do not yet know how reliable it can be, whereas – forgive my saying this – you demonstrated the vagueness of the *I Ching* just before lunch."

Li Kwang bowed his head. "My daughter will excuse me if I make a philosophical point. Ultimately, it does not matter whether or not the *Book of Changes* is 'true' in any empirical sense. Those who consult it value the way the book speaks to the older, less logical areas of the mind. It is a map to behaviour, not behaviour itself. Whereas you are producing, or trying to, a behaviour substitute. Further, it does not matter whether our map is 'truthful' or not since, if all accept the co-ordinates, then the map becomes reliable through general concurrence."

"Are you saying that if the map is inaccurate and leads you to fall into a ditch, you will all pretend there is no ditch?"

"No. I am saying that if all agree to believe in a certain god, then his power over men's minds is the same whether he exists or not. We do not believe in a god, but we have a belief in belief itself. That remains comfortably constant. Whereas you would be perpetually altering your procedures, adding new scraps of knowledge, new theories of chance… "

"Sir, that's not a valid objection. It simply means that new models would be needed from time to time – to the benefit of our clients, our shareholders, and the corporation. I hope your fundamental objection is not that we shall make money?"

"That is part of my objection, yes. All over America, to this very day, you still come on piles of old scrap automobiles or washing machines. And the useless motorways, mile after mile. All obsolete technology that exploited people in various ways to benefit corporations. In the World State, we plan to live with conservation, as China has always done. There will be no extravagant gadgets."

Clutching his head, Maine groaned. "You mean you're actually legislating for poverty! You'll have a world full of peasants in one generation..."

"Ah, but in the second generation, we can build from a position of equality."

"You'll drive out all the initiative to the zeepees. There will be nobody to build for you."

"I'm sure you know the answer to that, Mr. Maine. We shall build for ourselves. Nobody has ever helped us, and nobody has to help us now. Western know-how will be very welcome but it will have to concentrate on the things that are real, and not on illusions."

"You are looking at all this from a very Chinese point of view."

"In case you think I am indulging in an idle East-West hassle, let me say that you could easily come to appreciate that point of view yourself. You admit that your attitude to life is not your firm's. One understands that you personally are not exploitative or aggressive, if I may say so – although you are a unit of an exploitative and aggressive society. I read in you characteristics of humility and endurance which would find ready welcome here. You should not waste them on a corporation which battens on your talents while secretly despising you."

Maine stood up. "Sir, I have taken up too much of your time. I can see that you are dead set against my invention and the capitalist society. I will report what you say to my managing director when I get home."

"As you will. Can the lin tell you a pleasant story before we part?"

"Thanks, but no thanks." He turned and left the room, marched out of the front door, through the yard, and into the road. The rain had stopped and the late afternoon sun shone brightly. He walked briskly to the square. As he went, he heard running steps behind him.

Presently, Felicity caught up with him and took his arm.

"Oh, Edward, father has made you angry! I'm so sorry! He didn't say a definite No. You should have discussed longer with him and reached an accommodation."

"I'm sorry, Felicity, I don't want to talk about it. Of all the stubborn and difficult old – oh, I know it wasn't up to him personally. He was just speaking as a Minister. Jees, how hidebound can you get? This is just too difficult to believe, Felicity. I mean even fifty years ago I might have expected to meet up with such awful anti-Western nonsense..., and all that old crap about the mystique of China... China! What's so special about China? How's it any different from America?"

"Some say that the Americans raped their continent, whereas we have always had to serve or be raped by ours."

"Whose side are you on?" he asked, and then broke into angry laughter. "Let's get away for a while. My head is bursting. Let's go and look at the sea."

"It's farther than you think. It may be dark before we get there."

"Stop talking in that defeatist Chinese fashion. Let's go." They took the ochre-walled lane down from the square, and came along by one of the canals. Then the track took them away among the fields. They climbed a hill where slack-eyed peasant women walked home pushing babies and radios on the handlebars of their bicycles. Where merging tracks joined, an aged man sat by a small locker on wheels, a paper umbrella above his head. Felicity bought two ice creams from him, but Edward was nervous of his and threw it away.

As they climbed the slope, planting their feet firmly on the well-trodden ochre soil, Edward said, "You know what will happen? I can predict quite easily. In a way, your father's view makes sense; I have to admit it. His is basically the view of conservative people everywhere. But, pushed to its logical conclusion, such a view stifles initiative. The World State will kill initiative."

"End of Renaissance?"

"Very definitely. China never had a renaissance, I gather?"

"We had a revolution."

"Maybe your renaissance is to come... What is going to happen is that more and more positive-thinking people will migrate to the zeepees. And from there they will be driven outwards, to look for new fields to explore."

There was a small silence. Then she said, "My father is not a fool. He knows that what you call positive-thinking people always move outwards. He relies on that."

"He has a funny way of showing it."

"He has the only way of showing it. Men have dreamed of a World State for centuries. Now it is coming. It must have time to settle down, to get into working order. For a while, it needs stasis rather than progress. How can you achieve that without smothering the progressives? Why, by driving them out. They'll survive and profit by isolation."

"Like little city states," he said. Irreconcilable points of view existed and were necessary: maybe what was unnecessary was that either side should lose by the conflict.

Their way was downhill now, and the sea glittered through spring foliage. As they trotted forward, they lost the sun behind the shoulder of the hill to their rear. The track took them round a copse of flowering tung trees, and the ocean stretched ahead.

On it were three sailing ships, their sails still tinged with sunset pink, although the water was grey.

"Oh, that looks so wonderful!" Felicity cried. "That's what we came to Earth for!"

"Better than your artificial oceans?" He took her slender arm.

"Yes, and those are the automated windjammers I told you about."

He counted the masts. Five masts apiece, most of the metallic sails out to catch the evening breeze.

"Heading for Shanghai or the ports of the Yellow Sea," she said.

They stood and looked at each other as the dark came on. "Do you think your father understands as much as you claim he does – that Western ideas are vitally necessary to mankind?"

"I'm sure he read it in his Khien hexagram. It is a fundamental truth that most wise people have always realised: East and West are necessary to each other, like yin and yang."

"Now you are speaking metaphorically."

She shook her head. "No, I was speaking personally, if you must know."

They lay down together on the edge of the cliff, and dark came on.

Out to sea, the sailing ships faded away, heading for unknown harbours. Overhead, as the sky darkened, the stars began to spread. Venus stood out sharply, and then the familiar constellations. But far eclipsing them was a great halo going clear into distance, comprising hundreds of brilliant points of light. The darker the sky grew, the more brightly the Zodiacal Planets shone, ringing in the Earth.

The World State would come into being. Every night, the eyes of its citizens would be directed upwards, above the high-rises and the sullen chimney-tops.

About Brian Aldiss

BRIAN WILSON ALDISS was born on August 18, 1925, in Norfolk, England. When he completed his formal education, Aldiss was drafted and spent four years in the Royal Signals regiment, seeing action in Burma. After nine years bookselling in Oxford and writing part-time for magazines and trade journals, his literary career was launched with the publication of *The Brightfount Diaries* in 1955. He was elected Most Promising New Author at the World Science Fiction Convention in 1958, and became a full-time writer, editor, and anthologist in 1959. Aldiss quickly became a leading figure in British science fiction, and was elected President of the British Science Fiction Association in 1960. He has since endured as one of the most important science fiction writers and scholars of our time.

Aldiss is known for his prolific output, his diversity of topics and genres, and his wildly imaginative literary stylings. Among his many accomplishments, Aldiss co-founded the first journal of science fiction criticism, *Science Fiction Horizons*, edited the highly successful series of *Penguin Science Fiction* anthologies, won the Hugo Award for *Hothouse* and the Nebula award for *The Saliva Tree*, and had his stories adapted to the screen in *Frankenstein Unbound* by Roger Corman, and *AI* by Stanley Kubrick and Steven Spielberg. Celebrating his eightieth birthday, Brian Aldiss's inventiveness, humor, and originality continue to win him new fans throughout the world.